IRRESISTIBLE

Andrew J. Peters

A NineStar Press Publication

Published by NineStar Press
P.O. Box 91792,
Albuquerque, New Mexico, 87199 USA.
www.ninestarpress.com

Irresistible

Printed in the USA
First Edition
August, 2018

Print ISBN: 978-1-949340-48-8

Also available in eBook, ISBN: 978-1-949340-40-2

Warning: This book contains sexual content, which may only be suitable for mature readers, and depictions of graphic violence and deaths of secondary characters.

Brendan Thackeray-Prentiss is an Ivy League-educated trust-funder who Gotham Magazine named the most eligible gay bachelor in New York City. He lives for finding his soulmate, but after walking in on his boyfriend of three transcendent months soaping up in the shower with an older female publicist, he's on a steady diet of scotch, benzodiazepines, and compulsive yoga. Men are completely off the menu.

Callisthenes Panagopoulos has a problem most guys dream of. With the body and face of a European soccer heartthrob, the vigorous blond hair of a Mormon missionary, and a smile that makes traffic cops stuff their ticket books back in their utility belts, he's irresistible to everyone. But being a constant guy-magnet comes with its discontents, like an ex-boyfriend who tried to drive his Smart car through Cal's front door. It makes him wonder if he's been cursed when it comes to love.

When Brendan and Cal meet, the attraction is meteoric, and they go from date to mates at the speed of time-lapse photography. But to stay together, they'll have to overcome Cal's jealous BFF, Romanian mobsters, hermit widowers, and a dictatorship on the brink of revolution during a dream wedding in the Greek isles that becomes a madcap odyssey.

A gay romantic comedy of errors based on Chariton's *Callirhoe*, the world's oldest extant romance novel.

Dedication

My thanks to the NineStar Press team for taking a chance on my over-the-top invention: my meticulous and wonderful, cheerleading editor Elizabetta McKay, managing director Raevyn McCann, and cover designer, Natasha Snow. Thanks also to my early readers Elizabeth Welsford and Sarah Reeves who helped me get the manuscript in shape.

Who else would this book be dedicated to besides my true love, my husband, Genaro Cruz. You make it all worth it.

Chapter One

BRENDAN THACKERAY-PRENTISS was not interested in finding a boyfriend.

He reminded himself of this whenever he passed by an attractive young man on the Upper East Side streets, or when this or that friend took to social media to proclaim a change in their relationship status, or when he clicked through an especially earnest e-mail driving for donations to help gay couples maintain their legal status in the Deep South Bible Belt, and most of all when people asked him, "How is it possible the most eligible gay bachelor in New York City is still single?"

Brendan had made a vow, and it had received the endorsement of his therapist, Dr. Clotilde Trapp. He was taking time off from sex and dating in order to clear his head, and to renew, and to rise up from the ashes like a phoenix, if he wanted to be dramatic about it, which he truly had earned the right to be.

Thiago, a model and an erstwhile compulsory homosexual, had thoroughly shattered Brendan's belief he knew anything about love. After three full months of practically living together—including traveling together to St. Barts for the most we-belong-together weekend ever experienced by two sexually attracted, socially, intellectually, politically and morally compatible people in the universe—the fantasy had dissolved to black and been unveiled as a waking terror when Brendan returned to his apartment one afternoon and walked in on Thiago and a fortysomething, obscenely nippled fashion publicist in the shower. Thiago's only words— "You can join us if you want."

Brendan was on a detox from the gays (and those who styled themselves as "gay-adjacent") for at least thirty days. His hookup and dating media had been deactivated. His libido had been psychically stowed up in bubble wrap and locked away in storage. No flirting with the coffee shop barista when he purchased his daily macchiato. Eyes on his own business in the locker room at the tennis and racquet club. No "what-if" conversations with himself about a new guy in the neighborhood who kept the same schedule for picking up his groceries. Brendan was entirely committed to an asexual lifestyle, drawing on the same well of discipline that had seen him through his presummer purge of sugar, bread, and alcohol.

That was until he opened the tinkling bell door of The Golden Fleece Antiques and Curio Shop on Lexington Avenue, and a young man at the cashier's desk looked up at him with the buoyancy of a hand-raised golden retriever.

"Hi!" the clerk said.

He had a preternaturally handsome face of Mediterranean origins and the vigorous, cherubic hair of a Mormon missionary. He wore a teal, graphic T-shirt, which augmented the stunning aquamarine color of his eyes. The T-shirt rode up his upper arms, which were well defined like an Olympic diver or a god of Mount Olympus for that matter. The shirt was emblazoned with a triple-scoop ice cream cone and a question: "Want a lick?"

Brendan's mouth hung open. He couldn't produce a word or even budge. Helpfully, the shop clerk didn't act like he was a mentally impaired patient run free of his caretakers.

"Sorry to startle you. I guess I overdid it with the welcome. I haven't had a customer all morning. Take a look around and don't mind me. Or go ahead and mind me if you need any help."

Brendan smiled, nodded, and took a stumbling step toward the nearest display of bric-a-brac.

The shop felt like a cage in which he'd been ensnared. Brendan tried to fix his attention on the chintz teacup sets and art deco tumblers, but his awareness of the clerk was too much. Was he supposed to pretend he wasn't sharing the same space with the most deathly adorable creature he had ever seen in his entire life? Brendan's heartbeat accelerated to the range of near cardiac arrest, and he was reasonably sure he was sweating through the armpits of his burgundy gingham shirt.

He drifted discreetly behind a shelf of African fetishes to consider his options. He could make a sprint for the door and fast-track down the street, never to step within ten blocks of the shop, praying to never run into the clerk again. The alternative was to have to face that otherworldly, beautiful man as a garbling, awestruck lunatic.

Brendan clamped down on his panic. He was twenty-eight years old, far removed from his scarring teenage years at boarding school, charting out routes through campus to avoid running into his torturous crush—Jacob Chandler, captain of the lacrosse team, who used to punch his shoulder and call him "Brendawg," which sent him into withering, red-faced fits of aphasia. Brendan now held his own with men. He had no reason to feel inferior. He kept his body in shape. He wasn't too modest to acknowledge his WASPy good looks claimed attention at times. *Gotham Magazine* had named him the most eligible gay bachelor of 2018.

For all he knew, the clerk was one of those oblivious heterosexual types who didn't notice when other men took an interest in them. It made no difference anyway. Brendan had sworn off sex and dating. Even if the clerk was amused or offended by his shrinking, girlish behavior, they were nothing but passing strangers.

A reasonable plan came together. Brendan would grab the first thing in reach, pay for it at the counter, and exit the store with the dignity of having conducted himself like a normal customer.

"Looking for anything in particular?"

Brendan seized up like a jailbird caught in searchlights. That friendly, innocent voice. A hint of a lazy, Upstate accent? A cool wash of awareness passed over Brendan. Was he really plotting schemes to rush out on a stranger whose shop he'd entered quite willfully? Brendan came around the shelf, holding it together for the moment.

"My grandmother's birthday," he said. "She collects cameos. I've been buying them for her since I was a kid." Brendan tried something breezy. "I saw the name of your store and thought I might be in luck."

The clerk set down a leather-bound book he'd been reading. "We're Greek, but we don't have any cameos *that* old. I mean, the store's Greek. My uncle owns it. My great-uncle actually. I'm only half Greek. The other side's Polish and German. But we do have some Victorian cameos in the cabinet." He stood up from his chair and waved Brendan over to a glass-enclosed jewelry case.

Ornamental pins and pendants swam in Brendan's vision. His gaze bobbed stubbornly up to the clerk on the other side of the cabinet. He was as adorable as a puppy. Barely out of college, Brendan guessed. Was he a cuddly puppy in bed? Christ. Brendan's imagination had burst free from its hinges, and he couldn't stop himself from stealing glances at the clerk. His pectorals filling out his T-shirt. The golden hairs on his anatomically perfect forearms. The flecks of sun on his long, broad nose. His supple, berry-brown lips. "Want a lick?" Yes, please. At the crook of the clerk's neck, and his armpit, and his nipples, and every blessed place between his legs. A smoldering image blew up in Brendan's mind's eye. The clerk's mouth opening wide to swathe his tongue around a triple-scoop ice cream cone.

"I'll show you what we've got."

Brendan buried his gaze in the floor while the clerk unlocked the cabinet. A blush seared his face. He felt like a pervert and never more happily so.

The clerk brought out a double cameo silver hair comb and two cameo brooches and set them neatly on the glass counter. Brendan awakened to the world of the antique shop. Grandmum's birthday. *Focus Brendan.* He looked over the jewelry. A gold-framed brooch with a cherub carved on its oval plaque caught his eye. His grandmother had an extensive collection of ladies' silhouettes. The cherub was special.

"I like that one too," the clerk said, looking from the brooch to Brendan with a grin.

"It's gorgeous," Brendan said.

"Is your grandmother romantic?"

Brendan smirked. "I suppose. She's been married three times."

"It's Eros. The god of love. That's why I asked."

Was there a defensive tone in the clerk's voice? Had Brendan been too brusque? The thought of hurting his feelings shamed him. "It's really exceptional," he said.

"She's lucky to have a grandson like you."

Brendan shifted this way and that like a bashful boy.

"I mean, a lot of people, when their grandparents get old, they hardly pay any attention to them at all." The clerk said it like he was sharing shocking news from an investigative report. So sweet and unpretentious. Brendan's insides turned to goo.

He came back together. "Oh. My grandmother and I are very close. She practically raised me. I'm closer to her than my mother and father."

Their glances met for a breath and then darted away.

"You know, you're a really sweet guy," the clerk said.

Brendan ventured a glance at him. "You barely know me."

"I think you are. I mean, how many guys take off from work in the middle of the day to buy birthday presents for their grandmother?" The clerk tucked his hands into the pockets of his jeans and rocked back on his heels. His face darkened, and he looked askance with a self-reproachful snigger. "I shouldn't have said that. Probably made you uncomfortable. Never mind me. I'm always going on too much, talking to the customers."

Brendan shook his head. "I don't mind at all."

"So what'll it be? Is that the one?" he asked, giving Brendan a playful shrug of his blond eyebrows.

"Definitely."

The clerk grinned. "I'll get it wrapped up for you."

Brendan followed him to the cashier counter, where he brought out tissue paper and cellophane tape. With the impending termination of their transaction, a sorrowful ache worked through Brendan. His glance pivoted around. It was only lust. In which he was not permitted to indulge. But what if the clerk was "the one" he was meant to be with? What if fate had conspired to introduce him to his soul mate while he'd marked off a blackout period in his dating life? He had to take these things into consideration.

He noticed the leather-bound journal on the counter. *Lettres de Jean-Arthur Rimbaud.* The clerk was reading love poems by the most notorious, iconic homosexual who had ever lived? This was encouraging.

"You like Rimbaud?" Brendan asked.

The clerk looked up from his wrapping. "Yeah. I thought I'd try to read his work in the original French this summer."

"I minored in French literature," Brendan blurted out.

This earned him a smile of gleaming, white teeth. "I was a classical studies major."

"I minored in that too." Brendan tried to explain without sounding pretentious or mentally unbalanced. "I was an English major, but I couldn't really decide what I wanted to do. I ended up triple minoring in French lit, classical studies, and art history. With a certificate in dramaturgy."

"That's amazing. What do you do now?"

"Um, my family has a business. It's not anything related to my degree."

"What kind of business?"

This was always the hard part to broach with new acquaintances. Brendan usually made up something about the freight industry, which was reliably dull enough to scare away follow-up questions. It was terribly awkward to introduce himself as a trust-fund brat with a token job in his family's multibillion-dollar, international shipping company. But Brendan felt horrible about lying to him.

"Have you heard of Thackeray Worldwide Enterprises?"

"No. What's that?"

"It's a company my great-great-grandfather founded. We ship things around the world."

"Wow. That's great. I mean, you must get to travel to a lot of interesting places."

Brendan's glance slid away. "Um, sometimes."

The clerk laughed nervously. "I'm sorry. That was a really boneheaded thing to say. I don't imagine you go traveling around the world with the packages."

Brendan snorted mildly. "It's not such a glamorous business. Nothing most people have any interest in knowing about."

"Hey, my name's Cal." The clerk reached out his hand. "That's short for Callisthenes. From the Greek side of the family. I guess that's pretty obvs."

Brendan shook his hand, firmly like a regular guy. "I'm Brendan." The warm contact of their hands had his knees weakening. He couldn't think of what to say next. He couldn't even disentangle himself from the handshake.

"Nice to meet you, Brendan."

"Nice to meet you too." Brendan released the poor guy's hand. Damn, was he far gone. Forgetting how to do a normal handshake? He truly had regressed to adolescence. He'd happily stand there all day just to bask in Cal's aura. What was he to do when he finished paying? Brendan had to come up with something so he could see Cal again.

Cal finished taping the gift and brought out a shopping bag from beneath the counter. "Almost done here." He added with a touch of self-recrimination, "Probably would have helped if I'd told you the price first."

Brendan took out his leather wallet from the pocket of his chinos. "How much is it?"

"That one's three-hundred fifty."

Brendan scrounged out his credit card and handed it to him. "I see why you're called the Golden Fleece."

"Let the buyer beware," Cal said with a smirk.

They smiled at each other while Cal held Brendan's credit card. The last grains of sand were slipping through the hourglass. Brendan hoisted up some courage.

"Would you like to get together sometime?"

Cal grinned big. "What did you have in mind?"

Brendan shifted his weight. "I don't know. This might be a stab in the dark, but I'm thinking you like ice cream."

"I do." Cal glanced down at his shirt. "That's, like, uncanny you'd say that."

"Have you been to Frozen Zachary's?"

"No."

Brendan mugged woefully. "It's only the best ice cream in Manhattan. If not the world. Right in the neighborhood here. Third Avenue and Seventy-Ninth."

"I just moved to the city two weeks ago," Cal said. "I'm still finding my way around." He swiped Brendan's credit card, and a receipt churned out from the machine.

"Where are you from originally?"

"Upstate," Cal said. "Have you heard of Syracuse?"

Brendan nodded. "Sure."

Cal handed him the receipt and a pen. "I'm just here for the summer, watching the shop while my uncle is visiting family in Greece."

Brendan quickly signed the receipt. "Then you have to let me take you to Frozen Zachary's. It's a once-in-a-lifetime New York experience."

"Once in a lifetime, huh? Then I guess I'd be crazy to refuse."

Brendan lit up like a high-voltage light bulb. He had a date with the hottest and nicest guy in the world. They tapped each other's numbers into their cell phones and made plans to meet at the ice cream parlor the following night.

Chapter Two

LATER THAT EVENING, Callisthenes Panagopoulos met his roommate and best friend, Derek Foster, for a free, outdoor screening of the Mae West film *I'm No Angel*. The Bryant Park film festival of Hollywood classics was one item on a long list of things Cal had researched for them to do that summer. They only had twelve weeks in New York City, and Cal was determined to get as much out of the experience as possible. Derek had a seasonal job at a booth for discount theater tickets while Cal tended his uncle's antiques shop. Their paychecks had to go almost entirely to the rent of their one-bedroom, sublet apartment, but Cal had found a treasure trove of free entertainment in the city.

The small urban park was overfilled with picnicking families and couples. Cal scanned through the crowd and spotted a spare spot centrally located for viewing. It looked like a tight fit, but when he led Derek across the lawn to claim it, some very nice ladies with shellacked helmets of hair and Broadway T-shirts looked up at Cal and quickly shrugged back their blanket to make space. A pair of older gentlemen stared at him dreamily and scooted back in their lawn chairs so Cal would have some room in their direction as well.

Cal unrolled a tatami mat from his college backpack, and he and Derek seated themselves hip to hip. Cal unpacked two fried egg sandwiches and a sixteen-ounce can of Budweiser, which he portioned into paper coffee cups liberated from a nearby deli. They chomped on their sandwiches as the opening credits blared from the giant screen.

Mae West had always been a campy curiosity to Cal, but he found his attention drifting away from the film. Was the guy he met in the store earlier that day for real? It felt like it had been a dream. He wasn't supposed to be fishing for dates while he was working, but he hadn't been able to stop himself. Brendan was gorgeous and smart and really sweet and considerate, and he knew about Arthur Rimbaud, and he'd minored in classical studies. He was a native New Yorker, which made him something like five thousand times more interesting and worldly than anyone Cal had met before. And like a total airhead, Cal had asked him if he did a lot of traveling, working in the shipping business, as if he freighted the goods across the Atlantic himself. Brendan probably had some high-powered executive job. Cal winced, thinking about how dumb he'd acted.

Meanwhile, his companion was having a hard time paying attention to the movie for different reasons.

"I know we're homosexuals, but do we have to live out every gay cliché known to man this summer?" Derek said quietly.

Cal whispered back, "What do you mean?"

"Last night, it was the Jackie Onassis Hat and Apparel exhibit at the Fashion Institute of Technology. The day before was the Breakfast at Tiffany's walking tour of Greenwich Village. Tonight, it's Mae West?"

"You said you liked the walking tour."

"I did. But I'm beginning to feel like I'm turning into Truman Capote."

Cal guffawed. Derek looked nothing like Truman Capote. He was a slight guy with jet-black hair who looked like he worked at a tech company and skateboarded to work. Cal trapped his mouth with his hand, hoping his laughter hadn't annoyed anyone nearby. The Midwestern housewives were timidly watching him like they'd spotted a celebrity. One of the older gentlemen leaned forward and asked Cal if he'd like one of his chocolate-dipped strawberries. Cal thanked him and declined. He gathered that side conversations at a reasonable volume were acceptable during the outdoor film.

"I'm glad you mentioned Truman Capote," he told Derek. "It reminds me—Columbia has a free lecture this Friday on the art of writing the nonfiction crime novel."

Derek gave Cal a lopsided grin. "You really can't stop yourself, can you?"

"We have seventy-one days left until the end of the summer," Cal said. "We're budgeted at forty dollars a day, max, and that includes meals. I want to get in as much as possible." At the end of the summer, Cal would be starting a master's degree program in classical studies. Derek would go back to his odd jobs as a math tutor and working at the health insurance call center.

Derek's shoulder leaned against his. "Don't forget— I want to go to the beach."

Cal grinned. He and Derek had been best friends since freshman year in college. In fact, Derek had been his only male friend for the past five years. With other guys, complications had always cropped up. They acted like they wanted to be friends, and then it turned out they wanted to jump Cal's bones, which wasn't bad in and of itself, with the right guy, or even the semi-right guy if Cal was in the mood. But it seemed like the only thing guys ever wanted was sex, and Cal had a knack for attracting the most intense and possessive types. That was why Derek was so great. They could hang out all the time and do regular things without any sexual tension and drama.

"There's a beach on Coney Island," he told Derek. "You can walk to it right from the subway. I looked it up. The subway fare's only two seventy-five. The first sunny day both of us are off from work, we'll go."

Derek grinned and leaned into Cal some more. "Hey, what about going down to Little Italy tomorrow night?"

"Oh. I can't."

Derek gave him a double take. He was aware Cal closed up his grandfather's shop by seven o'clock at the latest. They'd never made plans without the other. Neither of them even knew anyone else in New York. "You can't?"

"I met someone." Cal's face bloomed. "We kind of have a date. Or, I think we have a date. Or, it could just be getting together as friends."

"When did you meet someone?"

"This morning. At the store."

"A customer?"

"Yeah." It felt like sunshine was spreading over Cal. "His name is Brendan Thackeray-Prentiss."

"Jesus. Did his family come over with the first gay pilgrims?"

Cal giggled. He evened out his enthusiasm. "He's probably too perfect to be real. And it's only going out for ice cream. I think he was just being friendly."

Derek shot him a crooked glance.

"What's that for?"

"Cal, you can be so oblivious when it comes to guys."

"I don't think I'm oblivious," Cal objected. "It's not a hookup. I didn't get that impression at all. You think after everything that happened with Steve, I'd be giving out my phone number to random strangers?" He sat up straight, self-righteous. "I've actually been super conscious about not giving off any sexual vibes."

Another crooked glance came back at him. "You've been super conscious about not giving off sexual vibes," Derek repeated flatly. "Wearing a T-shirt that says 'Want a lick?'"

"It's ironic," Cal said. "The whole T-shirt is meant to be ironic."

"There's nothing ironic about you, Cal. That's the problem." Derek dug his cell phone out and started tapping on the screen. His face twisted up skeptically in the blue light of the phone, and he turned the display screen to Cal. "That him?"

Brendan's strong-jawed, handsome face sparkled in Cal's vision. Cal took the phone so he could admire the photo more closely. Brendan was wearing a tuxedo for some society event. His wavy, dark brown hair was shorter and perfectly groomed. He stood in a ballroom filled with people who looked like they owned islands in the Caribbean. A modern-day prince.

"How did you find him so quickly?"

Derek took back his phone. "Brendan Thackeray-Prentiss is not exactly a common name." He swiped and tapped at the screen. "And there's, like, a zillion articles about him." Derek read from one of them. "*New York Magazine*— Heir to Thackeray shipping magnate hosts fundraising gala for LGBTQ homeless teens."

"Really? That's so sweet." Cal reached for the phone. Derek held him back as if Cal were a toddler trying to grab his lollipop.

"Stalk him on your own time," Derek said.

Cal took his arm and nuzzled up close. "But I want to stalk him with you."

"Don't come purring up to me," Derek scolded him mildly. "I turn my back for a half second, and you've got guys luring you into ice cream parlors to get down your pants."

"Brendan's not like that. He buys Victorian cameos for his grandmother. And he was really shy about his family being wealthy. It was cute." Cal brushed his hand through his thick, wavy blond hair. "I don't know. I've got this really great feeling about him."

Derek took a long, stiff draw of his beer. "That's great. So what's going to happen? You two are going to run off and make genetically gifted babies, and I'm stuck hanging out in New York all summer by myself."

"No," Cal said. He squeezed Derek's arm. "I'd never do that to you."

"It's cool, Cal. I mean, it's not like I can expect a guy like you to stay single for the rest of his life. You walk down the street, and people are falling over each other to try to inhale the air you breathe."

Cal gazed at Derek steadily. "That only happened once." A smile crept up his face, which earned a mild chuckle from his friend. Cal nudged Derek on the shoulder. "We came down here to experience New York together. I'm not going to renege on that. Brendan and I have known each other for, like, five seconds. It's nothing serious. You want me to text him and cancel for tomorrow?"

"Yes."

Cal's heart sank in his chest, but he rummaged in his pocket for his phone.

Derek caught him by the arm. "No. I was kidding."

"Are you sure?"

"I'm not going to be a total dick," Derek said. "Hey, maybe I'll do you one better and meet some billionaire to take me out for an actual dinner."

"Thanks, Derek. Have I told you lately you're the best friend in the world?"

"No, you haven't."

Cal kissed him on the cheek. "You're the best friend in the world."

"You still owe me the beach, you frickin' ho."

They scowled at each other, and then they tucked in to watch the rest of the black-and-white movie on the giant movie screen.

Chapter Three

AFTER STROLLING AROUND the block three times, Brendan arrived at Frozen Zachary's thirty-one minutes in advance of his date with Cal. That was not cool, and starkly not letting-things-happen-at-the-universe's-own-pace as Dr. Clotilde Trapp had advised. In his typical fashion, Brendan had overbudgeted on time and underbudgeted on sanity. His neurotic fugue had begun when he left the antiques shop thirty-two hours earlier.

After a pleading phone call, Dr. Trapp had agreed to squeeze him in for a second appointment that week. Brendan needed to process his chance meeting with Cal and obtain a professional green light to try dating again. During the session, he traversed the emotional landscape from manic exuberance to sobbing despair. This, Clotilde Trapp pronounced as "promising," and she'd ushered him out the door to face the world beyond her office's Danish modern furnishings.

Forty-five minutes of free weights, two maximum-resistance courses on his elliptical machine, two Klonopins, and a tumbler of scotch later, Brendan was flipping through channels on his sixty-five inch, flat-screen smart TV. He became fascinated by a series marathon of the Hallmark Channel's turn-of-the-century period romance, *When Calls the Heart*. Curled up in his bed, staring at the screen while shucking edamame, the only thing his nervous stomach was able to hold down, he finally passed out in his workout gear while the TV blared.

He woke up in a panic at ten o'clock the next morning when *The Golden Girls* had overtaken his TV. His date with Cal was to take place at eight o'clock that night. He had to pick up his laundry. He had to balance his chakras with his daily yoga workout and meditations. He had to brush up on Rimbaud and ancient Athenian history and Greek tragedians in case those topics came up in conversation. Not to mention, he had to shower, shave, groom, and pick out an outfit.

All of this, Brendan accomplished by five minutes past noon.

Trying to distract himself with a bit of routine, Brendan took lunch with his grandmother at the Sutton Place townhouse and later coaxed his best friend and squash partner, Louis Jeffries, to skip out of work early for a quick match at the tennis and racquet club. Brendan's play was aggressive and unreliable, and after losing the first ten points in the game, he broke down in a regrettably maudlin scene wherein he confessed to Louis if things didn't work out with Cal, he wasn't sure his life was worth living.

Louis then shouldered him to the lounge, deposited him into a Chesterfield chair and called out to the bartender with a tone of urgency for two very dry martinis. When the drinks arrived, Brendan managed to swallow one sip before looking at his watch and taking flight like the White Rabbit in *Alice in Wonderland*. He arrived back at his apartment at five-thirty.

Then, after taking a thirty-minute shower, moisturizing from head to toe, reexamining his nostrils for wayward nose hairs, hiking up a brand new pair of gleaming white briefs, flossing and brushing his teeth, lacquering his armpits with deodorant, stepping into distressed designer jeans, buttoning up a tailored, peach, micropaisley Oxford, pulling on black cotton socks over his cold and sweaty feet, and stepping into his favorite pair of horsebit loafers, Brendan paced the apartment.

He still had an hour and a half to spare.

Obsessive worries bore down on him. The elevators in his building might be out of service. They had been, just eighteen months ago. He had to budget time in the event he would have to take the seventeen flights of stairs down from his apartment.

Had he heard something on the news about a section of Third Avenue being closed for gas line repairs? Circumventing the construction area could cost him who knew how much time? His building was only ten blocks from his rendezvous with Cal, but Brendan ventured out of his apartment at seven fifteen, leaving nothing to chance. With his mental state as fragile as a Tiffany ornament, he envisioned a thousand obstacles. If he arrived late, he would hurt Cal's feelings. Cal would come to the conclusion Brendan was not serious about wanting to get to know him. He might give up on waiting for him and decide he never wanted to see Brendan again.

Now, Brendan stood in front of the glass-paned ice cream shop. He was bitten by a new swarm of worries. People were queued out the door. The prospect of claiming a table in the tiny shop was beyond discouraging, and how would they make conversation while standing around with their ice cream cones dripping down their hands? Going out for ice cream had been a horrible idea. Brendan was apt to be a total klutz. He might lose hold of his cone and drop it all over himself. He might drop it all over Cal.

It was now 7:35 p.m.

Brendan rechecked his text messages to make sure he'd given Cal the right address. He should have provided a link to a Google map in case Cal had trouble finding the place. Cal had said he was new to the city. He could easily get lost. But if Brendan sent the link now, Cal might think he was an impatient worrywart, which Brendan undeniably was, but no one liked an impatient worrywart. Wandering behind a curbside tree, he discreetly tried to sniff his armpits and breath. He popped another breath mint and cracked it with his molars, sparking a shooting pain into a filling that had him clasping his jaw.

That agonizing gaffe made for a time-killing distraction. But as the throbbing pain wore off, minutes ticked by, and anxiety returned to him in the proportions of vertigo. Approached by passersby, Brendan practically jumped out of the way. This had all been a very bad idea. He was too emotionally brittle. Cal was an eleven, and he was—on his very best days, with the right photo filter—an eight. It was too soon after he'd been psychically mauled by Thiago. What if he couldn't hold it together? He envisioned throwing himself at Cal's feet, begging Cal to love him.

Brendan texted Dr. Trapp an urgent message, confessing all of these things as lucidly as thumb-typing would allow.

A short reply dinged back: *Leave it to Jesus.*

He stared at his therapist's text bubble. What did that mean?!

"Brendan!"

Brendan startled at the voice, and his cell phone flew out of his hand and into the tree's little square iron-fenced plot, which was filled with pink spotted impatiens. He dropped to his knees to scrounge it out, and a pair of tan suede sneakers appeared in his peripheral vision on the sidewalk beside him. He slowly gazed northward of those sneakers past a pair of perfectly formed, blond-hair dusted ankles, farther up to cuffed denim joggers, all the way to the entirety of the heaven-spawned young man that was Callisthenes Panagopoulos.

Cal stooped down to help Brendan retrieve his phone. "I'm so sorry," he said. "I saw you, and I got excited. You must think I'm the biggest dork. Same thing I did to you yesterday at the store." Cal rooted the iPhone out from the flower bed and examined it. A grin spread across his face. "Hey look—not even a scratch! You got lucky."

Brendan grinned back. Somehow, the awestruck jitters that had nearly paralyzed him when they first met sublimated into the twilight. Which was not to say he wasn't happy to see Cal. Cal looked even more handsome dressed up for a date in a tropical pattern button-down, with his wavy hair still damp and fragrant from the shower. Brendan took the phone from him. "Thanks."

They stood, Brendan a few inches taller at six-foot-one, Cal practically vibrating with his infectious energy.

"Wow. You really look great," Cal said.

"You look great too."

"You didn't seem like the kind of guy who dresses down a lot. But I figured, it's an ice cream parlor. Can't get too dressed up for that."

"I love your shirt."

"I love yours." Cal looked to the store. "Guess you're right about this place. What a line!"

"It moves pretty fast. C'mon." Brendan led him to the queue, and they stood side by side, like boyfriends going out for ice cream. There must have been a glow of happiness radiating from both of them. Two teenage girls passed by, and they made "aw" faces.

"How was your day? How was work?" Cal asked.

Brendan hesitated. "I think you should know. I don't really work much."

"Oh."

"I mean, my grandfather runs the company. Along with a lot of other people. Some of my older cousins are involved. I'm kind of...superfluous."

"Does your father work there as well?"

"No," Brendan said. "The company belongs to my mom's dad. My mom does some work with the company's charity organization."

"That must be where you get your interest in charities," Cal said.

Brendan's brow pinched up. He had no idea what Cal was talking about.

Cal blushed. "I guess I have to fess up. I cyberstalked you. Only a little. Really, it was my best friend, Derek. He's kinda protective of me."

"Is he?" Brendan said, easing into a playful grin. "So what did you and Derek find out about me?"

"I didn't snoop too much," Cal said. "I swear. Stop looking at me that way." He turned his head to hide from Brendan for a moment. "I'm terrible with the Internet. I'm not even on Facebook anymore. You can ask Derek."

Cal's embarrassment was adorable. But Brendan didn't want to let him off the hook just yet. He put on a deadpan face. "I think you better tell me what you found out."

Cal drew a breath. "Honest to god, it was just one article. About you raising money for homeless kids. Homeless gay kids." His bright aquamarine eyes snuck back to Brendan. "I thought that was really amazing."

Now Brendan hid his face. Cal's shoulder brushed against his, sparking shy warmth through Brendan's body.

Cal was an irrepressible flirt. It already felt like the best date Brendan had ever had in his entire life.

When they made it up to the counter, Brendan ordered cones for both of them—a triple-scoop pistachio for Cal and a triple-scoop peppermint stick for himself. Cal dug out some cash to pay, but Brendan waved him off. It had been his invitation. And it was just ice cream. Even so, he felt proud to buy something for Cal.

While Brendan was dealing with the cashier, Cal scored the two-seat table right by the window. How was that possible? The shop was wall-to-wall people. Brendan walked over with his cone and a wad of napkins from the dispenser.

"You're a keeper," he told Cal.

"The people saw me looking for a table, and they said I could have it. New Yorkers are really nice. The rest of the country's got it all wrong about you." Cal took a soft nibble from the top of his cone, and Brendan waited out his reaction. "I think you're right," he said. "This is the best ice cream in the world."

Brendan grinned. He took some bites and licks from his cone. After twenty-four hours of not having an appetite, it had returned with a vengeance.

"So you told me about your mom," Cal said. "What about your dad?"

An "mmm" sound came out while Brendan swallowed down a mouthful of ice cream.

"I know. I'm a nosy pest," Cal said. "You don't have to tell me about your family if you don't want to. But you've got to talk some so I get a chance to eat."

Brendan wiped his mouth with a napkin. "My parents split up when I was five. My dad moved to Los Angeles after the divorce. He's the kind of person who changes his mind about what he wants to do with his life every other day.

Anyway, back then my dad had this idea he was going to be an actor. He got a couple of roles in TV shows and films, but it never really took off for him."

"Has he been in anything I'd know?"

"He had a bit part in an episode of *Chicago Hope*, and he was on screen for about two seconds in *Fight Club*. He usually got roles like Cop Number Three, who gets shot in a big action scene. But he hasn't acted in a long time. He started a documentary film company a few years back, and he keeps busy with that."

"What about you? Did you ever want to be an actor?"

Brendan smirked at the thought. "Not really."

Cal lowered his cone and looked at Brendan very seriously. "If you could be anything in the world, what would it be?"

Brendan hedged.

"You can't think about it. Just the first thing that pops into your head."

That wasn't the kind of thing Brendan was good at. It was much more in his comfort zone to analyze a big, personal question into a slow, meaningless death. Though talking to Cal was easy. He felt like he could be honest about himself.

"I don't know," he said. "I'm interested in a lot of things, but I guess the most important thing for me is finding someone to settle down with."

Cal lapped at his cone. "Would you be a househusband?"

Brendan snickered. "Yeah, I guess. I mean, I'd like to do something. Something more meaningful than brokering deals with clients to ship industrial equipment around the world. Something that makes a difference, y'know? I haven't figured it out yet. What about you? What do you want to do?"

"Mmm." Cal swallowed some ice cream. "Well, classical studies is pretty limited. Especially on the archeology side. My capstone project was on Apollonian sculpture from the sixth century BC. After I get my master's, I suppose I could teach. Do research."

"I thought the idea was to say the first thing that pops into your head," Brendan corrected him mildly. "What would you do? Be a superhero? Start a franchise of your uncle's antiques shops? Open an ice cream parlor?" He slid up in his swivel chair so that his knees touched Cal's.

"I guess I'm not playing by my own rules," Cal said. "To tell the truth, I have absolutely, pathetically no idea what I want to do with my life."

Brendan's eyes soldered on his. "I don't think that matters. I like you a whole lot the way you are."

"I'm twenty-four years old," Cal complained. "Don't you think I should have some clue about what I want to be when I grow up?"

"I'm twenty-eight, and I have no idea," Brendan said. "I can be your role model."

Cal crunched down on his sugar cone and inhabited a thoughtful phase. "I like kids. Sometimes, I think I might be good working in the education department at a museum."

"Kids would fall in love with you."

"You think so?"

"Absolutely." The inside of their knees leaned against each other. Brendan reached his hand across the table and touched Cal's elbow lightly. "Thanks for coming out with me."

Cal grinned. "You were awfully shy. I thought I might have to slip my phone number into your shopping bag."

"Do you do that with customers a lot?"

Cal gave him a wizened glare. "No. I never hit on customers. I haven't met anyone I wanted to date in a long time. Before I met you, I actually was planning on swearing off dating for a while."

"Why?"

Cal finished his cone and wiped his mouth. "Ex-boyfriend drama. I've been trying to figure out why I always attract the wrong kind of guys."

That puzzled Brendan. What kind of guy was not attracted to Cal? In the ice cream shop alone, glances kept darting at Cal from people of all ages and all genders. Brendan had been with good-looking guys before, even models, but Cal was in an entirely different category—like an angel fallen from the sky. And Cal was his that night. At a nearby table, a prim, Upper East Side middle schooler was staring at Cal with his mouth hanging open. Brendan gave the boy a knowing look with an unspoken message.

That's right, kid. Being gay can be good.

He munched down the rest of his cone.

"It's so easy talking to you," Cal said. "Like we've known each other for years."

"I feel the same way."

"I should tell you, my friend Derek...he wasn't so crazy about me going out with you. It was my idea for us to come down to New York for the summer, and we said we'd do everything together."

"Should I be jealous?"

Cal shook his head. "We're just friends. He's been my best friend for, like, forever. 'Sexless boyfriends,' he calls it. We're housemates in Syracuse, and we got this tiny sublet for the summer in the East Village. Derek's really amazing. He's the only gay guy I know who can have a platonic relationship without any weirdness. I feel kind of caught in the middle. I wanted to go out with you like mad when you asked me, but I felt rotten when I told him."

"Maybe I should meet him," Brendan said. "Then we could all be friends." He moved his hand along Cal's forearm, smoothing down the sun-whitened hairs, picking gently through his braided bracelets, which suited his earthy personality. Brendan settled his hand lightly on Cal's wrist.

"That's a great idea. Derek's dying to go to the beach," Cal said. "The three of us could make a day of it. Have you ever been to Coney Island?"

"Never."

"I think you'll really like Derek. He's really funny, and he's brilliant in math. He ought to get a PhD, but for now, he tutors high school students."

Brendan turned Cal's hand over to roll his thumb over his palm. Every part of his companion was a wonderland. He told Cal absently, "He sounds like a great guy."

Gradually, he became aware of their surroundings. People were still queuing into the shop. Folks were standing with their ice cream, glancing hopefully around the seating area for a place to park themselves.

"You want to take a walk?" he asked. "I can show you the promenade by the East River. It's a great view. You can see the bridges and Roosevelt Island."

Cal's face lit up. "Sure."

THEY HEADED CROSSTOWN and walked under the whirring FDR Parkway, emerging to the breezy waterside and the rippling void of the East River. An asphalt path for pedestrians and bikers edged along the bank of Manhattan and its jutting cliffs of high-rises. Across the water, the peculiar urban enclave of Roosevelt Island was a towering palisade of brick and steel. Cal wandered to the guardrail of the walkway, pivoting around to take in everything.

Brendan felt like a little kid again, watching him. Everything about New York City was still a wonder to Cal. Imagining the city through his eyes made it wondrous again. The leviathan island of skyscrapers. At night, it wasn't exactly peaceful, but it was definitely majestic with its colossal vistas and infinite panorama of sparkling lights. He drew up beside Cal and rested his hand on the small of his companion's back.

"You're so lucky to live here. To be able to see this anytime you want," Cal said.

"I guess I've gotten used to it. I hardly notice how beautiful it is most of the time."

"What's that?"

He followed the trajectory of Cal's outthrust arm, his pointed finger. "It's the sky tram to Roosevelt Island. Did you see the first Spider-Man movie with Tobey Maguire? That's where Kirsten Dunst gets stuck when she's attacked by the Green Goblin."

"Wow. I'd like to go up on that."

"Our second date?" Brendan suggested.

Cal turned to him, and his mouth enveloped Brendan's. Fireworks dazzled behind Brendan's eyes, and the world may as well have peeled away, leaving him in some dream realm where nothing bad could touch him. Nothing bad was even possible. The kiss broke off gently, and Brendan remained shuttered from the world, head spinning. When he opened his eyes, Cal's face was downcast.

"Was that too soon?" Cal asked. "I have a problem with impulse control." He stole a glance at Brendan. "But I guess I did pretty okay, considering I've been wanting to do that ever since you walked into the store."

Brendan held Cal by his firm and narrow waist and pressed up close. "I wouldn't have minded. I've been a basket case wondering about you since we met." He nuzzled his nose against Cal's and kissed him softly on the cheek. Cal's hands found the sides of Brendan's shoulders.

"It's up to you to make sure this doesn't go too fast," Cal told him.

That made Brendan chuckle.

"I'm serious," Cal said. "I'll ruin it completely. You know how gay men are—jumping into bed before they get to know each other."

"I want to get to know you." Brendan brushed his nose against the side of Cal's head, breathing in his freshly washed hair, claiming an olfactory memory of him. "Where in heaven do guys like you come from?"

"Chariton, originally," Cal said. "It's a Podunk town near Ithaca. That's where I was born."

"Like Penelope in *The Odyssey*. I bet you've had even more suitors."

"We only lived there until I was ten," Cal said. "My dad got a job at an air conditioner factory in Syracuse, so we moved there. I never left. I even went to college in town. Syracuse University."

Brendan led him by the hand to the walkway so they could stroll a bit while talking. That kiss had gotten his motor running, and he needed to move around and catch some air to help him be a gentleman like Cal had asked him to be. They headed downtown, toward the sky tram Cal liked, and kept to the pedestrian side of the walk while late-night joggers and bikers whooshed past them.

"Do you have brothers and sisters?" he asked.

"Seven. Can you believe that? I'm the youngest."

This was curious territory for Brendan, who had practically grown up as an only child. His half sisters through his mother's remarriage were over a decade younger than him. "What's it like growing up in such a big family?"

"Crowded," Cal said. "In Chariton, we had one room for the five boys and one room for the three girls. The house in Syracuse had a basement and a finished garage that my dad subdivided. We thought that was paradise. We only had to bunk two to a room."

"Which one of your siblings do you like the most?"

"I like them all. I'm closest to my sister Genie. She's one year older than me. My oldest brother, Sandy, can be a jerk sometimes. He's the only one who had a problem when I told everyone I was gay." Cal glanced at Brendan. "What was your family like?"

"It was a nonissue. My family is kind of that way. No one complains, and no one asks questions. I never really came out to my grandfather, but he doesn't treat me any differently. I guess the real test will be when I bring a boyfriend home for Thanksgiving."

"I bet your grandmother would love that," Cal said.

Brendan exchanged the hand that was holding Cal's so he could reach around to hold him by the waist. "She would love you."

"Has she ever met a half Greek, quarter German, quarter Polish mutt who lives with five housemates so he can pay off his student loans?"

"She wouldn't care about that," Brendan said. "Does it bother you that my family has money?"

"I don't think so," Cal said. "Do a lot of guys come on to you because you do?"

"Sometimes. Probably not as often as most people think."

They were quiet for a while, and then Cal posed a question. "Does it bother you that my family doesn't have any money? I mean, we're poor. Besides my uncle who owns the shop, none of us has ever been out of debt. I used to think that was normal. Like everyone in the world had to decide each month which bills they would pay and which bills they could let lapse. We never went on vacations, except to Greece a few times to visit family. I knew I couldn't afford to spend this summer in New York, but I did it anyway. I figured it would work out somehow."

"That doesn't bother me." Brendan drew Cal from the walkway to an overlook where they could gaze out at the glassy river again. They stood at a railing, clasping each other's shoulders. Out on the water, a police dinghy clipped along the waterway beneath the giant girders of the Fifty-Ninth Street Bridge.

"I'm not going to be an asshole and say it's hard being rich," Brendan said. "But I don't meet people who I can be myself with very often. There's kind of everything and nothing expected of me at the same time. If that makes any sense. My grandmother always kept me grounded. She told me my only obligation in the world is to make it a better place. And that's not something you can only do with money. Everyone's contribution is important."

Cal stared at him. "That's beautiful."

Brendan admired the way Cal's wavy hair got tussled in the breeze. Desire overwhelmed him. He captured Cal's mouth with his. They turned to face each other, and they necked like teenagers until they were breathless.

"I'm not doing very well at taking things slowly," Brendan said.

Cal gathered his breath and grinned. "I haven't made out like that since high school."

"What was his name?"

"Victor Saltaformaggio. We lived on the same block, but we traveled in different circles. He was on the football team. I was secretary of Latin club. We did really popular things like make up Jeopardy questions in Latin to compete in tournaments with other schools. Anyway, Victor and I ended up walking home from school one day after the teams and clubs got out. Somehow we ended up in the old playground of our elementary school, and Victor dared me to kiss him behind the backboards."

Brendan combed his hand through the side of Cal's hair, imagining him as a younger, adorable nerd. "Victor was a lucky guy."

"Not so lucky actually," Cal said. "Victor was a total closet case. He even had a girlfriend named Brianne, and they were both seniors. I was just a sophomore."

"Scandalous. So what happened to poor Victor Saltaformaggio?"

"Brianne found out, and she told everyone at school. Victor couldn't handle it. He had some kind of mental breakdown, and he had to get his GED in New Jersey where he had relatives. He used to send me messages on Facebook. Creepy messages. With photos of his penis. I blocked him, but he kept using fakes names to find me. That's part of the reason I quit Facebook." Cal's attention drifted away. "Come to think of it, it's not such a romantic story. Probably freaks you out a bit, huh?"

"You destroyed the guy," Brendan teased. He clasped Cal by the ribs. "You're just too irresistible. How many other guys have you destroyed? Are you going to destroy me as well?"

Cal squirmed from his tickling touch. "That was like nine years ago. And it wasn't my fault."

Brendan held him gently. "You've already destroyed me, Callisthenes."

Cal brushed the hair from Brendan's forehead, gazed at him piercingly. "What do you want from me, Brendan Thackeray-Prentiss?"

He'd been doing so well holding himself together, but all of a sudden, Brendan's eyes clenched shut. His heart was hovering over a blade.

"I want to take you home," he said. "I want you to want that too. I want us to wake up in the morning without any second thoughts and knowing this is for real. And I know that's impossible. We only just met, and neither of us can know for sure. But I wouldn't hurt you, Cal. I wouldn't stalk you. Or send you inappropriate photos." His eyes burned, and a teardrop rivuleted down his cheek. "I'm not that kind of guy."

Cal's finger traced his teardrop. "You're going to make me cry too."

Brendan wiped his eyes with his sleeve. "I really know how to kill a moment, don't I?"

Cal pulled him close and laid his head on Brendan's shoulder. "Just this, Brendan; hold me tight. I feel like I'm falling. Is it normal to feel that way?"

Brendan shut his eyes while their bodies were crushed together. "I don't know. But it's good. As long as we don't both collapse."

Cal giggled. "That would be kind of funny. Someone would have to call the paramedics, and what would we tell them?"

Brendan nuzzled against his ear. "Callisthenes," he said. "I love saying your name."

"I love hearing you say it."

Brendan's heart grew so big and warm, he wasn't sure he could withstand it. He needed Cal that night, not just because his body was revved up like a Grand Prix motorcycle. Cal made him feel so happy, so special, like there really was something good and loveable inside of him, powerful enough to save the world. "Callisthenes, can I take you home?"

Cal hooked his hand and grinned. "You bet."

NO SOONER THAN the door to Brendan's apartment eased shut behind them, they pressed together, tore at shirt buttons and tugged at pants to free each other of their clothes. The cautionary refrain of Cal's still, small voice: "You'll kill this relationship if you move too fast," was drowned out in a crescendo of wonder and desire. He and Brendan belonged together. Cal felt it in his soul. What else did two people do when they discovered that kind of connection? It had to be validated. It had to be celebrated.

They kicked off their shoes and left their pants and shirts on the hallway floor. Cal followed Brendan into the apartment in a shuffling dance as they grasped at each other and fumbled for each other's mouths. The apartment was dark. It felt vast and smelled of polished wood, and Brendan himself, which was a scent that was hard for Cal to describe—something like lightly worn clothes and a citrus-crisp deodorant, and whatever pheromones Brendan gave off that reached into Cal's gut and yanked him like a magnet. Brendan's naked body was firm and defined, though he felt slighter in Cal's arms than expected, strangely fragile, maybe from working out too much and not eating enough.

Brendan cornered him against a wall, stooped to his knees, pulled Cal's boxer briefs down to his ankles, and devoured him between the legs. *Whoa-ho, that was nice,* though Cal exercised some restraint and guided his eager Romeo up to his feet. He had absolutely nothing against blowjobs, but their first time together called for something more special than a quickie in a dark hallway. If things worked out as Cal hoped they would, they had a lifetime of blowjobs ahead of them. He stepped out of his briefs and told Brendan, "Shouldn't you show me your bedroom first?"

Brendan took his hand and led him through the shadowy apartment, down carpeted hallways with framed artwork, past rooms in hollows of darkness. He was clearly too single-minded to give Cal the grand tour, and traipsing along in his birthday suit, Cal didn't mind. They arrived in a spacious room that smelled even stronger of Brendan. Brendan flipped a light switch by the door and stepped aside.

Cal's eyes nearly popped out of their sockets. The room was easily the size of his and Derek's entire apartment, and it was furnished like a five-star hotel suite, or at least the ones Cal had seen in movies. The bed was like a throne—king-size, with an enormous walnut headboard and carved posters. It was dressed with a big, fluffy down comforter. Cal smirked at Brendan, and then he lunged for the bed, crash-landing spread-eagled on his back.

Brendan skulked toward him with a playful, predatory grin. He pounced on top of Cal. Play wrestling gave way to kissing, with thighs sliding over each other, hands finding nipples, and the turgid parts between their legs grinding together.

Cal rolled over Brendan and snuck down his body to peel down his briefs and repay his favor in the hallway. That was luscious and inspired bigger ideas.

He rustled up on top of Brendan and straddled his hips. Shy anticipation flooded his body, making him dizzy and breathless. Cal could count on one hand the number of times he'd gone all the way with guys. He'd never been so bold as to do it on a first date.

Brendan searched his face. He was such a gentleman, confirming Cal's consent. Cal's throat was dry and tight, and his head was suddenly too heavy to lift to make eye contact. All he could do was joggle his head.

Brendan stretched a hand to the drawer of his bedside table and brought out a condom and a little bottle of lubricant. Cal took the lubricant to do his business, and he put the condom on Brendan's not so little soldier. His eyes burned when Brendan entered him, but as he gasped out and adjusted, the pain peeled away.

Grinning now, Cal opened his eyes. Brendan's facial expression was adorably gobsmacked, like a boy who'd never fathomed that his man part could do such a deliciously raunchy thing. Cal drank him in, and then they worked at it together, and Cal moaned, and Brendan groaned, and thank god he was a groaner because Cal cried and whimpered like a porn star during sex, which, really, was half the fun. Together, they made loving oaths, and dirty oaths, and high-pitched gasps of disbelief. When they both started stuttering, Cal directed Brendan's hand so they could come together, which they did in a babbling, bucking clamor.

This was fucking at its earnest and loving best.

Cal nestled on top of Brendan. He gripped his lover's sturdy thigh between his own while their chests heaved and their heartbeats pounded.

Brendan brushed his fingers brushed through Cal's hair. "Callisthenes, will you be my boyfriend?"

Cal kissed him on the chest. "Do you promise we can do that every night and day, whenever I want?"

Brendan propped himself up on an elbow and turned to Cal. "I've never had sex that good before. But that's not why I asked. I think I'm falling in love with you."

His face was grim and pained. Cal felt like an all-star asshole for being so flip. Though everything about the way he looked and the way he lived made him seem powerful and self-assured, Brendan was a gentle, vulnerable man. Cal wanted to tend and nurture him. He didn't fully understand how Brendan had been hurt before, but he wanted to show him the world could be beautiful.

He gazed into Brendan's slate-blue eyes. "You're stuck with me now. You couldn't get rid of me if you tried."

Brendan cradled Cal's head and crushed their lips together.

Chapter Four

CAL HAD TO leave in the morning to change clothes and open up his uncle's shop. After the night they'd shared, Brendan didn't want to let him go, but he perked up with a grin when his cell phone dinged with a text message no more than a minute after Cal was out the door. Cal was texting from the elevator to say he missed him.

They texted each other all morning. After taking a shower, Brendan sent an e-mail to his grandfather to say he wouldn't be making it into the office. Appearances were kept up about Brendan's place in the company. But they both knew unless there was an important client coming in who might need to be impressed by a boardroom full of well-bred Thackeray heirs, Brendan would spend the day surfing the Internet in his oversized and underutilized office. He texted Cal to offer to bring lunch to the shop, and he headed out to pick up felafel sandwiches from his favorite Lebanese restaurant.

He strode down Lexington Avenue with a take-out bag swinging from one hand, smiling at passersby and glancing at familiar storefronts, which shone anew in Disney-movie Technicolor. He was as fresh as a daisy even though they'd barely slept last night. Between rounds of making love in every delicious permutation they could improvise, they'd curled up at the head of his bed, talking into the early hours of the morning when exhaustion had finally claimed them. Brendan had shared his disastrous relationship with Thiago as well as his many unachieved ambitions. He told Cal about his big dream to start a foundation for homeless kids, which he hadn't confessed to anybody for fear he'd sound like every other limousine liberal who thought he knew better than anyone else how to solve the world's problems. Cal hadn't thought that. He told him it was a great idea, said there ought to be more people like Brendan, asked him when and how he was going to get started on it.

Brendan's heart had led him astray before, attaching too quickly to guys like Thiago, believing they'd had something that never existed. Still, he couldn't help feeling like the connection he had made with Cal was different, pure and true. He felt more like himself with Cal than with any guy he had met in his life.

At the shop, Cal waved him behind the counter, and they shared the single chair while Brendan unpacked their sandwiches. Tucked up close, they fed each other and swiped tahini sauce from the corners of each other's mouths. Brendan couldn't help kissing Cal's neck and lips and feeling the wondrous contours of his shoulders and his back, the tender, whiskered skin on the inside of his thighs. Thankfully, store customers were few and far between.

A little later in the afternoon, Cal passed him a mischievous glance, stepped out from the counter, turned over the sign in the window, and locked the door to the shop. He led Brendan into a back room, which smelled like an attic and was filled with mismatched furniture in various states of disrepair.

They shucked their clothes and devoured one another like prisoners on a conjugal visit. Feeling hopeful, Brendan had stowed the necessary accoutrements in his Bermuda shorts before leaving his apartment. They took turns plundering each other against a red velvet turn-of-the-century settee, while moaning out adoring oaths.

Brendan suffered two nights apart from Cal, who needed to gently break the news about their relationship to Derek. After that, they arrived at an agreement—one night on and one night off from sleeping over at Brendan's apartment. Happily, that plan soon fell apart.

They'd tried, for Derek's sake, to exert some restraint, but the pull between them had been too much. On their first night "off," a Sunday—and after a string of text messages: "I miss you," "I miss you too," "I miss you more," "I miss YOU more," and so on—Brendan's doorman called to announce a visitor at half past midnight. Cal materialized at Brendan's door, his eyes bloodshot and swollen.

Their need for each other was easy on Brendan. He had no obligations to family or friends that couldn't wait a while, so he and Cal could be together as often as they liked. But he recognized it was hell for his boyfriend. He brought Cal over to the sofa in his living room. Cal only drank wine and beer, so Brendan fetched a bottle of Bordeaux and two long-stemmed wine glasses. He then sat to hear about Cal's big fight with Derek.

"All week, we talked about going to a concert at South Street Seaport. He knew we had to head out early to get good seats, and I just mention, lightly, we should get a move on, and he totally flips out on me. He said he's tired of being my 'backup plan,' and he stormed out of the apartment. I know he's hurt by us getting together, but he's never been that cruel."

"I waited for him to come back to the apartment. I thought maybe he just needed some time to cool off, and when he got back, we'd talk things out. He never came home, and he won't answer my texts. What was I supposed to do? Wait for him all night?"

Cal took a long draw from his wine glass and set it down. "I know he feels betrayed. The summer was supposed to be our vacation, and he spent a lot of money so we could hang out together. But he won't even let me apologize and try to explain. It's like he wants me to choose either him or you, and he won't be satisfied with anything else. How am I supposed to do that?"

Cal broke down in tears. Brendan reached around his shoulders and held him. He didn't judge Derek, and he didn't pressure Cal one way or the other. That Cal cared so deeply about his friend made Brendan love him even more.

He realized, though, something had to be done. After he made love to Cal that night, he brought up his previous suggestion about meeting Derek and trying to break the ice.

Cal looked up from where he rested on Brendan's chest. "He's really angry. I don't know if it's a good idea right now. He told me he might go back to Syracuse since I ruined the summer for him."

Privately, Brendan wondered how good a friend Derek was. Punishing Cal because he'd found a boyfriend instead of being happy for him? That didn't seem like something Cal needed to hear, however. He brushed the wavy hair on the crown of Cal's head. "Maybe we should get together sooner rather than later then. So he sees he's not left out."

"What if he's mean to you?" Cal said.

"I suppose he has every right to be," Brendan said. "I've been taking you away from him."

Cal hugged him tighter. "I'm scared I'll lose both of you."

Brendan kissed his forehead. "You'll never lose me, Cal. And I can handle being the villain if that's what Derek wants to believe. He probably just needs some time to get used to the situation."

Cal's gaze snuck away from him, and he picked at the russet hairs on Brendan's manscaped chest. "There's something else that's been bothering me. What's going to happen at the end of summer? I'll go back to Syracuse, and you'll be here."

Brendan had been worried about the same thing. Maybe it was crazy to think so far ahead in the future, considering he and Cal had only known each other for five days. But the feeling was there, a dreadful pit in his stomach. What would he do without Cal? It would be like having one of his limbs ripped from his body.

"Would you let me come up and visit?" he said. "Would you come down to stay with me sometimes?"

"I've never had a long-distance relationship." Cal's knees tightened around Brendan's thigh. "I want it to be like this every night."

"I want that too. This is where you belong. I found you, and I don't want to let you go. Even for a night."

Cal traced the whorls of hair below Brendan's abdomen. "The classical studies program has online classes. If I did that, I'd only have to be on campus a couple times during the semester."

Brendan's face bloomed. "You'd do that?" A wave of self-recrimination hit him. "What about your friends and family back in Syracuse?"

"Maybe it's time for me to grow up. To make my own life." Cal clasped his shoulders. "This feels so right to me. I wouldn't be giving up my friends and family altogether. But this, *you*, are more important to me."

Brendan rolled on top of him and cradled Cal's head. He looked down at Cal, his angel. So many emotions sang inside him—happiness and gratitude and even a weak, aching voice that said he didn't deserve so much.

Cal hugged his sides with his knees, beckoning him for another round. Brendan put on a condom and happily obliged. God, he could live inside Cal all night and day. Afterward, he would ask Cal to do the same to him. They were equal that way, which made their connection even deeper, not to mention making the sex even more spectacular.

With Cal, he could be every part of himself. It was more than a sexual attraction. Brendan realized that had been the extent of things with Thiago, and really, as he thought about it, every other guy he'd dated. He'd been obsessed with guys, and it had felt like love at the time. But what he had with Cal was so much more.

In his short-lived Buddhist phase a few years back, he had read in an old Tibetan text that falling in love was really an experience of gaining self-knowledge rather than giving to or taking from another person. The Buddhists called love: coming home. It was realizing one's capacity to love, which brought forth the possibility of loving oneself. That had all seemed strange and hokey at the time, but it was exactly how it felt being with Cal. He was home, a better man, worthy of being loved and admired, no longer afraid he would never be good enough to have a boyfriend, or anything else he wanted in life. Cal had unlocked a place in his heart that had been there all along.

Chapter Five

THEY MADE PLANS to go to Coney Island with Derek the following Monday when Cal's shop was closed and Derek had the day off from work. Brendan could have gotten a car and a driver to take them there, but out of respect for Cal and Derek's friendship, he suggested they take the subway together as they'd planned, and he would meet them on the boardwalk.

He took a company car with a driver as he always did though it made him self-conscious about flaunting his money. His grandmother had insisted on it ever since he'd been old enough to travel by himself. Desperate people kidnapped children from wealthy families. It was an ugly fact of life. He had the driver drop him off and wait in the parking lot of the Coney Island Aquarium. From there, he walked the short distance up the boardwalk to their meeting place.

He wasn't nervous about meeting Derek. In a strange way, he felt sympathetic toward him. He knew what it was to feel like a third wheel. When his pal from college, Betsy Schoonover, had gotten married, it had ended an era of meeting up on the spur of the moment for lunch and drinks, texting throughout the day, and being each other's date to dinner parties and charity events. Even though they tried to stay in touch, spending time together with Betsy's husband and two little kids around wasn't the same. Change was inevitable, and Brendan knew it also hurt something wicked.

Generalized anxiety gripped him, however, as he waited on the boardwalk, up the ramp from the subway station concourse. Vaguely ill at ease was his default setting, though he'd been much better since meeting Cal. As usual, he had somehow conspired against himself to arrive at their meeting place ahead of schedule, even though he hated waiting. He worried a little that the day would turn out with *him* feeling like the third wheel. Cal and Derek had been best friends for five years, after all.

A herd of people trundled down the subway concourse toward the boardwalk. A train must have just gotten in. Through a dizzying scan of the approaching mob of beachgoers—all breeds of New Yorkers, from baby-carriage pushing parents to swaggering bros, to urban hipsters, aging hippies, chattering teenage girls, and every type in between—he finally spotted Cal. He shone like a diamond in his tank top and his thigh-length swim shorts and his bronze-tinted aviator sunglasses, which he'd picked out at a street fair with Brendan over the weekend.

Naturally, a group of guys surrounded Cal on the concourse. They were a groomed and shirtless tattooed tribe who looked like they went from posing at the gym to posing at the beach, and to posing at whatever gay nightclubs were trendy these days. The guys had probably started chatting Cal up on the train in from Manhattan, hoping to coax him to spend the day with them, or at least to get his phone number. That didn't bother Brendan. Cal couldn't help that he was irresistible. He didn't even notice the attention he stirred up.

Cal saw Brendan standing by the boardwalk railing, and he lit up with a smile and waved. The muscle queens said their goodbyes, apparently adding things up. Now Brendan put together who Derek was in the crowd. A skinny kid with dark hair, dark shades, and a black T-shirt emblazoned with a skull and crossbones skulked behind Cal. His face was bland, giving off the unmistakable vibe of "I'm being dragged along for this?"

It was going to be an interesting day.

Cal climbed up the ramp and gave Brendan a great big hug, which Brendan tried not to return too enthusiastically so Derek wouldn't be uncomfortable. Cal stepped aside and made introductions. When Brendan held out his hand, Derek shook it weakly and peered around the boardwalk as though he was looking for something more interesting.

Brendan let the two decide on a spot to claim on the crowded, littered beach below them. Cal suggested a prime location near the surf. Derek sneered and said there were too many people in that area. Cal pointed out another option farther down the beach. But Derek gazed off in the opposite direction and said they should try that side. Never one to put up a fuss, Cal shrugged, and they followed Derek down the ramp to the beach and onward for a long hike through the hot sand to a sparsely populated area.

It was a hot and brilliant day, perfect for the beach despite Derek, the storm cloud who had come along. Brendan laid down a blanket he'd brought for the three of them. Derek sat at a far corner of it, pulled off his T-shirt, and dug out suntan lotion from his faded canvas backpack.

Derek called out to Cal, "Are you going to do my back?"

"Sure." Cal scooted up behind him and rubbed suntan lotion into his fair-skinned, freckled back and shoulders. Brendan brought out a beach towel and three frozen bottles of water from his suede tote. He handed one bottle to Derek.

"This is your first time at an ocean beach?" Brendan asked.

"Yep."

"There's a beach on Onondaga Lake in Syracuse, but it's nothing like this," Cal said. "Derek and I were at the lake just about every weekend last summer."

Derek said nothing.

"This is my first time at Coney Island as well," Brendan said.

"I couldn't believe it," Cal said to Derek. "He grew up right here in New York City."

"I believe it," Derek said. "You're more of a Hamptons kind of guy, huh?"

That was true to an extent. Brendan's family never went to city beaches, and his mother had a house on the water in Southampton. Though Brendan didn't spend a lot of time there. His mother had bought the house with his stepfather, and over the summer, it was a compound for his teenage half sisters and their friends. That story didn't seem worth mentioning. By his flat tone, Derek's insinuation was pretty obvious. He thought Brendan was a snob.

"I'm happy in most places," Brendan said. "It's good enough for me to just be invited." He hiked up some more friendliness. "Cal told me you guys Jet Ski. There's a place you can rent them in New Jersey. You can ride all around New York Harbor and see the Statue of Liberty and Ellis Island. We should all do it sometime."

Cal smiled at him favorably.

"How old are you?" Derek asked Brendan.

"Twenty-eight."

"Huh. I thought older. That's a swell suggestion, Daddy. But unless you're paying, it sounds like it's out of our price range."

Brendan tried to take his little dig in stride. "I'll find out how much it costs," he told Derek. "Hey, another thing you might like is Fire Island. That's where all the gays go around here. You can get there on the train and take a ferry."

"Ask Cal," Derek said. "He's the money-miser. He's got us budgeted to the penny."

Cal broke in. "We already talked about it, remember? We said we'd splurge over Fourth of July weekend when the shop's closed."

Derek yawned. "I don't recall."

Cal stared at the back of his friend's head in exasperation. "How do you not recall? It was the first thing we talked about when we decided to come to New York for the summer."

"You talk so much, how am I supposed to remember details?" With his back done, Derek leaned back on his elbows, kicked off his flip-flops and brushed his pale, slender feet together to get rid of some sand. "If you two want to go to Fire Island, that's fine with me. But don't pretend we had some huge discussion about it."

Cal heaved a breath. "Brendan and I never talked about it. It was you and me."

"Are you going to harp on this all day?" Derek asked.

That brought the conversation to a screeching halt. Brendan glanced at Cal sympathetically. They were both sitting behind Derek, so he stole a quick squeeze of Cal's shoulder. He'd never seen Cal get irritated. He was always gentle and magnanimous. Though Brendan knew codependent, gay male friends could bring out the worst in anybody.

Derek looked around the beach. "This place is kind of gross. I heard you have to watch out for hypodermic needles walking around here."

Cal shot him a glare. "You're the one who was dying to come to the beach."

"It's all part of the New York City experience," Brendan interjected. "You haven't had the real treatment until you've stepped on a hypodermic needle, or had your face slashed on the subway." He thought he caught a smirk pinch up on the side of Derek's face for a second.

"I'm starving," Cal said. He glanced at Brendan. "I saw a hot dog stand on the boardwalk. They call them Coney Islands, right? How 'bout I get us some?"

"That sounds great," Brendan said.

"Not for me. I'm trying to keep my carcinogen intake to a minimum," Derek said.

Cal stood up. "Two then. With sauerkraut?" he asked Brendan.

"Sure."

"Great," Derek said. "Then I get to smell you two farting all day."

Cal gave Brendan a helpless look, and then he wandered off to the boardwalk.

Brendan slid up on the blanket beside Derek. Rushes of Atlantic waves roared in front of them. Little kids were playing a game of running toward the ocean as it receded and running back before the waves broke and doused them. It brought back a memory of a summer long ago, when his parents were still together, and they had rented a house for the season on Martha's Vineyard. "I like your sense of humor," he told Derek.

"That's too bad. It alienates most people." Derek brushed some sand from his forearm and proceeded to apply suntan lotion to the front of his lanky body.

Brendan chuckled. He really did think Derek was funny. "That's a good one. So tell me, how did you and Cal become friends?"

"Is it so hard to believe?"

"I didn't mean it like that."

Derek finished lotioning up, sealed the cap on the tube, and stowed it in his backpack. "It's a legitimate curiosity. Back home—at the gay student union—they used to call us Beauty and the Beast."

Brendan scoffed. It was hard to tell if Derek was being serious, especially since his eyes were hidden behind sunglasses. But he had no reason to feel that way. Derek wasn't a bad-looking guy. Plenty of gays went for edgy twinks. Unless the mean queens called him "beast" because of his personality.

"What you have to understand about Cal is that he's completely in denial about his vanity," Derek said. "He keeps me around to have someone to look better next to so he gets all the attention when we go out. Then, if nothing turns up for him, he has me to take him home and tell him how great he looks and what an amazing guy he is, and how it's not him, it's just gay men being bitches."

Brendan let that pass without comment, though an urge to defend Cal burned in his chest.

"Cal's vain. I'm self-loathing. It makes us perfectly compatible, actually," Derek said. "To answer your question, we met at Gay-mer Night during freshman orientation. When Cal walked into our little den of geekdom, I was the only person in the room who could muster the courage to talk to him. I actually felt sorry for Cal. But it was all part of his game."

"It's funny," Brendan said. "Cal tells such a different story about you two. He talks about how much you have in common. That he's always admired you. He says what a great friend you've been to him."

"That's not surprising," Derek said. "He's a narcissist. His mind warps things like a revisionist historian so he always comes out looking better. Anyway, if you already knew the story, why did you bother asking me?"

"I don't get it," Brendan said. "If you think so little of Cal, why do you waste your time being friends with him?"

"I told you. I'm self-loathing. Like a fly drawn to a bug zapper." He pantomimed the visual and made a big splatting noise.

"Maybe you should get over that."

Derek coughed out a sarcastic laugh. "Wow. That's really deep. You managed to take some psych courses while earning your triple minors and a certificate in dramaturgy? What's dramaturgy anyway?"

"It's the study of dramatic composition and its history and social context."

"Sounds really practical. But I guess it's a fine hobby when you don't have to do anything to pay the bills."

Brendan's face compacted like a glacier. He imagined for a moment his fist making sweet, brutal contact with Derek's smug face. He drew a long breath through his nose. Was Derek baiting him to do that so the day would be ruined, and he could blame Brendan for doing it? The kid was seriously disturbed.

Derek drew grooves through the sand with his toe, and his tone turned more genial. "You thought this was going to be easy meeting me? Like a trip to the beach was going to make us best buds?"

"I thought we could be friends."

"Thought? Past tense. I guess you made your mind up pretty quick."

Brendan hadn't meant to say it like that. Or had he? "I haven't made my mind up," Brendan told Derek. "But I don't like you ragging on Cal."

"Maybe I was harsh." Derek cocked his head to look at him squarely, albeit behind his glaring sunglasses. "Maybe I'm just as broken as you think I am, with that deadly sincere, pitying look on your face."

"I don't pity you, Derek."

"Let's change the subject. Why are you interested in Cal?"

Brendan shifted a bit. The question was most certainly a trap. Though he had nothing to hide.

"I fell in love with him. Harder than I've ever fallen for anyone before. It happened quickly, but it feels like the one true thing I know in the world."

"That's sweet," Derek said. "Have you had a lot of boyfriends, Brendan?"

"A few."

"Cal told me you just broke up with some hot Brazilian model. Something about infidelity."

"He was unfaithful."

"That had to hurt," Derek said. He took a slug of water from his bottle. "So how do you know that Cal isn't your rebound guy?"

"He's not my rebound guy."

"Might be worth checking in with your therapist about that though, huh? It would be cruel to lead Cal on. Especially when he's talking about uprooting his life to move down here with you."

Brendan felt like he was sprouting horns. Who was this fucking twerp? "You're really protective of him, aren't you? Almost sounds like you're in love with Cal yourself. What was it Cal told me you call your relationship with him? Sexless lovers?"

"That's a low blow, Brendan Thackeray-Prentiss," Derek said. "I thought you said you wanted to be friends. Or did you just make up your mind about me?"

Brendan didn't answer. He was over talking to the jerk. Some silence passed, and he looked to the boardwalk, hoping Cal would be quickly on his way back.

"I've been a little hard on you," Derek said. "You can understand. Cal's had a lot of psychopaths in his life. He told you about his most recent stalker—Steve?"

Brendan knew a little about Steve, though Cal had only said his ex had been possessive, not a stalker. Derek must have picked up that tick of dissonance on his face.

"They were set up on a blind date back in February," Derek told him. "Steve seemed like a normal guy. He's about your age. A good-looking boy-next-door type. The kind Cal usually goes for. He was an IT tech for a security company. That should have been a red flag, in my opinion, but Cal inherently trusts anyone who fawns over him. He sees the world as all rainbows and unicorns. Even after Steve just happened to keep showing up everywhere Cal went, Cal agreed to go on a second date with him. And he slept with Steve. That was all the encouragement Steve needed to amp up to full-on stalker mode.

"Steve made some kind of GPS tracker for Cal's cell phone. Like the kind the cops use. He knew where Cal was every minute of the day. When Cal got weirded out by all of his phone calls and pop-up visits, he broke things off. Steve didn't take that well. He started harassing Cal's friends and family, asking them what he could do to get Cal back. Cal changed his phone and his e-mail twice, but Steve still managed to keep tracking him down and begging Cal to give him a second chance. When that didn't work, he flipped out and made twisted threats, saying he was going to kill Cal and then kill himself."

An icy chill passed through Brendan. Was evil Derek making up the story to screw with his head? Cal had said Steve was bad news. Was he that bad?

"Cal made a report to the police, but they didn't do much except give Steve a slap on the wrist," Derek went on.

"I don't know about New York City cops, but the ones in Syracuse don't really know what to make of us homos, and they'd rather pretend we don't exist in any case. Steve got smarter about keeping an eye on Cal. He borrowed cars from friends to park down the street from our house. A different one every night, so no one would notice him watching Cal. He even rented cars sometimes.

"One night when Steve saw Cal coming home with a guy he didn't recognize, Steve went berserk. It was just one of our college friends visiting for the weekend, but Steve thought Cal was bringing him home for the night. He pounded on the door and wouldn't leave. When Cal wouldn't let him in, he rammed his car into the house. That night, when the cops came and took Steve away, Cal finally had something to pin on Steve they couldn't ignore. Cal got a restraining order. Steve violated it about twelve hours later, and they locked him up. Seems getting thrown in jail for a while cooled him off, but we still look over our shoulders sometimes."

Brendan was in shock. That was something Cal should have told him, wasn't it?

Derek took account of Brendan's face. "Yeah, there's a lot of things you don't know about Cal," he said. "My job is to help weed out the crazies who follow him around. But you actually seem like a decent guy."

"That's high praise," Brendan said. "But I don't know that I believe you mean it."

"I do think you're decent," Derek said. "Anyone who can put up with my bullshit without trying to smash in my face probably deserves a humanitarian award. I was fucking with you earlier. I can tell your intentions with Cal are honorable. To hear him talk, you're his dashing leading man, like Chris Hemsworth and Matt Bomer all rolled into one. I get you falling in love with Cal. I honestly hope it works out."

Brendan took a skeptical account of Derek. He swung from one side to the other, making it hard to keep up.

"The tough part for you will be keeping him," Derek said. "He thinks he wants to settle down, but he's got the attention span of a goldfish. You've probably noticed that a guy who looks like him gets presented with a lot of options. Besides, who settles down at twenty-four years old?"

Cal came shuffling back through the sand with two hot dogs loaded with sauerkraut. Brendan took his hot dog and tried to look casual, though his head was reeling.

LATER THAT AFTERNOON, Derek announced he'd had enough of the beach and was going to catch a movie. Cal didn't ask if he wanted company. Derek had been determined to turn the beach trip into a train wreck, and they were all better off with him going his own way.

The situation had Cal stunned. He wondered if this was the end of their friendship. Even though he had Brendan, Cal felt like he'd been carved hollow. As they walked Derek down the crowded boardwalk to the subway station, it was as though he was adrift in a sea of strangers.

Cal went home with Brendan in his chauffeured black Mercedes sedan.

When Cal emerged from his gloomy inner world, he realized he wasn't the only one who'd been stunned silent. Brendan hadn't said a word since Derek left, and he wouldn't even look Cal in the face. Adding to the tension, they had mad traffic all the way to the Midtown Tunnel.

Clearly, introducing Brendan and Derek had been a bad idea. Derek had been a total douchebag all day, and from the point in time Cal had left them alone, Brendan had been distant. Cal sensed there were accusations brewing in his boyfriend's head, but he had no idea what they were. The longer he thought about it, the more it felt unfair. He hadn't done anything wrong. Why couldn't Brendan just say what was on his mind?

Brendan broke the silence while they were idling at the toll plaza for the tunnel.

"Why didn't you tell me about Steve?"

"I told you about Steve," Cal said.

"You said he was possessive. You never mentioned you had to take out a restraining order on him, or that he threatened to kill you, and that he drove his car into your house."

Cal's nose twitched. "What? Derek told you that?"

Brendan nodded.

Cal rolled his eyes. "I took out a restraining order on Steve, but he never said he was going to kill me. And as far as driving a car into my house, he had a Smart car. When it hit the stoop to the porch, the airbag knocked him unconscious, and the whole thing toppled on its side." He giggled from the memory. "I actually felt a little sorry for Steve. That kind of thing is a big deal in Syracuse. The news crews were there minutes after all the sirens from the police, the fire department, and the paramedics. They videotaped him being welded out of the car and taken by gurney into an ambulance."

Brendan blinked. Then his face drew up seriously again. "So Derek exaggerated. The guy still sounds pretty unbalanced."

"That happened a long time ago," Cal said. "He hasn't bothered me since." He knew it sounded weak. But he hadn't meant to hide anything from Brendan. It was just an embarrassing story to talk about. Who shares all the details of their past fucked-up relationships with someone they're trying to be with? Cal had Derek to thank for making him look like an asshole. "Derek had no right to tell you about it."

Brendan's shoulders sagged. He said nothing.

"That's why you've been giving me the silent treatment?"

The color had drained from Brendan's face. He looked like he was about to start sobbing. He muttered, "Derek said a lot of things."

"Give me a chance to make my rebuttal, Brendan. You're starting to scare me."

Brendan shook his head. The tears came. "I'm sorry. Maybe it's me." He wiped his eyes. "I shouldn't have let it get to me so much."

Cal slid closer to him on the seat. "You're going to tell me everything Derek said. And we're going to make it better, okay?"

Brendan looked at him. His eyes were blurry with tears. "You were going to let me know about Steve eventually, right? I mean, that's something pretty major, isn't it?"

Cal didn't know what to say.

"He could still be stalking you and wanting to hurt you."

"He hasn't tried to make contact with me in months. He can't leave Syracuse. He was sentenced to three years' probation. He has to check in with a probation officer three times a week." Cal gazed at Brendan steadily. He could see he had more things on his mind.

"Derek said there were other guys like him."

Cal huffed out a breath. "You can't possibly realize how embarrassing this is."

"Don't you think I should know?"

"I don't know, Brendan." Cal slid back to the other side of the car and pushed his hair back. There were things he didn't understand himself, so how was he supposed to explain them to Brendan? Anger bit at him. "Derek is supposedly my best friend. He knows everything about me. How do you think it makes me feel having him tell you private things about my life before I'm ready to talk about them?"

"You're right," Brendan said. "It wasn't fair for Derek to tell me. But he did. And now we're moving in together, and I'm scared, Cal. It's like there's this huge part of your past I know nothing about."

Cal chewed at one of his fingernails, an old habit he'd been trying to break since grade school. "You make it sound like I've been hiding a secret identity from you."

"That's not what I meant."

"Or maybe you're looking for a reason to break up with me."

"That's not what I meant either," Brendan said. "I know Derek had his reasons for telling me things you didn't want me to know. But this is a big commitment we're making. If there's stuff in your past that could affect both of us, I ought to know. You've got to see that, don't you?"

"What did Derek say?"

"He told me about Steve, and he said you had other stalkers in your past."

Cal snorted. "Great best friend I have, huh?"

"That was all he said. It's kind of warped, but I think he really cares about you. Like he's your protector, and he wanted to make sure I'm not another psychopath."

"That's a generous way to put it."

"Believe me—I'm no fan of Derek," Brendan said. "But if you have guys stalking you, it doesn't sound like a bad idea he's been looking out for you."

Cal's neck stiffened. "I don't need anyone to look out for me."

Brendan had so much concern pouring from his face, he looked like Cal had just been released from the trauma unit at the hospital. That pissed Cal off more. "I'm not a child," he said. "I can take care of myself."

"I know, Cal."

"I've been dealing with 'Steves' my entire life," Cal told him. "If that bothers you, I guess it's good you found out from Derek, sooner rather than later."

"Why are you getting angry at me?"

"Because I know this conversation. I've had it before. You'll say you feel really bad about what happened to me, and maybe you'll really mean it. But in a day or two, it's going to hit you that being with me is a lot more than you signed up for."

"Now you're not giving me a chance."

Cal wanted to believe Brendan would be different. No boyfriend had ever treated him so lovingly, but Cal had been fooled before. By guys who couldn't handle jealousy. Or guys who thought he was a freak or too much drama to deal with. Given the present circumstances, Cal's choices were to clam up like a five-year-old, bolt from the sedan to ford through the bumper-to-bumper toll plaza (to walk through the Midtown Tunnel?), or tell Brendan the truth. It hit him then how screwed up it was he was even considering the two former possibilities. Brendan deserved to know, and Cal needed to start facing the truth himself.

"Do you believe a person can be cursed?" he asked.

"What do you mean?"

"People who keep getting into the same crappy situations no matter what they do," Cal explained.

"I don't know if that's a curse," Brendan said. "But tell me more."

"You've heard the expression—rolled in dog shit? Maybe that's what happened to me. I don't know." A sigh heaved out of him. "It wasn't just Steve. It started all the way back in middle school." Brendan's gaze locked in on him. Cal began the story.

"Trinity Maypole. She was always taking photos of me. We were in eighth grade, and I thought it was just for fun, because we were friends, and she really liked me. I didn't know she was posting every photo of me on her online diary and saying I was her boyfriend and we were having sex. Her parents went ballistic and nearly got me kicked out of school.

"High school got worse. At a sleepover at my best friend's house, I caught his mother standing at the door to his room, staring at me in the dark while she thought I was asleep in my sleeping bag. She used to steal things from me, like a glove or my schoolbooks, and text me to come over to get them when no one else was home. I had to break up with my best friend because his mom freaked me out.

"I told you about Victor Saltamaggio, Then junior year, my art teacher, Mr. Jankovic, offered to give me a ride home from school one day when we got let out early because of a snowstorm. Outside the house, while we were sitting in his car, he got this weird look on his face, and he tried to kiss me. When I told my parents, they went to the principal to get him fired. Meanwhile, a bunch of kids at school spread a rumor we'd been having an affair for months.

"My parents made me go to a psychologist. Mr. Goldschmitt. He seemed normal for a while, and then he started asking me all these sexual questions and saying he wanted to see me three times a week. We got hang-up calls at the house late at night, and I noticed he put away the photos of his wife and kids in his office and started dressing up and wearing cologne for our appointments. I stopped going to see him, though I never told anyone about any of that."

Cal felt small and brittle. He'd thought about this history sometimes, but Cal had never voiced it in its entirety, even to Derek.

"I thought college would be different. But it wasn't. Guys got aggressive if I said I wouldn't go out with them. I found out that my first boyfriend had a secret webcam in his dorm room to record the two of us fooling around. Every guy I liked played games, as though I had to prove I really liked him, which I never could. They just wanted to put me down and show me they were too good to be with someone like me. Or, they wanted to know where I was every second of the day.

"Sophomore year, a real dickhead, Mark Buffalino, kept trying to get me alone in his room. When I wouldn't, he spread a rumor that I came over, and we had a sex party with a bunch of his friends from out of town. I barely left my dorm room for months after that."

Brendan looked stricken. "I'm so sorry, Cal. I don't know what to say."

"Say that you believe me. Say I'm not some kind of mental case or pervert."

"Of course, I believe you. Those other guys are the mental cases and the perverts."

"Then why does it keep happening to me? Every guy I meet just wants to conquer me, or hide me from the world, or despise me because I can't love him back. It happened with Steve. It happened with everyone." He added in a small voice, "It's probably going to happen with you."

Brendan was quiet for a while. "I don't know why, Cal. You're an attractive guy. That's not an excuse for anyone to treat you that way. But a lot of people—they're going to fall for you."

"Sometimes I wish I was hideous."

Brendan eased up close to him. He pushed Cal's hair back from his face and grinned. "I'd still love you if you were hideous."

Cal snorted.

"Y'know, when we first met, I was blown away," Brendan told him. "You were so beautiful I was afraid to even talk to you. But that's not why I wanted you to be my boyfriend. You're even more beautiful on the inside. You're kind. You make me laugh. You're smart."

Cal looked up at him. "It doesn't bother you that my life has been a total mess?"

Brendan shook his head. "You've been a victim. I hope you understand that. There's no such things as curses. There's just...people who do shitty things to other people."

Cal thought on that for a while. He'd said similar words in his head before, but they'd never really rung true. Hearing Brendan say them made it feel true. As if he was a good person, not some magnet for psychos.

"I don't care that you've had stalkers and bad relationships," Brendan told him. "I don't even care that you turn heads wherever you go. I don't want to hide you away or show you off like a trophy. This is who you are, and it's perfect. You're the guy I want to be with for the rest of my life."

His meaning sank in, and Cal's eyes grew big. He'd wanted to hear those words for as long as he could remember, but a wave of fear rocked through him. When Brendan clasped his hand, his gaze steady and sure, he made it hard to believe it wasn't possible.

"So what do you say? Will you marry me?"

Cal hesitated for a half second. "Really?"

Brendan chuckled mildly. "Yes."

Cal took Brendan's hand in his, massaging it, staring at his ring finger. He looked up. The corners of his eyes burned. "Yes. I'll marry you, Brendan Thackeray-Prentiss."

They sealed it with a kiss.

Chapter Six

THEIR WEDDING PLANS proceeded directly, and Brendan would admit it all looked impulsive, rushed, and even delirious from an outsider's perspective. It was only two weeks after their first date, and they were engaged. They chose September, just eight weeks later, for the wedding. His grandmum said the news was wonderful, though her aged, sagacious eyes worried around her for a moment, the same way they had when he'd explained he needed to go back to college for a sixth year to finish his triple minors and dramaturgy certificate. Still, she recovered from the awkward moment in her inimitable way and brought out a smile as though she'd been waiting all her life for Brendan's happy proclamation. Then she went straight to work itemizing what had to be done next.

His pal Louis Jeffries was less subtle about his doubts. When Brendan snuck in the big announcement on the squash court one weekday afternoon, Louis stepped away from the serving line and approached Brendan with his racquet and the ball still welded in his hands.

"Married? Brendan, at the beginning of the summer, I pretty much had to shovel you out of your bed where you were laid out for funeral viewing after breaking up with Thiago."

"I know," Brendan said with a huge grin. "It's amazing. That feels like it happened to another person. And now I'm in love with the greatest guy in the entire world."

Louis's well-bred, shaven, angular face screwed up in a skeptical frown. "So how about giving this relationship a little time to breathe? I thought only lesbians shacked up after the first date. I'm not trying to be a buzzkill here, but you've got to admit, it's a little dramatic."

"I knew you'd see it that way. But I've never been surer of anything in my life." Brendan added, "You know that's just a stereotype about lesbians, right, Mr. Gay Rights Ally?"

"I love lesbians," Louis defended himself. "Anyway, that's not the point. You were sure about Thiago. Before that, you were sure about my cousin Trevor who you dated for, let's see, seventy-two hours? You were sure about that guy in college. What's-his-name? That redhead who always wore those really awful bow ties?"

"Clinton," Brendan helped out.

"That's right," Louis said. A distant, wistful gaze. "Clinton. What a tool. I never told you this because I didn't want to hurt your feelings, but I couldn't stand that guy."

"Cal's nothing like that. He's really down to earth. You'll love him."

"Don't be so sure. You decided to get married, and I never even met the guy."

"You will," Brendan said. An idea hit him. "We have an appointment to shop for tuxes on Saturday. How 'bout we get together for dinner that night? You can bring that girl you've been seeing—Isabel."

Louis looked askance. "Afraid not. Things got a little weird with Isabel. I don't know if it's the same in your 'world,' but you let one little thing blurt out of your mouth while you're getting a blowjob and suddenly you're a disgusting, sexist pig."

"That's surprising," Brendan told him, deadpan. "You're such a paragon of women's empowerment."

Louis scowled at him. He shrugged his big shoulders. "So I'm a work in progress."

"No big deal. It'll be the three of us then. What are you in the mood for? Steakhouse? Italian?"

His friend gazed at him squarely. "Brendan, how much do you know about this guy?"

Brendan shrugged. "We spent just about every day and night together for the past two and a half weeks. I think I know pretty much everything."

"Where'd he go to college?"

"Syracuse."

"Has he got a job?"

"Right now, he's running his uncle's antique shop here in the city. He's starting a master's degree program in classical studies after the wedding. He's like a genius in Hellenic archeology."

"What do his folks do?"

"His dad works for an air conditioning company. His mom's a medical secretary."

That seemed to signify something to Louis. "Whose idea was it for the two of you to get married?"

Brendan caught his drift. "It was mine. Totally mine. Christ, Louis, give me a little credit."

"I'm only looking out for you, buddy. You put some thought into a prenup?"

"I'll work that into the conversation while we're picking out tuxes," Brendan told him flatly. "You're such a goddamn cynic, Louis. I wish you'd meet someone like Cal. It might restore your faith in humanity."

"And you see the world through a kaleidoscope of hearts and rainbows," Louis said. "I love you for it. It's like having Sam Smith as my best friend, and I don't even have to fuck you." Brendan gave him a cease-and-desist glare. "Actually, you're a lot better looking than Sam Smith. If you really, really wanted me to, I'd fuck you."

"I think I'll pass," Brendan said.

Louis came over and gave him a big hug. "Congratulations, Brendan. I really am happy for you."

Brendan hugged him back. Louis had his faults, a work in progress as he said, but he had also been Brendan's most loyal friend and fiercest defender, getting him back up on his feet numerous times after life punched him in the stomach, letting every guy back in boarding school know what's what if they considered giving Brendan flack about being gay. Louis' approval meant a lot to him, even though he could tell his friend still had reservations. But Brendan was done with overanalyzing things. All his life, every decision he'd made had been vetted through friends and family and mental health professionals, and even then, his choices had still spun around his head, never locking at a place of certainty. This relationship with Cal felt right. That was the only thing that mattered.

Sturdy Dr. Clotilde Trapp had also agreed, though Brendan wouldn't have changed his mind if she hadn't. He was beginning to suspect the absentminded, old Neo-Freudian was starting to fall off her game. She'd admitted she never read his SOS text before his first date with Cal, and her reply, "Leave it to Jesus," was meant for her husband, who was bringing home leftover saltimbocca she wanted him to feed their Chihuahua Jesús.

As for his parents, the news was met with predictable reactions. When he told his mother, she was detached, as though he was calling about a change in plans for the weekend. His father sobbed on the phone from California and turned the conversation to the litany of regrets he had for not having been in Brendan's life as much as he should have.

Everything was falling into place in its familiar, dysfunctional manner. Brendan felt like he was on top of the world. He'd put aside his crutches of compulsive exercise and pharmaceuticals. He didn't need them anymore. He'd gained seven pounds since dating Cal, which normally would have bothered him. But people told him he looked better, healthier, and Brendan felt it.

He and Cal decided on a no-frills wedding at City Hall and a bigger ceremony and reception in Greece where Cal's humongous extended family could attend. Brendan's grandmum insisted they publish an announcement in the *New York Times* as she had with all of her married sons and daughters and her grandchildren. He suspected she regretted she couldn't oversee a sparkling society reception in the city, but that wasn't important to Brendan and Cal.

Their families and their closest friends would celebrate with them in Greece, and then they'd be off to a two-week honeymoon in the Mauritius. They'd return to New York City where Brendan's apartment would be their home. Cal had found online courses that would allow him to start his master's program in the spring.

There was just one nagging matter to sort out. Brendan decided to broach it one night after he and Cal had finished a bottle of Loire Valley Cabernet Franc and were cuddled up on the couch in their sleeping boxers, looking over their guest list.

They had a table for Brendan's family, eleven tables to accommodate Cal's, and one designated for friends. The latter table was starkly absent of any of Cal's friends. It was a sensitive matter. Cal had friends in Syracuse, mostly girls, but he'd said none of them were in a position to afford to fly to Greece for a wedding. It didn't seem right that Cal would have none of his own friends take part in their celebration, particularly the guy who, in a way, had helped bring them together by partnering up with Cal to come to New York City that summer.

Brendan was embanked with Cal, bobsled style, and holding up the guest list on a handwritten notepad for them both to review. He brought out carefully, "Have you spoken to Derek?"

"No," Cal said. He left the issue hanging in the air, probably hoping it would drift away.

Brendan set the notepad down and tickled the back of Cal's neck with his nose. "Don't you think you should?"

"Why?"

"He's your best friend."

Cal dropped his head onto Brendan's shoulder. "He texted me the other day. I didn't answer."

"What did he say?"

"'Don't be mad at me'," Cal recited. "He said he'd had a 'bad day.' He wanted to know if we could talk."

"Sounds like he wants to apologize."

"I'm not sure I'm ready to hear it."

Brendan sat up a bit, minding that his fiancé was still supported comfortably. "He's your friend, and it's your call. I just wouldn't want you to regret leaving him out of the wedding, later."

"He tried to sabotage our relationship."

"I know. He was a real jerk. But he could never do that. I bet he knows it too."

"You think he deserves a second chance?"

"Do you?"

Cal breathed out a weary sigh. "I miss him. And then I remember what he did, and I get angry at myself for missing him. I don't know. I'm confused."

"Maybe it would help to hear him out."

Cal thought on it a while. "I guess I haven't been a very good friend myself. He's always been there for me. I ought to cut him some slack." Cal drew into himself again for a moment. "Though I can hear him already when I tell him about the wedding. He's going to say I deliberately left him out since there's no way he can pay to fly to Greece."

"Tell him I'll pay."

"You'd do that?"

"Why not?" Money was no object for Brendan. He just wanted to make their wedding as special as it could be for Cal.

Cal chuckled. "I don't know how Derek will react to that. He's got a lot of pride."

"He can turn down the offer if he wants to," Brendan said. "No hard feelings."

Cal nestled into the crook of Brendan's arm. "I'll give him a call tomorrow morning."

Chapter Seven

TWO MONTHS LATER, Cal and Brendan were on the island of Hydra in the Aegean Sea. That was where Cal's grandparents lived, along with many of his uncles, aunts, and cousins. The rest of his Greek relatives were ferrying in from Athens, a short distance away.

They'd booked a five-star resort on the beach for the wedding and the reception. Cal's grandparents had wanted the entire wedding party to stay with them in town, but Cal explained, as tactfully as he could, that Brendan's family and guests weren't the sort of people who slept on cots and floors in a farmhouse.

Brendan would have been fine with it, and he probably would have insisted on everyone staying there and having whatever country-style wedding Cal's family preferred. That was Brendan's noble nature. He was actually worried Cal's family wouldn't approve of him even though Cal had told him for working class people the question of approval pretty much ended when they heard his husband was an heir to a multibillion dollar corporation. Cal had reassured him no one would be offended by holding the event at a hotel. It was easier for the Panagopoulos clan to be comfortable in the kind of setting Brendan's family was accustomed to rather than the other way around.

The Royal Phoenician Resort and Spa was a gorgeous property with gleaming white bunkers of ocean-facing guest suites, stone-laid terraces, a giant kidney-shaped swimming pool, and a quarter mile of private beach, all carved out of a jutting spur of the island's sun-scorched, rugged coastline. It had an open-air pavilion for the reception, a chapel for the ceremony, tennis courts, a gym and a spa facility, a dock for water taxis, and even a helipad. Brendan and Cal had booked the presidential suite, which had a wraparound sundeck and "his and his" showers and baths.

When they first arrived, Cal worried they'd overreached. He imagined his locally grown family arriving by mule cart, for there were no cars or even mopeds permitted on the rustic island. They would descend on the place with their loud voices, brash manners, homemade pashminas, and mismatched outfits, and shatter the pristine elegance in one fell swoop. Cal felt like he was walking through a museum, and he had no idea how to handle the hotel staff, who stood around smiling at their stations in neat, white uniforms, just waiting to be helpful. Naturally, he let Brendan take the lead with checking in and tipping the guy who brought their luggage up to their room. Then, a strange thing happened as he stood with his fiancé on their deck, admiring the glistening resort sprawled out below them, like princes overlooking their kingdom.

Cal realized he truly belonged in this fairy tale of a destination wedding. It was the perfect culmination of a perfect love story with the most perfect man on the planet. And if his family brought a little ethnic flavor to the hotel, the place would be better for it. Cal gave Brendan a kiss on the cheek and lured him into their suite to get in a quickie before the guests began showing up.

They had a day to settle in. The next day would be the wedding, and the reception with all the traditional dances, the Ouzo, the money pinning, and the honey and almonds for good luck. After that, he and Brendan would spend five days visiting with Cal's family, and then they'd have their private celebration on an island in the Indian Sea.

It was surreal that first day, greeting the guests as they materialized in the hotel's posh lounge, steps down from the reception foyer. Arriving on the first ferry from Athens, with a transfer from the main harbor by water taxi, Cal's father came in bickering with Cal's brothers Sandy, Yannis, George, and Demetri. His brothers always seemed to regress in time when they were together, fighting for bragging rights over who knew their family history best and who knew the quickest route from here to there. Cal's mother came along and turned brittle and weepy at the sight of Cal, as though she beheld a mirage that was slipping out of her grasp. His sisters Ana and Lucy swooped in on Brendan flirtatiously while their beleaguered, jetlagged husbands barked after their children who ran footloose through the hotel. His sister Genie, who was the only unmarried one, caught Cal up on all the comical details of the family's transatlantic voyage.

Brendan's family began arriving a short interval later, on schedule from his grandfather's chartered jet and a private helicopter connection to the island. First, it was his grandfather Harry and his grandmother Millie, who looked to Cal like people who got invited to White House dinners. They'd met before, back in New York, and Harry was polite, if a little brusque. Millie was sweet and lovely, just as Brendan always talked about her. She was full of compliments about the island as though Cal had discovered and colonized it himself.

Next came Brendan's mother, stepfather, and half sisters, who had dallied behind the grandparents. This was a first meeting. Though Brendan had vehemently asserted it was they, not Cal, who needed to mind making a good impression, Cal stood straighter and tried to imagine himself as the sort of person who knew about polo and private yachts.

Brendan's stepfather, Roger, turned out to be an easygoing guy, albeit in expensive sports clothes. He gave both grooms friendly hugs of congratulations and was eager to chat while his wife and daughters were preoccupied on their cell phones. The two girls, Daryl, seventeen, and Riley, fifteen, eventually presented themselves in their sunglasses and summery gowns, each one fussing with a toy terrier cradled in their arms like a baby. They made a show of fussing with their handsome older brother and then turned their attention to fussing with Cal. Riley declared Cal looked just like her best friend Ashlyn's boyfriend, who apparently was some sort of European supermodel. Instagram photo taking quickly ensued.

Then, Brendan's mother, Belinda, glided over while wrapping up her phone conversation. She looked like a former model, blonde and elegant in a wide-brimmed hat and a wraparound dress, and every bit as intimidating as Cal had imagined. Belinda scolded her daughters about pestering Cal with photos, gave her son two pecks on the cheek, and offered Cal her slight and manicured hand in what he supposed was a ladylike handshake. After pushing up her sunglasses like a visor to take a better account of him, she left him with a horrifically awkward head-to-toe gaze, and then she harassed her flock onward to their rooms, declaring she had a terrible migraine.

Brendan had spoken of his father in not so gracious terms, but when Donovan Prentiss arrived with his much younger Venezuelan actress girlfriend Gabriela, Cal was fascinated by the man, and sort of instantly sympathetic. For one thing, Brendan was the spitting image of his father. He had the same piercing, earnest, slate-blue eyes. Though Brendan wouldn't have liked him saying it, it was also obvious Donovan had passed along his endearingly excitable personality to his son. He probably had the money to rent out the entire property, but he awkwardly fumbled through check-in, and then stumbled down to the lounge with his shirttails somehow sprung free from his pants through the exchange. He halted, trembling and tearing up, and staggered forward to embrace his son as though Brendan had just been rescued from a burning building. Then he took ahold of Cal with nearly as much exuberance. Emptying his designer suitcase onto the floor to rustle something out, he returned to them brandishing a silk-screen T-shirt he'd designed for the wedding, which read, "My gay son is getting married."

Brendan's friends arrived later: Betsy Schoonover and her husband, Brendan's best man Louis Jeffries, and a host of other Ivy League types who chummed up to Cal with curiosity—the guy who'd stolen their buddy's heart.

While Brendan was working out some mix-up with the rooms up at the reception desk, Derek ambled into the hotel with his army-style rucksack thrown over his shoulder. Cal waved both his arms to call him down to the lounge.

"You made it."

Derek removed his sunglasses from his pale, stubbly face. He looked disoriented but was such a welcome sight Cal grasped him in his arms in a bear hug.

"You thought I was going to renege on you?" Derek asked.

"No. I'm just glad to see you."

They'd made up over the phone a while after the Coney Island incident, but it was the first time Cal had seen Derek since that day. Derek had gone back to Syracuse for the rest of the summer. Truthfully, Cal had been worried his friend wouldn't show up.

Derek rubbed his face. "I feel like I just woke up after a night of boilermakers and beer bongs."

"It's jet lag."

"No kidding," Derek grumbled. "Nine hours to Athens, an hour on the bus to Piraeus, two and a half hours on the ferry to Hydra, and then a water taxi ride from hell that nearly had me puking out my guts over the side of the boat." He glanced around, taking account of their privacy. "Y'know, your cheapskate boyfriend could've ponied up the money for business class."

"He wanted to," Cal said. "I told him you'd feel less obligated in coach."

"Obligated? You overestimate my integrity. I would have leafletted for the Republican Party for some legroom and a chair that reclined more than a quarter inch."

Cal took his hand. "You're here now. The hotel is amazing. Every room has an ocean view. The beach is, like, five seconds away. After you get settled, you can come down for the rehearsal dinner. We're having lobster and chocolate soufflé."

Derek disentangled his hand from Cal's.

"You're getting married now," Derek said.

Cal gave him a strange look. "Holding your hand doesn't bother Brendan. He knows we're just friends."

"Maybe it's a little too touchy-feely for me."

They were quiet for a moment. Cal tried to make allowances for the remark. His friend was ornery from the long trip.

"Let's go see your room," Cal suggested. "You can get unpacked and relax a bit before dinner. You even have time for a quick nap if you want."

"Not a chance," Derek said. "I've only got four days for this vacation. Which way to the slutty Greek boys in loincloths? Someone who can rub me down in olive oil and feed me peeled grapes."

Cal giggled. "You can get a massage at the spa. But I'm not making any promises about getting a happy ending." He remembered something. "We booked a deejay for the hotel nightclub who does all the party circuits in Europe. Ibiza. Amsterdam. Mykonos. Maybe you'll meet some gay guys there."

Derek nodded, though his face was suddenly downcast. "You're really doing this, aren't you?"

"What do you mean?"

"Marrying Brendan."

Cal beamed. "I am." He raked his hand through his hair. "God, I am. I'm still not sure if I believe it. He loves me, and we're getting married."

"It doesn't bother you that he pays for everything? You'll spend the rest of your life as a kept man."

"It's not like that," Cal said. "We can't help that he has more money than me. And it's just money. It doesn't make me a kept man. I'm still going to have a career in classical studies. I start the masters program in the spring."

Derek skirted his gaze. "Sometimes I wonder what he has that I don't."

Cal held him by the shoulders. "Hey, we'll always be friends, Derek." His face drew up in a smile. "What do you think I'd do without you?"

Derek leaned in and kissed him on the lips very suddenly and forcefully. Cal froze, baffled by the desperation conveyed in that kiss and frightened someone might have seen it.

Derek backed away, heaving a breath and gathering himself. He came back to Cal, trying out a nervous grin. "That was just for good luck." A pained expression returned to his face. "I love you, Cal. No matter what happens, know that. I'll always be there for you."

Cal took a dry swallow and nodded.

"I'll get out of your hair," Derek said. He strode off with his rucksack and disappeared down a corridor leading to the guest rooms.

Chapter Eight

DEREK SHOULD NOT have come to Greece. It hit him like a blunt axe cleaved into his gut. He'd been there for ten seconds and attacked Cal with a kiss on the lips like a desperate lunatic. Derek hated himself for that. And now he was trapped for four days in a nightmare world where he somehow had to act like he was happy Cal was getting married when his vital organs were bleeding from the pain.

He fast-tracked to his room, head down, brooking no acknowledgement from passing guests, and he fidgeted his key into the door and let himself in. A few steps inside, the solitude of the spotless suite pressed in on him from all sides. He stumbled to his bed and curled into himself on top of the comforter. For the first time since high school, Derek wept until his rib cage ached.

He wished he could disappear. He wished he could escape his life, being a pathetic loser who broke down in tears because his best friend was getting married. But for five years, the one thing that had kept Derek going had been the possibility that Cal could love him as he loved Cal. He had stood by, in and out of Cal's disastrous relationships, always believing one day Cal would see they belonged together. Derek fully understood how fucked up and deluded that was, but his feelings for Cal were too strong to control. He could set them on a dimmer for a while, but they came back, flaring, demanding to be dealt with. He had suffered through Cal pining for other guys, hooking up with other guys, all the while afraid to say how much he loved the kid, just waiting like a dumb fool for a sign the time was right.

In his warped mind, Derek had imagined Cal's wedding would be his chance. Cal had gone out of his way to invite him, and it had felt like a sign he needed Derek, maybe because he wasn't sure about Brendan. Maybe he realized deep down his heart belonged to Derek. And Derek would be there to tell him he'd always felt the same way. Like a pop song cliché, Cal would see that true love had been waiting right in front of him all along.

It had to happen. Derek didn't believe in god or fate, but life had to offer some kind of justice to even out the scales. He asked for so little and had been handed so much shit. Born a gay weakling who had no place in the world. With an older brother who had made it his mission in life to verbally and physically crush his soul since they were kids. Parents who let that happen because he was nothing, and his brother was a star athlete and the perfect straight son they had always wanted. Tortured by kids in school so much they put him on antidepressants so the thought of killing himself only occurred to him once or twice a week. How much was he supposed to take? What had he done, besides being born, for the world to hate him so much?

Squalls of laughter traveled from the courtyard beneath his window. Families happily reunited. Friends hyped up about the big party to come. Derek listened, slowly dying. He couldn't face those people. To put on a fake grin and pretend his insides weren't shattered? Why bother? No one in the wedding cared about him. It was all phony bullshit.

He could slip out of the hotel, grab a water taxi to the ferry pier and sleep on the dock all night if he had to, waiting for the next ferry to get him off this horror show.

Cal would be pissed, but not really. Cal never gave a shit about him. Their friendship had been about passing the time until something better came along.

His cell phone groaned in his pocket. Languidly, he retrieved it and squinted to read the screen in the room's fading daylight. A text from Cal.

You coming down? You're at the table with Genie. Dinner's starting.

Derek laid the phone facedown on the bed.

A vision of Cal sitting with Brendan at the rehearsal dinner, nuzzling and showing off how much they were in love—it was like shards of glass to Derek's heart. It wasn't fair. They'd only known each other for three months. Derek had been devoted to Cal for five years.

Brendan was a spoiled, pretentious, useless human being, and he had hooked Cal on a line like a fish with his penthouse apartment, chauffeured cars, and his prep school idol good looks. Even though Cal had done him wrong, protective emotions overcame Derek. Brendan didn't deserve Cal. Cal was too good, too sweet, too innocent for him. He was probably the only good guy left on earth. Just being around him made Derek feel like he was someone important. They were meant to be together. And Brendan had the fucking gall to take that away from him?

A cold reckoning washed over Derek. He could bolt from the wedding, or he could fight for what was his. Running away would be exactly what Brendan wanted. Fighting would be desperate and messy, but what did he have to lose? He might walk away with nothing, but he was assured to walk away with nothing if he skipped out of the wedding like a coward.

He sat up and collected his thoughts. Then he went to the bathroom, washed his face, and pulled from his rucksack a button-down shirt, which had held up pretty well through his flights, and a pair of his best jeans. Avoiding his reflection in the mirror like it might turn him to stone, he dressed and brushed his teeth. Then he ventured out of his room and found his way to the noisy hotel restaurant where everyone was gathered.

In retrospect, he would describe the dinner as a dissociative experience. He was aware of everything and grounded in his body, but some persona emerged that night as a screen to his disordered state. He was a talented Mr. Ripley, chatting easily with Cal's sister Genie, who'd always shared his cynical observations about the world. He even regaled the table of Panagopoulos siblings and spouses with witticisms. All the while, he kept a furtive eye on Cal and Brendan, and clinking his wine glass with a spoon, he stood and offered them a toast. Brendan's vaunting sincerity did not chafe Derek's sociable veneer. He'd left "broken Derek" in his hotel room, a vague, distant relation. Strangers glanced at him favorably. He was the good-natured, eloquent, best bud of the groom.

When lapses of attention from his companions allowed, he took a precise account of the party's goings-on. He was surrounded by spirited conversations in Greek from the Panagopoulos side of the hall. Unattended children scarpered from table to table, vacating their chairs for the freedom of the margins of the room where games of tag and roughhouse play broke out. Brendan's guests on the other side of the room were a comical contrast, stiff and bland and impeccably dressed, preoccupied by their inner worlds.

Derek glimpsed a waiter, standing by the swinging door to the kitchen, who looked similarly bemused by the proceedings. He was tall and thickly built, a young Mediterranean as handsome as a star footballer. On closer examination, Derek noticed the waiter's gaze had pinned to Cal, who was chatting and grinning back and forth with Brendan's best man—a smirking frat-house type who had asshole written all over him. The waiter's gaze was desirous, betraying his professional comportment. Spying that Cal's wine glass was only half-filled, the waiter hastened to his table, taking up a wine bottle to smoothly fill it. Cal gave him a word of thanks, and a shy smile bloomed on the waiter's face. For a moment, he lost track of his duty to attend to the other guests at the head table. Brendan looked at the guy with a hint of ill humor.

This was a juicy intrigue.

Meanwhile, the frat house bro threw his arm over Brendan's shoulder and gave his friend a strangely intimate caress of the underside of his chin.

Genie, who must have noticed Derek watching the exchange, interrupted him from his thoughts to explain. "It's a tradition for the best man to shave the groom on the morning of his wedding day." Misreading Derek's interest, she added in a low voice, "I know. It's kind of hot to imagine in this case, huh?"

Derek gave her a dirty smirk, though other thoughts were churning in his head. After dessert and coffee, he gently disentangled himself from the party, claiming his eyes were crossing from jet lag.

Before retiring to his room, he discreetly found his way to the hotel's back offices, slipping past the single attendant at the front desk. He skulked down the main artery, past locked doors, until he came to what appeared to be a cloakroom. Everything was dark. Likely, there was only one night manager for the place, and he or she conveniently was nowhere to be seen or heard. Derek clicked on a light switch, illuminating a little alcove with staff lockers and a rack of uniforms. He quickly rifled through the rack, grubbed out a waiter's bow tie, and stowed it in his pocket. He flipped off the light switch and snuck out of the private corridor as quietly as he had come.

Back in his room, Derek stripped down to his underwear and lay in bed, contemplating the deed that lay ahead of him in the morning. He felt strangely powerful, a criminal mastermind. He gazed all night at his darkened window, listening to the gay festivities echoing through the open-air hotel, thirsting for the light of dawn. His hand groped between his legs, attending an absentminded need. When he was close, he retrieved a condom from his rucksack, wrapped it on himself, and lay on his bed, palming himself to climax.

Derek didn't sleep at all that night, possessed by a monomania, which was fueled in part by the distortion of his body's circadian rhythms. He waited until the resort came alive again with sunlight, observing the rustle of staff moving about the grounds, the clinking of trays of glassware being carried into the breakfast room, the light, ambient music cueing up from the property's stereo system. Derek pulled on a pair of shorts and a T-shirt and stepped into his sneakers. The digital clock on his bedside table read 8:00 a.m., which may have been too early, but he would have a tight window of time.

He emerged from his room and charted out a stealthy route through empty colonnades and stairwells to the topmost tier of suites. The prior night, he'd noticed that the grandest rooms with private balconies were up there, and one of those master suites had to be occupied by the two grooms. At the foot of the final stairwell, he climbed over a shallow stone wall and smuggled behind a bank of shrubbery.

A short while later, a footfall traveled up from below. Peeking out from behind the dry, groomed vegetation, Derek spied Brendan's polo shirt–clad best man spryly taking the stairs up from the lower tier. The smarmy hunk climbed onward to the crown suite and disappeared from view for a moment until Derek carefully rooted out a hidden vantage from which to watch his movements. The guy knocked loudly on a door and waited, hands shoved into the pockets of his linen pants, rolling back and forth on the heels of his leather sandals, his big shoulders tensing and easing. The door opened, revealing a bed-tossed Brendan, sporting a sheepish grin. His dumb-ox friend commandeered him out of the room and shouldered him down the stairs for his wedding-day shaving.

Everything was proceeding like clockwork.

Derek emerged from the foliage and crept up to the crown suite. The door, like his own, probably locked when closed, but if Derek knew Cal, there'd be a sliding door on the wraparound deck that he'd probably left unlatched in his carefree manner. Derek sidled along one side of the deck, worried slightly about the open-air design of the resort but attracting no notice from anyone below so far as he could tell. It was still an early hour for most guests, and breakfast was taking place in a lower pavilion looking out to the beach.

Curtains were drawn over a plate glass wall, but Derek found a spot to eke out a view to the inside. It was the bedroom. Derek drew back from the sight of a bare back beached in a tangle of sheets on a king-size bed. He knew that clear, light-olive-skinned back. It was Cal, still sleeping.

Now, Derek's timing was crucial, and he had to pray for a little luck. He waited in a corner of the balcony, shadowed by an eave. His heartbeat drummed in his ears. People were venturing out on the grounds below. A group of children stormed into the central courtyard around the pool to take a swim before breakfast. Anyone could spot him if they looked up and scanned the crown suite deck closely enough. Derek stood as still as a statue for about thirty minutes—or maybe only five—while sweat dripped down his back.

He noticed some kind of ship far out on the water, like a tugboat sitting on the sea. To heaven, he prayed it wasn't headed to the hotel dock, readying to blast a horn to herald its arrival so that everyone would come out of their rooms to check it out. He glanced back cautiously to the stairwell. If he'd misjudged this plan and Brendan came strolling back, he was doomed.

A faint displacement traveled from the bedroom, and then came the triumphant sound of a shower squeaking on. Derek waited a few breaths and proceeded to the sliding door, which was graciously unlatched. With the touch of a diamond thief, he eased the door open just enough to slip through sideways. Then, he stole up to the bed and brought out the pilfered bow tie and his used condom.

For a tenuous moment, the villainy of what he was about to perform held him paralyzed. Cal would be devastated, and he would have to somehow explain to his family why the wedding had been called off when they'd traveled across the Atlantic Ocean and spent a lot of money. Derek steeled his heart. It was the perfect scenario for Cal to surrender himself to the comforting arms of his best friend, the one person who truly understood him, the one person who would believe him. The guy who loved him ten thousand times more than Brendan ever would.

Derek placed the condom and the bow tie on the bed, and he slipped out of the room.

Chapter Nine

FRESHLY SHAVEN AND a touch slaphappy from the shot of Ouzo Louis had pressed on him, Brendan strode back up to his suite. The whitewashed seaside resort shimmered under the fierce Mediterranean sun, nearly blinding, yet invigorating. And the roar of waves was like a celebratory ovation—as if the whole world was singing for him on his wedding day.

He was marrying Cal. That refrain had been echoing in his head for weeks, halting his breath, making him briefly dizzy, and ultimately enlivening him like a wide receiver who'd just made the game-winning catch in the end zone. Now, the actual day had come. Glancing around to take everything in, he decided it could not have been more perfect: This cliffside palace where they were getting married. The bright, warm early autumn day, tempered by a fresh, seaborne breeze. He and Cal would say their vows in the open-air chapel perched over the sea, surrounded by all of the dearest people in their lives. Brendan had won at life. That was the only way he could think to describe it. He took the final stairwell to the presidential suite, two steps at a time, and let himself in with his key.

The shower fizzed in the bathroom. Brendan carefully closed the door behind him and licked his lips with the thought of quietly stripping down and sneaking in there to surprise his fiancé with a little wedding morning romp. He stepped lightly down the hall while pulling his polo shirt over his head. It was easy to pass through the living space to the bedroom. Then he would have to be even lighter with his step to slip into the adjacent bathroom. Moving into the bedroom, he undid the button fly of his chino shorts while keeping an eye on the open bathroom door. Quietly setting his shirt on the bed, he then wriggled his sandals off and stepped out of his shorts and underwear. He placed the last of his clothes on the bedspread bunched up at the foot of the bed. Then a stray glance landed on something strange.

Sitting on a spot of the bed uncovered by the sleep-tossed sheets was a balled-up, white bow tie that Brendan gradually recognized as the kind the hotel wait staff wore. He grinned, thinking it must have been mixed in with the sheets, unbeknownst to him and Cal while they'd climbed all over each other last night. Then his gaze drifted to the bedside table. There, he spotted, in all its foul ignominiousness, a used condom.

It belonged to neither Brendan nor Cal. They'd stopped using condoms after being tested for HIV. Brendan jumped back a step as it occurred to him he might have strolled into—and was now standing buff naked in—the wrong suite. But his key had let him in. His sunglasses case and tablet were on the table. He didn't want to believe the inevitable conclusion. His throat closed up like he was going into anaphylactic shock. What else could it mean?

The shower cut off while Brendan stood staring at the condom, frozen by fear and disgust. Cal appeared at the bathroom door toweling off his wet mop of hair. Despite the fact that Brendan's heart had dropped out of his chest, Cal brightened at the sight of him. When Brendan didn't respond, Cal gave him a strange look.

"What's wrong?"

Brendan turned his head and pointed to the condom. He asked Cal in a trembling voice, "What is this?"

Cal came closer to the bed to take a look. His face grew wide with shock. "I don't know," he said. "It wasn't here before."

Was Cal really going to lie about this to his face? Brendan's legs were weak. He stumbled to sit down on the room's overstuffed chair. Cal wrapped the towel around his waist and came over to him.

He grinned nervously. "Brendan, you can't possibly think—"

"Tell me what I'm supposed to think."

Cal drew back from the anger in his voice.

Brendan's hands shook. This wasn't happening. On their wedding day. From the man he had trusted more than anyone else in his life.

He looked up at Cal. "How could you do this? Was it all a lie?" He glanced at the bed and snorted bitterly. "You could have at least covered it up a little better."

"I can't believe this is what's going through your head."

Brendan stood, enraged. He went to the bed and scooped the tie up in his hand. "What's this, Cal? Do you think I'm a fucking idiot?" Cal shrank back to the other side of the room, which only fed Brendan's anger. He demanded, "Which one of the hotel staff was it? The waiter from last night?" The bow tie slipped out of his trembling hand. He crossed his arms, cradling himself. He suddenly couldn't bear even looking at Cal. "Did you guys plan it all along? The moment I was out of the room?" He shivered. "Were there others, Cal?"

"Brendan, you need to get a grip," Cal told him.

"Don't tell me to get a grip," Brendan shouted.

Cal went to the bedroom bureau and started dressing. He muttered, "This is fucking bullshit."

"You're going to stand there and lie to me? For Christ's sake, Cal, it's our wedding day."

Cal pulled a pair of cargo shorts over his underwear. "It *was* our wedding day. Until you ruined it."

Brendan spat out words, "I ruined it? Are you out of your skull? I'm not the one who got caught fucking someone in our bed on the morning of our wedding."

Cal finished buttoning a madras shirt, now fully dressed. "You've been waiting for this moment all along, haven't you? To accuse me of cheating. To show me I'm not good enough for you." He grabbed his wallet and his passport from the bureau and gave Brendan a hateful glare. "Congratulations, Brendan. You got what you wanted."

Brendan had never before been possessed by an urge for violence. But some heinous, primal instinct took over in that moment, eclipsing reason, humanity, even his surroundings, like being buried by a cold, crimson blanket. He stormed at Cal, reaching to grab him by the collar. "So that's it? You're going to throw this in my face and walk out of here?"

Cal pushed him back, but Brendan wrangled a grip on his arms. Cal stumbled against a standing lamp, knocking it over. Cal's voice: "You're hurting me."

That jolted Brendan back to himself. Cal twisted free, huffing breaths, afraid. Brendan crumbled to his knees. Of all the nightmares in the world, he could never have imagined things with Cal would end like this. He stared up at his fiancé, defeated. "Why? Just tell me why?"

Cal shook his head. He pulled off his platinum, diamond-set engagement ring and placed it on the bureau. Then he walked out of the suite, leaving Brendan clutching himself beneath the weight of a fallen sky.

Chapter Ten

FOR A BLANK stretch of time, Cal walked along the shore of the Aegean Sea like a dazed survivor of a shipwreck on a deserted island. He had nowhere in the world to go. He couldn't face his family. As he left the hotel suite, he'd sorted out a back route to the beach, thinking he might find solace by the water. The roaring surf enveloped him, and he was alone with his thoughts. He headed toward a towering bend in the coastline where he'd be hidden from everyone in the hotel.

The fight with Brendan echoed in his skull. It was as though a demon had possessed his fiancé, but there weren't such things as demons. It had been all Brendan, or at least a dark, deluded side he'd never shown before.

Cal could not fathom how the condom and the bow tie had gotten into the room. It had to have been the most bizarre of mix-ups. A maid came by while he was in the shower, and she unearthed those items, left by the room's past occupants, and went absentmindedly on her way? But Brendan hadn't considered any other explanation than Cal having suddenly, blatantly lured some guy into their room at the first opportunity to fuck around behind his back. He'd made Cal feel like a depraved sex addict.

He thought he'd known Brendan so well, and still a part of him didn't want to believe his fiancé would hatefully accuse him, even rough handle him. When would everything fade away and come back into focus, revealing it had been a dream, or a comet throwing off the world's orbit, warping space and time and briefly making possible the unimaginable?

Cal sat down on the pebbled beach and buried his face in his hands. It was supposed to be their wedding day. Everything had been so perfect. Some cruel god was laughing in the heavens, having blessed Cal with his perfect soul mate only to wrench that fantasy out of his hands and leave him a wretch. And now he had to come up with something to say to his parents, his grandparents, and all of his relatives. His relationship with Brendan was just another disaster like every other attempt he'd made to find someone to love him.

He stood and retook his route down the beach, drawing breaths, trying to refind his composure. Maybe this was fixable. It was a misunderstanding. Were they really going to throw away everything they had together? Cal needed to talk to Brendan. Brendan had a history—that Brazilian model who'd cheated on him—and the situation must have triggered that betrayal, Brendan's insecurity. Cal would give him time to cool down, give himself time to cool down, and then he'd go back to the hotel, and they'd have a rational conversation about what had happened. Brendan would realize he'd gotten worked up over nothing. Cal had been rash, too, bolting out of their room, not giving Brendan a chance to talk things out. They'd both been on short fuses because of the pressure of the wedding. A snort rushed out of Cal's nose. He could picture the two of them talking over each other to apologize, and after a while, they'd laugh about it. Cal's heart warmed, imagining Brendan embracing him and telling him he'd been a fool, that what they had was real and much too strong to fall apart because of a stupid fight over nothing.

God, Cal needed that to happen. He walked on, feeling steadier and reawakened to his sun-flooded seaside surroundings. He was surprised by how far he'd traveled from the hotel. The bend back to the resort was four, maybe five football fields away. Here, the waves frothed up tall and forceful, untempered by the hotel's protective cove. Up ahead, he noticed two men alighting onto the beach from a dinghy with an outboard motor. Strange—they didn't look like fishermen or locals for that matter. They were outfitted in shirts and slacks and had thrown off their suit jackets to accomplish their sloppy landing. Far offshore, a tugboat wallowed on the horizon, perhaps the larger vessel from which the men had launched.

Cal strode up the beach toward the men. Maybe they were lost, looking for the main harbor, or had encountered some problem with their boat. As he got nearer, he noticed they were both big guys, like bodyguards or chauffeurs, with rounded faces and builds, maybe Eastern European. They didn't look like any of the hotel guests or staff Cal had met, but an odd thought occurred to him. Had Brendan sent these guys to look for him already? Only steps away from where they stood with their beached dinghy, he hiked up a grin and waved his hand.

"Hi."

The big guys exchanged a glance. Neither one cracked a smile, and the way they were looking at Cal reminded him of schoolyard bullies sizing up smaller prey. One of the guys stepped toward him and spoke in what Cal recognized as a Romanian accent, "Mr. Thackeray-Prentiss?"

Cal halted. A premonition of danger flashed before him like a neon sign.

"We have business with you," the man told him.

His companion fidgeted with something in his pants pocket. This could be nothing good. One of the guys staggered toward him. Cal turned and ran for his life. He imagined gunshots in his back. The nearest safety was the hotel. Cal stumbled in that direction, not helped by the flip-flops he'd set out in, fighting for traction on sand and pebbles.

One of his flip-flops sprang loose, and he stepped down on hard stones with a yelp. A sharp edge had punctured his skin. That threw off his pace, and he heard the toughs scrambling behind him. Cal limped forward, and one of the guys grabbed him hard by the shoulder, jerking him around and grappling to try to cuff Cal's wrist in his big hand.

Cal cried out for help. His life depended on it. Would his voice carry to the hotel? He wrenched his arm away from his attacker, shearing off one of his bracelets that had gotten hooked in the bastard's fingers. The other guy caught Cal from the side in an iron grip. Both men were built like linebackers, strong enough to rip him apart. Cal struggled to break free, and then a wadded cloth smothered his mouth and nose and scored his sinuses with medicinal vapors. His lungs clenched for air, and the strength drained from his body. He plunged into a dark void.

Chapter Eleven

TOWARD EVENING, BRENDAN was balled up on his couch in a hotel bathrobe with a menagerie of people installed in his suite.

Louis had brought over a bottle of scotch, which he kept trying to get Brendan interested in while he'd emptied the bottle to the halfway mark over the course of the afternoon. Daryl and Riley had somehow decided the suite was a fitting place for them to spend the day, flipping through European TV shows on the big-screen television and squealing to one another in foreign accents. Betsy Schoonover and Cal's sister Genie had found their way up to the room, both dressed uselessly in formal gowns. They were taking account of Brendan at intervals like nurses on suicide watch. Brendan's father paced the room in his "My gay son is getting married" T-shirt, laughing strangely and telling everyone that everything was going to turn out fine. More realistically, Brendan's grandfather and grandmother had appropriated the glass dinette table and were playing two-handed bridge while drinking gin and tonics. From the courtyard below, a gathering of Cal's Greek relatives was starting to sound like a mob stumping for blood.

Brendan prayed for aliens to abduct him into outer space with a tractor beam.

Grandmum discovered the room-service menu, and called out to her grandson, "Let's order up some eggplant dip, Brendy. It's always been your favorite."

Grandad threw down his cards. "We've got a five-course meal waiting for us in the dining hall. Already paid for."

Brendan shrank further into himself. He was an abysmal human being. Dragging everyone to Hydra just so they could witness his coup de grace to botching up his life.

His father came over and placed a hand on Brendan's shoulder and said to Grandad, "No need to rush things, is there Harry?" He then gave Brendan a loosely tethered manic grin. "Cal will be back any moment, and the two guys will set things right."

"Oh, let's be practical, Donovan," Grandad grumbled. "The boy's been gone for seven hours. He's flown the coop." He turned to Brendan. "There's a time to cut your losses, Brendy. Handle this like a man. Go down there and give his family your regrets. Then we can all have our lamb chops and octopus carpaccio and call it an evening."

Donovan whinnied out a laugh and then drifted away to the bedroom. A dull thudding of skull against compressed earthen wall carried from the room shortly thereafter.

"Maybe Brendan wants his privacy," Riley piped up. "Did anyone bother to think of that?" She was, as usual, completely unaware of the irony of her statement, camped beside her brother on the couch in sweatpants and a micro T-shirt, while her teacup terrier, Piper, gnawed on the terry cloth belt to Brendan's robe.

Louis crouched in front of Brendan, trying to nudge out eye contact, and he lay his hand on Brendan's knee. His boozy voice, "Whatever you want us to do, Champ. We can go. We can stay. We can hunt down Cal and bring you back his private parts as a trophy. You just tell us what you need."

"Jesus, Louis," Betsy Schoonover protested. She shooed him away to take over. "We love you, darling. And we support you, no matter what." She shot a look at Louis. "That's what I think Louis was trying to say."

Brendan looked up at her blearily. "I destroyed everything."

Betsy took his cold hand and warmed it with hers. "No you didn't, darling. It's just wedding nerves. It happens all the time."

Brendan winced. If his body had any tears left, he'd have started crying again. Instead, a sort of hiccupping croak came out. He wanted Cal back. He hated himself for laying his hands on Cal. What the hell had been wrong with him? Brendan abhorred violence, and to think he could have hurt his fiancé— He was a monster. Brendan still wasn't sure what to make of the condom and the bow tie, but he'd come to realize he'd grabbed blindly for the very worst conclusion. Even cynical Louis, who knew the full story, had suggested Brendan had been rash. He'd driven away the man he loved. Cal would probably never speak to him again.

Daryl climbed behind Brendan on the couch, leaning against her brother's back. "Betsy's right. Marina stood up Chad at the altar, and he never saw it coming. But Marina picked him for a date at the Second Chances resort in Jamaica, and six weeks later, they got married for real."

Grandmum: "I don't think I know Marina and Chad. Who are they, dear?"

Daryl rolled her eyes. "Season eleven of *The Bachelor*. The destination-date episode was filmed right next door to the house in St. Kitts."

Genie ventured into the Thackeray jabber. "This isn't like Cal. He would have come to talk to me if he was upset. He'd have come to talk to someone." She joined the crowded perimeter around Brendan. "He adored you," she told him. "Try to remember again. Did he say anything about where he was going?"

Brendan shook his head.

Grandad pushed up from his seat and looked to the balcony. "Someone needs to go down and talk to the natives before they decide to send in a Trojan horse and drag our dead bodies out to the beach on chariots." He grimaced. "As usual, it will be me standing in for Brendan at the office."

"Have some compassion for your grandson, Harry," Grandmum told him.

Grandad stood tall and unchastened. "Compassion is exactly what got him into this mess. Cal is clearly a man of no honor."

Brendan unraveled from his fetal position. "It was my fault, not his."

Riley broke out in a shrieking, hand-waving flourish from behind her cell phone screen. "Oh. My. God. My photo with Cal got over two million likes on Instagram. That makes us more famous than the Kardashians."

Grandmum propped her reading glasses on her genteel nose and discreetly gestured for her granddaughter to bring the phone over for a gander.

Genie put her hands on her hips and gave Grandad a murderous look. "Cal is a man of honor. He's the sweetest, most honest guy in the world."

"See what you did now, Grandad?" Daryl said. "You upset the in-laws."

Grandad shrugged and made a moue. "Young lady, your use of the word 'in-laws' is highly questionable under the circumstances."

Louis swayed over to the patriarch. "Mr. Thackeray, if I might suggest, you're not helping this situation right now."

Grandad took account of the room's miserable inhabitants. "Right-o. Not my area of expertise." He smoothed out his tie and herringbone sport coat. "I'll be off then to negotiate with the Panagopoulos strategoi." He wavered a moment. "Brendy— Any pharmaceuticals you'd like from your mother's top-shelf stash while I'm down there?"

"I've got Lexapro, if you want one," Daryl told her brother.

"Adderall?" Riley offered.

"No, sweeties," Betsy Schoonover told them. "This is a vodka and Darvocet situation." She patted Brendan's back. "What do you say? I've got them in my purse downstairs. I'll mix you up a nice sweet-dreams cocktail. Be down and back in a jiff."

Brendan nodded vaguely.

Louis swerved over to Betsy, attempting guile. "Spare one for an old friend?"

Betsy crossed her arms and looked him over. "I would, but I heard the emergency room closes at seven o'clock around here. Though I could ask around for a rusty hand pump later to clear your stomach if you'd like."

"Pretty please?" Louis tried.

Grandad offered his arm, and he and Betsy walked out of the suite together. Just as they left, Derek appeared at the door.

The young man's face was as white as a sheet. Brendan fixed in on him hopefully. Had he heard from Cal?

Their eyes locked. Derek shook his head and looked away just as an official from the hotel came walking in behind him carrying a transparent plastic bag.

Derek explained, "They sent one of the groundskeepers to look for Cal down on the beach." His face shrank up, and he moaned. "He found these by the edge of the water."

Brendan shot straight up from the couch. The uniformed hotel manager plodded over and handed him the bag.

Cal's flip-flop. Cal's woven bracelet. Retrieved from the edge of the sea.

Brendan stared at the bag with the terrifying sensation he was holding his fiancé's last remains. Had he pushed Cal into going off to do something desperate?

Chapter Twelve

CAL AWOKE FEELING as though he had been shot in the head. His vision was delicate and blurry, and besides his throbbing head, he was dehydrated, and his entire body was enervated as if he'd woken up with the worst hangover of his life. He gradually ascertained he was in a room faintly lit by a porthole that kept rolling up and down as though it were on the other end of a seesaw.

Actually, the entire world was seesawing. And Cal's memory was frighteningly blank. Had he been drugged? He could barely move, and he felt like some enormous terrestrial force was rocking him up and down. How had he arrived in the strange room?

He realized his hands were cuffed and bound to a metal beam. His ankles had been tied together with vinyl cord as well. Cal's strength and clarity returned in a panic, though he couldn't find any method to break his bonds or wrench his hands or his feet out of them. The two big lugheads dressed in suits had snuffed him out and kidnapped him. What did they want? To use him for some sick perversion? To sell him into white slavery?

Cal cried out for help and beat his feet against the floor. The rocking motion was now familiar to him. They'd taken him in their dinghy and stowed him on a larger boat, and then motored out to sea—who knew how far, and to who knew where. He could have been blacked out for hours.

The porthole revealed a mere dot of a fading sky. Stacked wooden crates lined the bulwarks of his prison. He was in the hull of some kind of freight craft. Cal had no idea if there was anyone aboard who would help him, but he put all the capacity of his vocal cords and movable parts into rousing a clamor to be heard throughout the entire steel-walled ship.

A watertight hatch door across from him clanged from a wheel turning and bolts sliding free. Cal's breath caught in his throat. The door swung open, and tragically, one of the thugs from the beach stepped through, and then the other followed. They stood like mobster bookends, staring at him impassively.

Cal was not much of a fighter, but he didn't appreciate being roughhoused and tied up when he'd done nothing wrong. If they had come to strangle him for trying to call for help, they'd get a piece of his mind first.

"You think you can get away with this? Two hundred of my relatives are waiting for me back in Hydra. They're Greek and highly experienced in vendettas."

His captors didn't budge an inch, or a moustache. Cal remembered the one guy's accent, and it occurred to him they might not speak English very well.

Another figure ducked through the door. That hiked up the temperature. Cal was tied up to a beam with three criminally inclined men taking account of him. The last guy was tall and brawny like his cohorts, but he wore a sharper pinstriped suit with a red handkerchief in the lapel pocket, and he was even rounder with a great globe of a belly preceding him. His face was almost entirely obscured by a thick brown moustache and beard. An unlit cigar sprouted from his lips like some weird appendage of his tough-guy anatomy. Cal also glimpsed a holster beneath the flap of his suit jacket, as a man might wear a handgun.

This was undoubtedly "the boss." A Romanian gangster, Cal surmised, based on the accent of his henchman. The guy's eyes brightened in cruel amusement at what seemed to be his first look at the bounty his thugs had brought him. As the light had faded even more in the room, he pulled a chain to switch on the overhead light bulb. He stepped closer.

Despite his earlier convictions, Cal slid back against the beam to make himself smaller. He kept his eyes trained on the guy. Oddly, the boss didn't look like he'd come in to deliver a pistol whip or a kick to the ribs to shut Cal up. He stopped short of arm's length away, popped his cigar out of his mouth, and scrutinized Cal. His eyes widened and narrowed in apprehension.

Words in Romanian coursed out of his mouth. He strode back to his henchmen and gave them each a smarting clip on the ear. Cal watched as he pulled a document out of his pants pocket, unfolded it, and waved it in the faces of the two men, barking all the while in his native language. Cal caught a glimpse of the paper. It looked like a black-and-white photograph.

The sense of calamity was unmistakable. The thugs gestured back and forth from Cal to the photograph and then to each other in an increasingly desperate conversation. The boss ended it with a jab of his pudgy finger into each of their necks. He shoved the photograph back in his pants pocket and pushed his two lackeys out of the cargo hold.

Alone, he wiped perspiration from his fat brow with his handkerchief, seeming to collect himself for a moment. The cigar went back in his mouth, and then it came out. He replaced it and took it out a final time, shaking his head and grimacing.

Pulling at his moustache, the boss leaned closer to Cal and spoke in slow and articulated English. "You are not Brendan Thackeray-Prentiss."

Cal shook his head.

The walrus-like man brought out the folded photograph again. He showed it to Cal, tapping a dirty-nailed finger on the image. "You are Callisthenes Panagopoulos."

It was a photograph of Cal and Brendan in tuxes that Brendan's grandmother had sent to the *New York Times* for their wedding announcement. Cal grinned. It was a great shot of the two of them. Then, coming to his senses, thoughts whirred in his head. Might he go free now? It was startling to think the mobsters may have been planning to kidnap Brendan for weeks. The announcement mentioned the wedding ceremony for Cal's family in Hydra. These international criminals must have intended to ransom Brendan for a good chunk of his grandfather's money.

Cal nodded. "My family barely had money to buy clean underwear for the wedding," he said. "I'm sure they'd like to pay for my ransom, but the best they could do is barter a goat and some used fishing equipment for my release." He waited out a response as long as he could. "Can I leave now?"

The mobster frowned and waved his finger. "This, not so simple."

"It can be," Cal argued. "I won't tell anyone. I swear. Just drop me off at the nearest port. I'll even take my chances swimming if you'd prefer."

For a moment, the man's gaze fell on him—gentler, perhaps yielding? Cal tried out a smile. It was really his only artillery. That brokered some more hesitation and even a face-palm from the guy.

The mobster shook it off. "You stay. We decide to do with you," the man told him, omitting "what." His command of English lacked proficiency, which posed yet another challenge for Cal. How the hell would he negotiate being set free?

The big guy propped his cigar in his mouth in a gesture of finality, though his glance lingered on Cal in something like fascination. He turned around, stepped through the door, and cranked closed its locking mechanism.

Cal was trapped. His fate wasn't looking so good. And what if the gangsters decided to make a second try to kidnap Brendan? Being kidnapped was terrible, but the thought of the gangsters getting Brendan and chopping off his ear to mail to his grandfather was even more terrifying. Cal had no way to warn his fiancé. He had no way to tell Brendan he was all right, albeit kidnapped and in need of a SWAT team rescue. Everyone back in Hydra had to be worried sick about him.

His only hope was that they'd find some clue he'd been taken, and the authorities might quickly follow a trail. Otherwise, he'd have to pull off some kind of impossible Houdini escape and hope one summer of lifeguard training on Onondaga Lake had prepared him for a gambit to land.

AFTER HE HAD rearticulated to his nephews Anton and Emil they were useless excuses for human beings, Dragomir Negrescu—who'd earned the name the Bear of Bucharest—retired to his above-deck cabin with a bottle of Armenian brandy. He hung his suit coat up, unstrapped his revolver holster, stripped down to his sleeveless undershirt, and unbelted and unbuttoned his pants. After laying the revolver on his bed, he sat on the cabin's single chair and lit his half-incinerated cigar with a silver Zippo lighter that had served him through three decades of smoking.

This job of ransoming the rich American freight company heir was to be his life's pension. He had toiled at all forms of illegal enterprise for forty years. At fifteen, he was taken under the wing of a corrupt Soviet Commissar to root out information on rabble-rousers in the Bucharest slums and garnered occasional work kidnapping children and bullying their families to empty their larders of contraband goods. Dragomir had moved on to running opium from Afghanistan into Romania to supply the recreational interests of army foot soldiers and then provided the names of the derelicts to the Commissar when his boss was in the mood to make an example of one of his underlings. It was dicey and modestly compensated work from a man whose paranoid nature made him an unreliable employer. By good fortune, the Commissar was shipped off to Siberia by his backstabbing superiors. That allowed the Bear of Bucharest to break out independently as a diamond smuggler, using the profiteering contacts he had established from his drug-running days.

When there was competition, the Bear crushed it. His favored method had been abducting criminal upstarts and tearing out their faces with a three-toothed gardening claw, which he found provided a deterrent to their associates and had the benefit of enlarging his reputation. Later, he diversified to smuggling artillery to Central Asian rebels. In the fat years of the 1980s, he operated a profitable casino and a brothel in Constanta on the Black Sea. But every boom had an expiration date. The revolution of 1989 shuffled the deck of government authorities he could bribe. They played favorites with a new breed of criminals who supported independence, with no regard for experience or tradition. There'd been lean years for sure, but Dragomir found his next opportunity in joining the cause of his country's urban rejuvenation by forging claims to abandoned lots and extorting hefty profits from big-moneyed foreign developers.

It was a career that took a physical and psychic toll on a man even as hardened and unprincipled as Dragomir Negrescu. He was now fifty-five years old, overweight, diabetic, with plaque-encrusted arteries. According to his physician, he had a chance of reaching fifty-six if he retired, forswore fried meats and pastries, and adopted a highly improbable regimen of cardiovascular exercise.

Dragomir had never married, so he had no sons to take up his trade. His nephews, Anton and Emil, had no such aptitude. They had bruised the few brains god had given them in street fights. Always, there were younger, hungrier men who were eager to claim territory in the world of criminal trade.

When Dragomir received an international call from an old friend who had moved to New Jersey, he'd been sufficiently dog-weary to entertain the proposal of a ransom. He was adrift in debt, and while he knew such operations were a risky game, he had a winning track record in kidnappings from the old days. The friend, Marin Vadova, had been scoping out the American billionaire Harold Thackeray, and his grandson's wedding trip to Hydra presented the perfect opportunity to snatch the society dandy. Dragomir had use of an old tugboat owned by a tobacco smuggler in Constanta. Marin knew a friend with a vacant apartment above a *taverna* on the minor North Aegean island of Psara. The plan was to hold the billionaire's son there and use the apartment as a base while Marin negotiated the transfer of ten million dollars to an untraceable bank account in Dubai. When the money was received, they would release the rich hostage, blindfolded in a busy market in the city of Izmir on the Turkish Aegean coast. They had agreed to split the money fifty-fifty, though Dragomir had already worked out some creative accounting of his expenses to push things in his favor. With his share, he would buy a palace in Albania overlooking the Adriatic Sea, where at least if he died of heart disease, he would enjoy a better view than from his back-alley facing apartment in Bucharest when he took his last glimpse of the world.

He took a long slug from the bottle of brandy. Now that dream was flushed down the latrine. They had stolen the target's boyfriend and could never return to Hydra for an encore performance. The wedding party would be as skittish as cats. They would soon make a report to the Hellenic Police, who were, if not particularly adept at investigation, at least prudent enough to question an unscheduled Romanian towboat making port near the scene of the crime.

Dragomir beat his fist against his knee. He had tasted the goddamn money. He had made a short list of Albanian properties and fucking calculated exchange rates. Instead, he would be returning to Bucharest where he was living on phony credit cards and dodging the Vasile clan for an unpaid gambling debt, until he cooked up a new extortion scheme. Prosperity was a fickle whore. Money cometh and money goeth. More goeth than cometh lately.

And now, what to do with Callisthenes Panagopoulos? The greenest street hustler knew there was no profit in kidnapping a Greek unless his family had struck it rich in America, and Marin, who had researched every angle of the operation, had reported the kid's family were peasants all the way back to the reign of Alexander the Great. Anton and Emil had insisted the two men in the photo were identical, but they were blind. Callisthenes was a man who could not be mistaken for anyone else.

Sweat beaded on Dragomir's temples. He stood and pushed open his porthole window to cool himself with some bracing nighttime sea air. That young man strung up in the tank of the boat had gotten him worked up in ways that were not advisable for a man of his age and failing physiology. His photograph had whetted the appetite, but he was many times more glorious in person. With curled, blond hair as it was said crowned the heads of angels. A face that inspired a thousand sighs, and a body that hit all the marks of masculine perfection. A smile from him had turned Dragomir's insides to custard. To touch his lips would be an ecstasy. To do to him what Dragomir's more base imagination pictured would be a sin worth being lashed by whips in the pit of hell for the rest of his days.

This was not his first infatuation with a man, but even the most desirable young hustlers Dragomir had hired in Bucharest, Sofia, or Ankara had been ordinary in comparison. All his life, he'd kept his proclivities discreet. Romania was not Denmark with its worldly sensibilities. People concealed their perversions, though they had plenty, and they bargained with priests for absolution or bargained with grain alcohol if they were atheists. To be known as a homosexual, particularly among Dragomir's gangster ilk, could end a man's career, not to mention his life.

Yet sublimely, ridiculously, Callisthenes Panagopoulos lifted him above those worries. How could anyone condemn him for loving the young man? He was the embodiment of beauty. He shone brighter than Apollo himself.

Anton and Emil had vented strategies for disposing of the boy. Anton had suggested putting a bullet in his head and casting him overboard to disappear in a deep trench of the Aegean Sea. Emil had openly wondered if they might get a little cash for him from an Arab sex trafficker such as they had dealt with from time to time.

This could not happen. Dragomir realized he needed to be careful about displaying his desires, but he would not allow any harm to come to the boy. In thinking about these matters, a terrible fear clutched his heart, and he stepped over to the greasy mirror on the wall of his cabin, searching his reflection with the horror of a man who did not know himself anymore. What fate had befallen him? His nephews had kidnapped the wrong man, and Dragomir could not cipher if Callisthenes was a seraph sent to deliver him to an afterworld of ecstasies or a Marţ Sara, an incubus disguised in beauty's form to lure him into carelessness and destruction. His mind was beguiled by a fantasy that Callisthenes would want him, and they would swear their hearts be sewn together in the manner of righteous lovers like Hadrian and Antinous. Dragomir would make a home, a life for them, however it pleased his beloved. He would spare no sacrifice to make him happy, even forsaking his criminal ways to make an honest living, lest the boy be imperiled by his misdeeds.

What foolish dreams had overtaken him! Dragomir was a fat, old, faltering ogre of a man. Callisthenes garnered proposals from handsome, young American aristocrats like Brendan Thackeray-Prentiss, a man who required three names. He would laugh at Dragomir's near-pederastic infatuation. Though it was hard to imagine Callisthenes being anything but virtuous, Dragomir was well aware of how vain, cruel youths regarded amorous old men. His heart would be torn to pieces if Callisthenes spurned him. And if he did not drop dead from that, any word getting out about him circling around the boy like a pink-feathered, old buzzard would destroy him. It was tight quarters in the tugboat. His nephews could easily spy or eavesdrop on something they shouldn't have.

Dragomir sank back down on his little chair, grazing a hand on his bearded cheek. Though all of these considerations spoke emphatically against it, he could not shake free from the possibility of having Callisthenes as his lover. He could, however, make a bargain with himself. If the young man showed some sign, some divinely generous inclination he could love him, Dragomir would spirit him away to a place where they would never be found, and they would be sheltered by their happiness. Tears stung his eyes, and a great, maddening despair shook his bones. If it could not be so, Dragomir swore to himself he would kill Callisthenes to erase this folly of his heart and to make it so no man could possess him.

Chapter Thirteen

THE NEXT MORNING, Brendan headed to town in a water taxi, accompanied by Cal's father, his four brothers, and Grandad Harry who could not be dissuaded from helming a mission of dire importance. They disembarked at the harbor of Hydra's quaint town of immaculate white-faced villas, roofed by terracotta tiles and bedecked with scarlet bougainvillea hanging from windowsills. It was the shoulder season for the Greek isles, and only a few dozen tourists threaded the cobbled streets, which were lined with boutiques and outdoor cafés.

The island's police station was a short walk from the harbor, and it was housed in a cozy ground-floor pied-à-terre with dark wood doors and latticed windows. Such dainty elegance was nice to look at it, but it set the mind to worry about the police force's experience with serious matters like kidnapping, or god help Brendan, suicide or murder. The Panagopoulos brood pushed themselves on the lobby's single clerk in a Hellenic umbrage. Brendan stood back in deference. He couldn't blame them for making a scene. They'd lost their baby brother. Alone, he might have thrown himself at the clerk with equal desperation. Though this seemed to be a garden-variety situation for the unflappable young man on duty in his tidy white cap and a uniform in patriotic midnight blue.

Grandad sorted out an opening in which to insinuate himself. He was, as always, surefooted yet civilized with the clerk, and managed to send things into orderly motion. Brendan was briefly touched when Grandad introduced him as the "fiancé." Documents appeared that needed filling out. The police lieutenant was called out from the station's back room to welcome and tend to the complainants.

While Cal's father and brothers carped about the paperwork and argued with each other over how to fill it out, Brendan introduced himself to Lieutenant Giannis Constantinides. He explained he had evidence that needed swift examination. The dapper officer welcomed him into a comfortable office of artisanal furniture and framed photographs of the local scenery. Brendan insisted on taking the interview alone in spite of the glare of forbearance from Grandad and the grumbles of the Panagopoulos brothers. But Brendan was Cal's betrothed and the last person to have seen him.

Lieutenant Constantinides was a slim, handsome, clean-shaven man with dark Mediterranean features and a pleasant aroma of aftershave. He looked to be Brendan's age if not younger. His English was accented but entirely serviceable, and he offered to make Greek coffee from a little brass pot on an electric burner that was set up on the office's gleaming sideboard cabinet. Brendan politely declined. As soon as they were sitting across from each other at the lieutenant's desk, Brendan brought the plastic bag with Cal's flip-flop and bracelet out from his beach tote and presented it to Constantinides.

The officer casually turned the items over, and Brendan explained where they'd been found. He proceeded to tell the man everything, from the embarrassing circumstances of his fight with Cal to their brief grapple, which had scared Cal away. He'd previously considered that in a missing person's investigation, the boyfriend or husband was usually the prime suspect. Grandad Harry had urged restraint, wanting to fly out his lawyer from New York before anything was said. But Brendan decided he had to report the unadulterated facts. Cal's life was at stake. How could he hide anything that could impede the investigation? His last accounting of Cal was a haunting, shameful memory, and if some detail inspired a theory about Cal's whereabouts, he would happily go to jail. The confession poured out of him, as though he was striking a bargain with a god he'd not believed in prior to that day, and by his honest contrition, a higher power would bring Cal back.

When he was done, the lieutenant smiled at him with a knowing glimmer in his eye. "This is a lover's quarrel."

He reached across his desk and turned a double-photo frame outward for Brendan's edification. One side of the frame held a photograph of a pretty, young Greek woman and the other side showed an infant, perhaps six months old. Constantinides interwove his knuckles on his desk. "I am married myself." He blustered out a razz that briefly unsettled his jet-black hair from his forehead. "This is a war that can never be won. Day and night, this woman is wanting to be fighting. 'Why cannot we be going on vacation, Giannis?' 'Why does my sister have help to watch the baby, and I have none?' 'Why do you not love me like you used to, Giannis?'" He leaned forward and smiled crookedly at Brendan. "Always, this is what my wife is saying to me."

The lieutenant turned the photo frame back to his advantage. "Yet we make a very beautiful baby, don't you think?"

"Yes," Brendan assured the young officer, though he was wondering how things had turned into two pals commiserating over married life. "But Lieutenant, Callisthenes has been missing for over twenty-four hours."

He looked to the faded, unmatched flip-flop, and a rush of sadness overcame him. "Why would he have left his shoe on the beach and torn his bracelet?"

"This bracelet, it is a gift from you? Could be he was angry and tore it from his wrist in spite."

Brendan shook his head. "No. He had the bracelet before we met." Now he was perturbed. He stared at Constantinides incredulously. "This doesn't look like more than some minor domestic dispute to you? Where would he run off to, wearing one sandal? He left the hotel in a short-sleeved shirt and shorts, with maybe forty euros in his wallet. There had to have been some sort of struggle on the beach. Or he went into the water." Brendan's voice trailed off fearfully.

"Mr. Thackeray-Prentiss, this is Hydra. We have no crime," the young lieutenant said. "And if your fiancé drowned, tell me—where is the body?"

Brendan froze up for a moment, wondering if it was an accusation. The lieutenant sat back in his chair, inhabiting the thoughtful manner of an actual law enforcement official. "This place where the shoe and bracelet were found, the island shoal is very rocky and the sea is very forceful. You say the hotel groundskeeper searched this place. If your fiancé had been swimming there and drowned, he would be washed up on the rocks, along with his shoe and bracelet, plain for anyone to see. The same if he was thrown in. So you see, my friend, this cannot be."

Brendan didn't know what to think. The lieutenant's deduction was, on the one hand, reassuring. But was this to be the extent of his interest in the matter?

Constantinides stood and came around his desk. "I am sorry for your troubles. On your wedding day of all things! It pains me that you and your guests should have such problems on our beautiful island." He looked down at Brendan, who was still seated in his chair, unable to move. "I do not believe any harm has come to your fiancé, but I myself will search this place where his belongings were found." He gestured to the plastic bag. "May I keep them?"

"Of course," Brendan said. He then remembered he'd brought a photograph of Cal, which he'd downloaded from his phone and printed out at the hotel business center. He handed it to the lieutenant.

Constantinides glanced at the photo twice. "A handsome man, your fiancé. In Greek, we call this *kouklos*. Like a teen idol, you would say. Inspiring the strongest and most stirring passion."

Brendan smiled weakly. He stood, and the lieutenant ushered him from the office.

LATER THAT DAY, Brendan hiked the beach to the place where the groundskeeper had found Cal's flip-flop and bracelet. He knew he was no police detective, but he needed to see the spot himself, to feel like he had the slightest use since Cal had disappeared. Clearly, the local police would do nothing. After his exasperating visit with Lieutenant Constantinides, Brendan had gone over to the ferry station with Grandad and the Panagopoulos men to canvas the employees with a photo of Cal, describing in detail what he'd been wearing. The ferry was the only way off the island, unless Cal had somehow hired a private boat. None of the ferry employees recognized Cal, and they didn't exactly do a brisk business at this time of the year. There were only two trips off the island each day, one in the morning and one at night.

Returning to the hotel, Cal's family mobilized a door-to-door search of the island, calling on their network of relatives and sending the brothers on foot and mule to comb the island's more rugged regions. Grandad had placed a phone call to a U.S. senator, an old, family chum, in order to exert international pressure on the Greek authorities. The rest of the hotel guests were holed up at the pool bar in varying states of languor and distress.

The hotel groundskeeper had staked a wooden post at the spot where he'd found Cal's things. Brendan stood there, looking out to the boundless seascape. It was low tide, and the shallows were indeed rocky and inhospitable as the police lieutenant had said. Brendan kicked off his sandals and walked into the surf.

Hard pebbles bit his feet, and he had to maneuver very gingerly around bigger, jagged stones, while the icy, weltering current had him swaying for balance. It was nearly intolerable, but Brendan waded in farther, searching for evidence of Cal. Why would Cal have gone swimming in the spot? Brendan trudged out a good ten yards from shore, and the water was only at his knees. It didn't make sense that Cal would have gone into the water and struggled, or intentionally tried to end his life, or that foul play had been involved. Beyond the fact that his body should have been easily found, as Constantinides had said, the shoal was a terrible place to wade into. If Cal had been determined to drown himself, he'd have picked an easier place to trudge into the sea. Any criminal who might have tried to wrestle him down would have had a very difficult time on the sharp rocks. Who would have done that anyway? Cal had no enemies, and the beach was so remote. A criminal would have had to have planned to follow and attack him. There was access to the beach from the hotel, but Brendan observed no trails down from the inland cliffs as far as he could see.

Glancing toward the shore, he spotted a solitary figure standing on the beach. Squinting, Brendan recognized Derek in a Syracuse University sweatshirt and baggy shorts, both of which were much too big for his skinny frame. Brendan waded toward him. The kid was downcast and shivering.

"Hey," he greeted Derek. The young man barely looked up at him. Though Derek was wearing sunglasses, Brendan had the distinct impression he'd been crying. Derek had to be wrecked by his best friend's disappearance. Brendan joined him at the water's edge.

He told Derek about his dealings with the police. "They're completely useless. They think Cal's sulking somewhere because we had a fight." Brendan was glad for Derek's company. He could tell Derek understood how ominous the situation was. They both knew Cal intimately— that he wasn't the kind of guy to run off sulking, kissing off everyone who cared about him.

Derek hiccupped tears. He groaned out, "It's all my fault."

Brendan looked upon him kindly. "How's it your fault? I'm the bastard who made him run away on our wedding day."

Derek fidgeted around like there was some kind of torment eating away at him. "You don't understand. I did this. I didn't mean to. It wasn't supposed to happen this way." He started hyperventilating. Brendan stared at him strangely. Derek blurted out, "It was me, Brendan. I put the condom and the bow tie in your room."

For a moment, a smile tweaked up on Brendan's face from the impossibility of Derek doing something so absurd, so unconscionably conniving. Then, arisen from a vulnerable place, he was beguiled by a sense of absolution. He'd lost it for a reason back in the hotel room with Cal, and neither he nor Cal was to blame. Those were fleeting impressions, however, as the sinister nature of Derek's confession sank in.

"Why would you do that?"

"I'm in love with Cal," Derek whined. "Always have been. I was afraid of losing him to you."

Brendan's body tensed up like a steel coil. A vein on the side of his brow throbbed. He stormed at Derek, ready to tear him apart. "Why would you fucking do that? You goddamn piece of shit."

Derek cowered away. "I'm sorry."

"You're sorry," Brendan spat out. He felt like a sheet had been pulled out from under his feet. He remembered Derek's delight while telling him about Cal's stalker, Steve. Could Derek have been a sexually obsessed psychopath all along? They say it takes one to know one. Could Derek's plot have been even more desperate?"

"Where is he?" Brendan demanded. "What did you do to him?"

"I don't know where he is," Derek said. "I thought the two of you would have a fight, and he'd just get upset."

Brendan grabbed him by the collar of his sweatshirt. "We had a fight. You made me accuse him of something he didn't do. You fucking ruined our wedding. You ruined Cal." Brendan was so disgusted he shoved Derek hard. Derek went toppling backward and fell on the pebbled beach. Brendan stood over him, thinking about a kick to the ribs or stooping down to punch him in the nose. Derek teared up and raised his hands pitifully. The burning embers inside Brendan cooled a bit.

"Go ahead and hurt me," Derek said. "I deserve it. I just had to tell you and say I'm sorry. I just want Cal back."

"You deserve a whole lot more hurt than I could ever give you," Brendan said. "And you never deserved Cal. You're a sick, demented, backstabbing fuckup."

"I know," Derek moaned. "I'd take it all back if I could. I'd confess it all to Cal and walk out of everyone's lives forever."

Brendan looked down at him with venom. "I never want to see your ugly face again. If you ever get anywhere near Cal, I'll make you wish you were never born."

The despicable runt wiped his eyes and muttered to himself. "Beat you to that. I already wish I was never born."

"Spare me the melodrama," Brendan told him. "Why can't you be a fucking adult?"

Derek gazed at him in what Brendan supposed was an attempt at earnestness. "I want to help, Brendan. You said the police are useless. I know you've got every reason not to trust me, but honest to god, you've got to believe me— I'd do anything to bring Cal back safe and sound."

Brendan snorted. "You're right about one thing. I've got no reason to trust you. How the hell do you think you're in any position to help?"

"I don't know," Derek said. He pushed himself up a little on his elbows, looking like a psychiatric patient who'd lost track of his surroundings.

Brendan noticed for the first time how frighteningly pale he was. It thawed him a little, though only so much.

"I saw something," Derek told him. "Yesterday morning. It couldn't have been much earlier than when Cal took off from the hotel. There was this tugboat out on the water. I didn't think anything of it at the time. Maybe it means nothing. But if Cal came around this way, and there's no other place he could've gone, I started thinking maybe it could've had something to do with him disappearing."

Brendan gave him a good look-over. More goddamn tricks? He'd never know for sure. But it brought to mind an idea.

He reached his hand to help Derek up and hoisted him to his feet with more force than necessary. "You want to help? This is what you're going to do. We're going back to the police station together, and you're going to tell them exactly what you saw. Then, when we get back to the hotel, you're going to tell all the guests, including Cal's family, what you did." He gave Derek a shove down the beach in the direction of the water taxi dock.

Chapter Fourteen

CAL POUNDED HIS feet on the floor of the freight hold and cried out, "I have to pee." He'd been holding his bladder for what had to have been hours because he didn't relish a visit from the Romanian crooks. But it was bad enough being bound by hand and foot without pissing himself.

He'd never known such agony. His back was spasming from being hunched over for so long, his wrists were torn raw from his attempts to free himself, and the hard metal floor bit into his tailbone. This was real, human suffering. His dental surgery for his wisdom teeth? A week in bed with the chicken pox? Cal dreamed about trading for one of those misfortunes.

Meanwhile, he had to find the courage to face the thugs and hope for some opportunity to free his hands and legs and make a break for it. Maybe a rescue attempt was in the works, but maybe it wasn't, and even if it was, his captors might decide to cut their losses long before help arrived. If he could work out a way to trick one of the guys to free his hands under the pretext of tending to his private business, he would give it a go to overpower the bastard. Based on his size in relation to the thugs, it would take the viciousness of an alley cat. He had to do it while he still had strength in his body. They hadn't fed him or given him water. One day and night at sea had passed, and by the fading light from the porthole, it was getting on nighttime again.

The vault door churned and clanged. Cal zeroed in on the entryway, which he'd noticed could only be locked from the outside. It pulled open, and one of the Eastern European gorillas appeared. He strode into the room, pulled the chain for the overhead light, and glared at Cal with umbrage. A metal pail swung from one of his big meat hooks.

"I've gotta go to the bathroom," Cal said.

The guy squinted. As it appeared he didn't know much English, Cal looked down at his lap and swiveled his hips, hoping to drive home the point. That little motion almost made him lose control of his bladder right then and there. He bit his lip. The big guy lumbered over and dropped the pail on the floor.

"How am I supposed to use that?" Cal said. He tried to beseech some mercy by maneuvering his arms around the beam, behind which his hands had been pinioned.

The thug looked him over, appearing to take account of the dilemma. He grunted something in Romanian and gestured with his hands. Loosely following, Cal twisted his legs under himself so he was slightly upright and leaning on his knees. The guy used his foot to slide the pail near Cal's crotch.

Cal stared up at him in disbelief. "You've got to untie my hands. Or at least untie my feet."

Horribly, the guy hunkered down in front of him, grasped the waistband of Cal's shorts, and fumbled open the button and his zipper.

"No. No," Cal pleaded. He tried to squirm away, but his mobility was pitiful. The goon yanked his shorts and briefs down to his knees. Then he rattled over the pail into aiming distance.

Cal felt like bawling, but the sight of the receptacle triggered a bodily need he could not contain. The water started streaming. He strained his hips to aim it into the bucket, but he was so confined, legs twisted and folded under, his piss went everywhere but the receptacle—the hammock of his briefs, his legs, the floor. Exquisite relief and bald humiliation all at once. He looked up to the thug as a child might search for answers from a stranger who had ground his face into a mound of dog shit. The mustached fink smiled at him in cruel amusement. He turned around and headed to the door.

Just then, the boss man came to the door. He peeked at Cal, who was contorted in abject distress, and he clipped the henchman hard on the ear. Romanian reprimands and curses flew from the big guy's mouth. His underling cowered from the vault, as much as a two-hundred-and-fifty-pound gangster could cower.

Cal buried his gaze in his shoulder. He was exposed and soaked in his own urine from his thighs downward. The man stepped near. His bearing was quiet and gentle. Cal glanced at him. He'd stowed his cigar in his breast pocket, and he held a mug of steaming soup in one hand and a bottle of water tucked beneath one of his lumbering arms. He looked stricken by the sight of Cal's discomfort. Did the gangster possess some humanity? Though Cal also noticed he'd brought along his gun, strapped to his shoulder holster.

The guy had sealed closed the portal to the hold, which seemed a gallant gesture to protect Cal's privacy. As he came over, Cal tried out a piteous expression, which wasn't too hard to do, given the circumstances. The man set down the water and the soup and mumbled to himself in rancorous Romanian. He looked to Cal's shorts and then up to his face in a gentlemanly way, skirting the parts in between. Cal nodded his head and maneuvered his legs so the guy would have an easier time pulling up his shorts. He stooped and did the deed.

"Drink?" the man said.

When Cal nodded again, he unscrewed the bottle cap and brought the top to Cal's mouth. The water was cool and fresh and heavenly. He downed the entire bottle, which the guy tipped back very gently. He even brought out his red handkerchief from his suit jacket to dab at the spillage on Cal's chin.

Catching his breath, Cal uttered, "How long are you going to keep me here?"

A musing look passed over the mobster's bearded face. "This is complicated."

"Tell me about it. You've got me tied down like prison furniture. It's not like I'm a flight risk. The door's locked, and the only other way out is a porthole I could barely get my head through."

The man raised the mug of soup. "Eat?"

Cal nodded. It looked like one of those fluorescent yellow, instant soup mixes, but the smell of food was wonderful. The man blew on it in case it was too hot. He carefully brought it to Cal's lips. The broth was perfect—not too hot, not too cold. Cal drank it down. Only after he was done did it occur to him to not take food from strangers. His insides shrank. Did he just help himself to a dose of tranquilizers?

It didn't feel like he had. The boss man crouched at his side, gazing at him happily. His friendliness was hard for Cal to reject outright. It was always nice to be liked, and in his present situation, it was arguably pretty vital. He tried a play for sympathy.

Cal looked down at his lap. "I haven't wet myself since grade school. And now I'm supposed to sit in my wet shorts until we get to some kind of port?" He shivered. It got pretty cold in the hold at night.

The boss man looked like he'd picked up the music but not the words. Cal jostled his bottom half. He grimaced. He was patient. Finally, a light bulb went off in the man's head.

"I bring you."

He raised himself to his feet with a groan and stepped stiffly from the room.

The guy was getting on in years. That could work in Cal's favor. Unless he collapsed on top of Cal while he was trying to get away. He had to be at least twice Cal's weight.

Alone, Cal's heartbeat raced. This was going to be his chance. He could appeal to the mobster's surprising good nature and ask him to give him the dignity of dressing himself. With his hands and legs free, he would figure out a way to grab the guy's gun and hold him back and race out the door. What he'd have to deal with out and about on the boat was even scarier to consider, so Cal left the plan at that. One desperate act at a time. He heard a clop of footsteps returning and composed himself sullenly.

The boss man brought in a handful of garments and stood at Cal's feet. He brandished the clothes proudly. "This for you. Make you good again."

Cal raised his hands feebly behind the beam. He winced until he felt a tear sprout from his eye. In his side vision, he saw the man's face deflate, and then his eyes fixed in on him with concern.

"This is all so demoralizing," Cal moaned. "I can't even dress myself."

"I help you."

Cal shook his head languidly. "What does it matter anyway? These ropes are so tight; my wrists are torn to shreds. I can't feel my feet. If I can't get out of these ropes and into a comfortable position, you might as well just leave me as I am."

The boss stepped around the beam to look at Cal's hands. He muttered a pitiful oath and came around to face Cal again.

"You see what you did?" Cal said with a pout.

The mobster's expression turned dark and grim. It was something like an old cartoon in which Bluto was being chastened by Olive Oyl. He gazed at Cal sharply.

"You be a good boy?"

A little glow grew inside Cal, but he did not let it show on his face. "I've been tied up for so long, I'm practically an invalid. I don't think you've got anything to worry about."

The tone of his voice appeared to convey his surrender to his fate. The boss went to the door and shut it all the same. Cal took a sly account of the bulge of his holstered gun inside the skirting of his jacket.

His captor lumbered around the beam. Blissfully, hands worked to unknot his bonds. The big boss had to nudge up close to do it. A reek of cheap cologne mixed with body odor assaulted Cal. Midway through the untying, the man spoke quietly, "You are handsome boy."

"Thanks," Cal said. Though his eyes worried around from the unexpected compliment. One hand was unfettered from the ropes. His free wrist throbbed, but the removal of the pressure was glorious. The gangster told him, with a touch of buoyancy, "You like the rich men."

That spun things into freakier territory. Cal held down a surge of panic. "Oh, I don't know that I have a preference," he tried out. "I've always been more attracted to what's on the inside." His second hand came free. Cal breathed out in relief. He massaged his aching, chafed wrists. The hairy mobster came around and looked Cal in the face.

"I, rich man," he said. "I make you very happy."

"That's sweet," Cal managed to say. "I feel a lot better already. How about you untie my feet?"

The mobster gazed at him in wonder. Something may have been lost in translation, Cal feared. But fortunately, the guy got down on his knees to unknot the cords around Cal's feet. He looked up at Cal. "I make you beautiful home in Albania. You like?"

"I've never been to Albania. I've never been anywhere in Europe besides Greece. I bet it's a beautiful country." Cal realized he was on the razor-thin edge of keeping himself in the guy's good graces and giving him the horribly wrong impression. What could he do? While the man worked on unknotting his ankles, he stretched into another topic. "Does your work have you traveling a lot?"

"Traveling?" the man repeated. "Where you like to traveling?" He grinned at Cal, giving off a slight hint of a younger, waggish version of himself with his wide and sparkling eyes. "You like to make party? I take you all the places. Mykonos. Bodrum. Tel Aviv."

Cal smiled. "You've been to all those places?"

"I am young man once. Make big party everywhere." He looked at Cal grimly. "I still know how to make big party with handsome Greek boy."

Cal turned his head and blushed. The old, behemoth Romeo was almost endearing. Cal was untangled from the ropes and tangled in a new, uncomfortable predicament. He flexed his unbound feet to get the blood coursing again. The man stood up proudly. Cal pushed his achy body up from the floor. An awkward silence passed while the boss man gazed at him, nearly giddy like a teenage girl. Meanwhile, urine saturated the crotch of Cal's shorts and was soaking into the seat. He looked to the pile of clothes the Romanian had brought.

The guy caught the cue. He gathered the clothes from the floor and handed them to Cal. Cal looked around the hold. It wasn't a very big space, but there was a dark corner that would give him a little discretion.

"I'll just go over here," he said, nudging his head in the direction.

Cal stepped away, and thankfully, his new admirer stayed put. Now he had to work out a way to get to the gun. Facing the wall of the hull, in a hollow of shallow, Cal took his time piecing through the articles of clothing he'd been given. He couldn't hurt the man. Cal was too softhearted to do that. Maybe the boss man deserved it for smuggling him into his boat, for conspiring to ransom Brendan, but Cal had seen a gentler side of the gangster, and didn't every criminal have a hard-luck story that was owed some sympathy? His family couldn't have approved of his life choices. Maybe they were destitute. Maybe he'd grown up in a neighborhood of violence and crime.

Cal could hear what Derek would say—Cal was being naïve and overly trusting. Had he developed Stockholm syndrome? He'd read about that in psychology class. If he ever expected to gain his freedom, he would need to harden his heart. Getting the guy's gun was his only chance.

His change of clothes was troubling. A pair of briefs that would fit him like a droopy diaper. Trousers that he could use to compete in a potato-sack race. Fortunately, the guy had provided him with a thin leather belt to hold up his pants. Cal doffed his drenched shorts and underwear and stepped into his new clothes. He laced the belt through the pant loops and found that the remaining ends needed to be tied up in a double knot to accomplish cinching his pants. He cuffed the legs in clownish wads. Adding to the absurdity, he had one flip-flop. Cal peeked over his shoulder and saw his companion had turned his back chivalrously. An idea hit Cal. It was something he'd seen in a spy movie.

He stepped out of the shadowy corner and presented himself to the Romanian. The man's face turned rosy, and he let out a throaty chuckle. "Big," he declared.

Cal pshawed. "They're perfect. Believe me; it's an improvement on what I was wearing." He gestured to the pants. "They're yours?"

The Romanian nodded bashfully. Cal stepped closer. He channeled the cool of an actor, while trying not to trip on the cuffing of his pants. He didn't end his steps until he was a mere hand's reach from his companion and could look him boldly in the face. "I don't know how to thank you."

The Romanian's eyes quivered. He was suddenly scared stiff. Cal put out of mind the smell and sight of him. The deed had to be done. He pressed up close and kissed the gangster on the mouth, even contriving a little tongue action.

The guy's lips were cold. Caught by surprise, he was nervous, even virginal. Cal extended the kiss while venturing one hand beneath his jacket, searching for the place where he had holstered his gun. Before he could reach it, the guy coughed into his mouth.

Cal drew back. The man had turned pale as a sheet, and he winced and clutched the left side of his chest. His eyes stabbed at Cal, and a Romanian gasp escaped from his lips. Then he foundered to his knees with a thud and collapsed onto his side.

Cal leapt down beside him with a hand drawn over his mouth. The guy's eyes were wide open, though unfocused, and his chest was moving with shallow breaths. A heart attack? The timing was miraculous, but to have been the cause of it was troubling.

"I'm so sorry," Cal said. He pried a revolver from the

man's holster. It was so much easier to do than he'd imagined. He fastened on the man again. "I'm so sorry about this. Really, I am."

Cal stood and looked to the door. A charitable little part of him suggested he call for help. He banished the idea. He had to be ruthless. The gun was his ticket off the boat, and the guy was still breathing. On his way out, he could alert the henchmen, and they would attend to him.

A fluster of movement gained up on the other side of the door. That hard fall the boss man had taken must have been loud enough to alert the goons. The door swung open, and the two mobster bookends appeared in states of high alert.

Channeling policeman drama, Cal launched his arm out at eye level and pointed the gun at the thugs. They glimpsed the gun, glimpsed their boss laid out, and threw up their hands like pussy willows.

Sweat sprouted from Cal's temples, but he held his cool. He gestured with the gun. "Get in."

The guys shuffled into the freight hold, and Cal stepped around them, keeping the gun aimed at their chests while he went. He passed through the portal and pushed it shut, and then he got to working on the wheel that closed up its bolts. It held fast. A steel trap, half a foot thick. Cal looked around. He saw a ladder to the deck. Lord knew, he had no idea of how a tugboat worked, but he guessed he'd find a cabin above deck where there'd be a radio and steering controls, and maybe by grace, a phone he could figure out how to work. He stashed the revolver in his sizeable pants' pocket and climbed the ladder.

Cal emerged to a murky night and a great chasm of sea all around the boat. A cabin and a bridge were aglow with light, and he saw antennas and a masthead, topped with a red flashing beacon. Cal climbed another ladder up to the bridge. That was where people captained their vessels. He knew that much. The cool, gusty air surprised him, as did the wave-tossed deck. Cal probably had all the time in the world with the three crooks in lockup, but it didn't feel like it. He staggered into the cabin on the bridge.

The bridge console was a helpless puzzle, with its dials, switches, blinking lights, and a screen showing numbers and bleeps in an inscrutable navigational language. Anything labeled was in Romanian.

Cal found an old-fashioned telephone receiver and picked it up. Dead silence, and he couldn't find a dial or switch or number pad that did anything to work the device. Static droned from a radio. He found its dial, but working the radio was another mystery. Faint, tinny voices drifted in and out as he tried to tune into channels. He found a handheld microphone and called out desperately for some response, trying English, Greek, and the universal "Mayday."

Panic overwhelmed him. He threw switches, punched buttons, twisted dials. Something he did triggered a floodlight from the bridge. It shone onto the waters up ahead. But Cal had no idea how, or even where, to navigate the vessel. He found a throttle that controlled its engine and something like a joystick that seemed to steer it slightly one way or another. Everything was very touchy and unreliable, like trying to commandeer a shuttle in outer space. He'd end up in a wreck trying to put the boat to land. The best he could do was cut off the engine when he got close to a harbor or a beach or even another boat. Then he'd use a lifeboat or swim the rest of the way to safety.

Glancing out of the bridge, he spotted a blinking light, straight ahead on the horizon. Cal wiped the sweat away from his eyes and stared at it. A tower buoy, tall as a house, some thirty yards away, directly in the tugboat's path.

Cal grasped the joystick to try to swerve around it. With his mental faculties entirely frazzled, he swung the throttle into higher gear by mistake. Pulling it back did little to decelerate the momentum, even after he cut off the engine completely. He batted around for anything to slow his course. Something triggered the cranking of an anchor from below. It was too late. They rammed into the tower in a violent clash of metal. It sent the boat shuddering and knocked Cal's legs out from under him.

In the aftermath, the vessel wallowed, and Cal gingerly lifted himself back on his feet. He looked out of the bridge to the floodlit scene. The tugboat was moored against the bent signal tower. Bumper tires floated around, ripped from the bow, and the boat groaned and rattled in duress. What a foray into seafaring! Within minutes, Cal had nearly sunk the vessel.

He worked the throttle to try to get moving again. The engine revved and strained, snared from below by the anchor which must have caught on the girding of the tower. Meanwhile, the vessel tilted heavily to one side, and surf doused the deck. Would the whole thing go under? Cal moaned from the situation. He broke out of bridge cabin, went down to the deck, and searched for a lifeboat.

Off the high side of the deck, he found the wooden dinghy the crooks had used to grab him off the beach in Hydra. Desperately, he unfastened its moorings. Waves rushed over the deck, steadily burying a greater portion of it. Would the whole ship sink with the gangsters trapped in the hold? Cal thought about running down there to let them out, thought about the possibility of a violent confrontation. The dinghy came loose and clattered down the side of the hull, and he was left with the choice of descending before it floated away or rushing back below deck on the chance he could inspire some teamwork for their survival.

Cal climbed over the gunwale and jumped down into the little boat. He'd hope for a naval rescue for the mobsters. Surely, some marine authority would be alerted to the busted beacon tower, and they'd come before the hold flooded with seawater. If the lifeboat had a radio, he'd call in the disaster. But first, he had to make sure he stayed afloat himself.

Orienting himself, he saw a pair of oars, life jackets, waterproof bundles of supplies, and most helpfully, an outboard motor.

This, Cal knew how to use. He had motored around Lake Onondaga with his brothers in the summertime. He attached the fuel line, gave it some pumps, unlatched the choke, got the handle in start position, and put his strength into pulling the wind to bring the engine to life. Gloriously, it sputtered and revved up to a vigorous churn.

Cal steered the vessel away from the wreckage, triumphant for a brief moment. Anxiety cramped up inside him soon enough. He was motoring through the pitch-black night across an enormous and unfamiliar sea and could be headed farther from land. He might not encounter another boat for days, and the dinghy likely had spare provisions and at best a flare gun to try to signal for help. Meanwhile, Cal noticed when he patted his trouser pocket that the boss's gun must have tumbled out when he jumped into the lifeboat.

Chapter Fifteen

BRENDAN MARSHALED DEREK through town to the police station and onward to Lieutenant Constantinides. They found the dapper, young Greek at his leisure, watching music videos of voluptuous Persian pop stars on the computer at his desk. He seemed completely unbothered by the intrusion, and clicking closed his day's entertainment with a winsome grin, he offered them Greek coffee. Brendan declined for both of them, and he nudged Derek to report what he'd seen the morning Cal disappeared.

This, Derek did straightaway, telling the lieutenant about the strange tugboat lurking on the water near the hotel. Constantinides took the story in with a troubling expression of amusement. When Derek was done, the lieutenant turned his attention to Brendan.

"This is now the two of you playing at detectives?" he asked.

Brendan's shoulders tensed. "It's a lead. Don't you think?" He ventured to lay his hand on the lieutenant's immaculate desk. "Cal hasn't turned up anywhere on the island. We checked the ferry. No one saw him leave that day. The only way he could have gotten off Hydra was in a private or a commercial boat."

Constantinides knitted his graceful hands together. "Mr. Thackeray-Prentiss, dozens of freight liners pass by Hydra every day. We are in the middle of the major seaway to Athens. You are suggesting to me that one of them saw your fiancé, waving from the beach near your hotel, and decided to set anchor so that he could climb aboard?"

"Or they took him by force," Derek said, trying to be helpful. "It looked suspicious."

"Why do you say this word, 'suspicious'?"

"It was early in the morning," Derek said. "It was just sitting there out on the water. And it wasn't a big freight liner. It was an old, rickety tugboat." He scratched his ear. "I don't know, Lieutenant. Maybe one thing has nothing to do with the other. But when Cal left the hotel, there was no one around for miles. Except for that boat. How can you explain him vanishing from the beach, leaving one flip-flop and a bracelet?"

Constantinides put on a deadpan face. "This is a most interesting theory. So you believe this tugboat quietly stole up on Mr. Panagopoulos while he was walking the beach, and a group of sailors stormed down from its deck, into the water, trudging to the beach, and caught him by surprise to drag him back to the ship?" He sniffed. "This would make a very excellent Hollywood movie." He turned to Brendan. "Perhaps one which your father would be interested in producing?"

Brendan realized his high-profile American family must have engendered gossip on the tiny island. He didn't mind Europeans resenting American tourists, as a general rule, but he'd had enough of the lieutenant's attitude.

"What exactly are you doing to investigate?" he blurted out. "Isn't it your job to find missing persons?"

The lieutenant's easy bearing changed. "Ah yes. How peasant-like of me to forget. Especially when I have already been reminded of this fact by a phone call I received from the Minister of the Hellenic Police. It appears he was handed down an inquiry about my handling of Mr. Panagopoulos's disappearance from the U.S. Secretary of State. This is a friend of your grandfather, Mr. Harold Thackeray, if I am not mistaken?"

Brendan blinked. Grandad worked fast. His call to his senator friend must have ratcheted up the matter. Though in this case, his methods had made an enemy of the local authorities. Brendan tried to take things more gently.

"Can't you check out this tugboat? Its owner could be questioned at least. Even if they weren't involved, someone aboard could have seen what happened to Cal."

Constantinides looked upon Brendan with a grimace. He picked up his phone and dialed. A pleasant-sounding conversation in Greek ensued. Brendan and Derek exchanged a glance. It would have been marvelous to actually understand the discussion going on, to hear whether Constantinides was dropping in the words "American fascists" or some such with his colleague. The lieutenant sounded like he was handling everything companionably. He said goodbye and replaced his phone.

"I have consulted with the Harbor Marshal," the lieutenant told them. "It appears there was a tugboat making port yesterday morning for the purpose of refueling."

Brendan brightened. "Did he say where it was going?"

Constantinides shook his head. "No. It was a vessel of Romanian origins. We will conduct a query based on its IMO number, which will lead us to its owner and its recent ports of call."

Brendan turned to Derek. "That's great." He looked to the lieutenant. "How long does it take to conduct a query?"

"This is all done through a computer database. One hour. Two perhaps."

"Thank you," Derek said.

The lieutenant frowned impartially. He glanced to the door. He was over the whole exchange. Nevertheless, Brendan asked to borrow his gold-plated pen and his notepad and wrote down his cell phone number.

"Can you call me when you find out about the boat?"

"I am at your service, Mr. Thackeray-Prentiss. Now perhaps you will allow me to attend to other matters which concern the public safety of the good people of Hydra."

Brendan and Derek stood and removed themselves from the office.

WHILE THEY WALKED back to the water taxi dock, Brendan noticed Derek smirking.

"What?" Brendan asked.

"The guy's kind of a dick, but you've got to admit, he's smoking hot."

Brendan smirked himself. "A *kouklos*," he said.

Derek looked at him funny.

"It means something like a teen idol in Greek," he explained. "Constantinides told me." His lightheartedness evaporated as he remembered how angry he was at Derek. "He's straight and married, so I'm afraid you don't stand a chance. Though like you said, him being a dick, the two of you would make a great couple."

Derek let his dig pass in silence. "At least he's going to look into that boat. You lit a fire under him." Derek said it with admiration. That was new.

They came up to the road that encircled the harbor. Some two dozen recreational boats lined the pier along the shore, and the big yachts had a separate quay farther out on the boatyard. Brendan spotted a docking station where a triple-decked fishing ship had anchored. The station had a pair of gas pumps on concrete platforms.

Brendan headed in that direction and waved Derek along. "I'm not so sure about Lieutenant Constantinides," he said. "He hates my guts. Wouldn't hurt to do some of our own investigating."

When they reached the fueling dock, Brendan noticed a short, bespectacled, white-bearded man in a fisherman's hat who looked like the attendant. He approached the guy in a friendly manner, introducing himself and Derek and explaining their situation. The fuel attendant looked like a decent guy. He was dressed in worn trousers and a long-sleeved pullover, and his face was weathered by age and the sun. Probably, he had worked at the fuel station for most of his life. Hydra was such a small island— Brendan figured the locals must have heard about his missing fiancé. The gas attendant was instantly polite, and one might even say solicitous. There was no denying there were benefits to being a wealthy tourist. The man seemed to follow everything Brendan was saying.

"We've been talking to anyone who might know what happened to Cal," Brendan continued. "We heard a tugboat from Romania stopped by here yesterday morning, around the time when he disappeared."

The old guy nodded his head. "Yes. I tell the warden this."

"Do you remember what time?" Brendan said.

"Every morning, I am opening at six. She was here when I arrive."

This was curious. Brendan recalled Louis had taken him down for his shave a little after eight o'clock. That was around the time when Derek had spotted the boat, before breaking into his hotel suite to do his dastardly deed. What was the tugboat doing hanging around the island two hours after it had stopped for fuel?

"Did they say where they were headed?"

A little wry twinkle lit up in the man's eyes. "They say they are going to Athens." He waved his hand dismissively.

"You think they had other plans?"

"I see this is not something they are wanting to say. So, well I am thinking, not every man is wanting to talk to strangers. And these are big Romanian men." He emoted with a little pantomime. "They speak no Greek. They speak a little English. So I say to myself, what calls these men to Hydra? This, you see, is a very rich and beautiful island. Their boat is ancient. I know all kinds of freight boats bringing goods to market. This is none of these kinds of ships. And so I ask this men, from what places do they come to Hydra? This, the man will not answer, and by this I know he is a dishonorable."

A shiver worked through Brendan. The story made him suspicious too. "How many were aboard the ship?"

The old man frowned. "There were two, the like of which could be brothers. Big, thick, with bushy beards. They dressed as businessmen. What business they had, I do not know." He looked to Brendan confidentially. "We have many of this kind in Greece. Romanians with drugs and contraband goods."

Brendan's eyes widened. Though he wondered if there were national prejudices at play. He had heard the same version of denunciation of Greeks while traveling in Spain. "Where would men like that go?"

The attendant shrugged. "Who can say? There are two hundred islands in the Aegean Sea. If they are having illegal business, there are the big cities in Crete and Kalamata. Could be they were returning to the Black Sea and their own country." He gave Brendan a clever grin. "Though I am hearing something to think different."

Brendan bid the man to go on.

"I know a little Romanian. When I was young, I served the Hellenic Navy and knew Romanian sailors from time to time. This, the men do not know while they are talking to themselves. They are saying this and that about their route through the Aegean. And I hear them say 'Psara.' This, a small island, to the north."

Brendan felt invigorated. The fuel attendant's story could be confirmed when Constantinides got back to him about tracking the tugboat's ports of call. He thanked the man effusively, and he and Derek headed to the water taxi dock farther out on the harbor.

A short while along, Brendan's cell phone rang. He pulled it out and saw a name in Greek on the screen. "This could be Constantinides," he told Derek. Brendan quickly took the call.

"Lieutenant Constantinides?"

"Greetings, Mr. Thackeray-Prentiss. I am afraid I have bad news about the Romanian tugboat. It appears the IMO number was a fake. They can find no record of it in our databases. But I must assure you we will do everything in our power to locate it. We have sent notifications to every jurisdiction of the Hellenic Police and Navy."

Brendan stooped down to a squat on the dock. He was sick to his stomach. Cal could be in the clutches of Romanian gangsters, being tortured, even killed. And now the unregistered boat had a day and a half lead on any pursuit, in a vast sea, with many hundreds of islands where the criminals could hide, and waterways to places much farther away, anywhere in the world. Frightening facts from TV crime shows thundered in his head: *Most kidnapping victims not recovered within seventy-two hours are never found. Most are killed within hours of their abduction. Nearly all of them are sexually assaulted.*

Chapter Sixteen

CAL SAT SLUMPED in the lifeboat with a tarp drawn over his head, wallowing on an endless plain of seawater as thick and lustrous as latex paint. The ancient Greeks had called the Aegean "the Great Green," though that seemed like a misnomer to Cal. The water was much more of a rich, almost Technicolor blue, darker in its troughs, aquamarine when the sun glowed through its frothy peaks. Meanwhile, he was Odysseus, abandoned by mankind and the gods, condemned to drift eternally on the deserted sea. This, he realized was a touch histrionic, but for a young man who had never ventured out on his own for longer than an afternoon's bike ride through the sturdy and predictable Central New York State countryside, the circumstances evoked a rather extreme grade of despair.

Against his hopes, he'd found no emergency radio in the dinghy, and then the outboard motor had conked out early in the evening, run out of gas. Cal had proceeded to shoot off every round from the flare gun, hoping to arouse a rescue from whatever naval force held purview in his location, but to no effect. To temper his panic, Cal had eaten all twelve noisome packets of doughy rations in the dinghy's survival kit and slugged down all but one can of water. He was a lousy survivalist.

The sky was just brightening. Based on the dusky conditions when he escaped from the capsizing tugboat, he'd only been lost at sea for ten, maybe eleven hours at the most, and he'd already run through all of his supplies. The dinghy was equipped with oars, but Cal saw no point in using them when he had no idea which way led to land.

His solitude provided generous time for self-reflection. How had his life come to this? Marooned in a boundless body of water when he was supposed to be enjoying the crowning moment in his twenty-four-year lifetime? Cal had never been prone to self-pitying, and he continued to resist it, even then. He could not lose himself to hopelessness. His family would never give up looking for him. As for Brendan, Cal didn't know what to think. But more than anything, he wished he would awaken from his nightmare to the sight of Brendan helming a motorboat, racing to his rescue, to scoop him out of the sea, and then he'd take him in his arms, apologizing for how wrong he'd been, how wrecked with grief he was since Cal had disappeared.

Cal searched the horizon. He searched the sky. He had to believe in miracles—a passing boat or a low-flying plane spotting him out on the water. The world was vast. He'd never realized how many voids of emptiness it contained, how easily a person could be lost forever. How long could a man live without food? How long could he live without water?

His glance landed on a speck on the horizon. Cal blinked, rubbed his eyes, and focused sharply on it, praying it was not some trick of sunlight against the glassy sea, a mirage. He unfastened the oars from inside the boat, hitched them to their casters, and rowed vigorously in the direction of that spot of hope.

Cal lumbered through the waves while the muscles of his arms burned and his shoulders throbbed. He was encouraged by his progress and the sight that grew larger in his vision. Another boat. Not much bigger than his own. Suitable for a single fisherman. He cried out toward it. He was going to be saved.

DURING HIS LABORIOUS trek, the owner of the boat must have spotted him and heard his cry. He motored over to rendezvous on the water. Cal rejoiced and tears sprouted from his eyes. His savior was a kind-looking, Old World fisherman, captaining a modest, aluminum skiff. What grace of fate it was that he had ventured out on the open sea so early in the morning.

The fisherman's boat came about, and the man looked him over with wonder and a touch of forbearance. Cal figured he had to look pretty scary after being detained in a tugboat freight hold for two days and spending the night on the open sea. Besides, he was wearing a rumpled, loud print madras shirt and oversized trousers that made him look like a hobo. The fisherman had a full head of white hair, a bushy, white horseshoe moustache, and a weathered complexion as dark as terracotta. Cal's Greek was a little rusty, but he tried to string words together as best as he could.

"Thank god! You won't even believe what I've been through. Oh, thank you, sir! I'm so glad to see you."

"Amerikanos?" the fisherman asked.

"Yes. But my grandfather is Greek. He lives right here in Hydra. Alekos Panagopoulos. Do you know him? I'm here for my wedding. I'm supposed to be getting married to my boyfriend, and I end up getting kidnapped and then stuck in a dinghy in the middle of the Aegean Sea. Can you believe that?"

The fisherman stared at him as though he was dangerous. Cal realized he was probably babbling like a lunatic and not getting half of his Greek phrases right.

"I'm sorry. I'm just so excited to see another human being. Wait until my family finds out I'm all right."

The fisherman garbled a question in Greek. Cal looked at him blankly. The man tried again, "*Travmaties*. Wound?"

"Wounded?" Cal said. He collected his Greek. "No. I feel healthy as can be. These Romanians had me tied up so my wrists are a little chafed." He showed the scrapes and bruises to his companion. "But that's nothing, really. I'm just happy to be alive. I'm pretty well fed and hydrated too. They don't advertise how awful lifeboat rations taste. I guess for good reason. But I ate them all."

The fisherman brought out a long wooden hook from his boat and caught the grab rail of Cal's dinghy to bring it up snug to his skiff. He waved Cal aboard. Cal climbed over the gunwale and into the hull. As soon as he'd righted himself, he threw his arms around the fisherman in a great big hug. The man smelled like wool, and tobacco, and a little bit like chum. All those familiar scents were wonderful.

"Thank you, my friend." Cal gulped back tears. He'd been afraid he would never see another soul again.

The fisherman gently broke off their embrace, patting Cal on the head. "I take you Samos."

"I've never been to Samos. That sounds great. Hey, if you have a radio, maybe you could call me in to the authorities? Everyone back in Hydra must be worried sick." Cal noticed a microphone on a cord in the boat's console. The fisherman stared at him, at a loss. Maybe Cal hadn't said it right. He didn't want to be rude and insist on using the man's equipment. His companion stepped around him and pointed to Cal's boat.

"You need anything?"

"Gosh no. Just leave the whole thing here. I don't mind if I never see it again."

The man guided Cal to the stern to sit at the skiff's bench amid the bait and tackle equipment. Then he got behind the console, motored on the engine, and they went hurdling over the water en route to glorious, solid land.

Chapter Seventeen

THE PREVIOUS NIGHT, back in Hydra, Brendan returned to the hotel and summoned all of the wedding guests to the dining pavilion for a town hall meeting of sorts. The information he'd uncovered about Cal's disappearance needed to be shared. Derek's testimony and confession was another item for the agenda, and though he offered Derek no forgiveness, he assured the twerp he would appeal for leniency if the Panagopoulos brothers demanded bastinado as punishment for his outrageous actions. The more important matter was for everyone to come together behind a plan for finding Cal. To the turncoat's credit, Derek offered no resistance to doing the noble thing.

The pavilion was packed with Cal's family on one side and Brendan's family and friends on the other. Even Brendan's mother showed up, masked by oversized sunglasses and ready to get to business after a two-martini lunch. Brendan had asked Lieutenant Constantinides to come, though he'd promised everyone an eight o'clock start, and by twenty past, the lieutenant was nowhere to be found. The mood was tense with swells of ill-humored murmuring like a suburban mob gathered for a referendum on a halfway house moving into the neighborhood. The only overt act of misbehavior came from Riley, who wanted to videotape the proceedings on her phone and post them on social media. Her father Roger quickly confiscated her phone and Daryl's, to the girls' pouty dismay.

Brendan stood on a dais, which was to be for the head table at the wedding dinner. He was joined by Derek, Grandad, and Cal's father. With it looking like Lieutenant Constantinides would never show up, Brendan started the meeting. He told the room of sixtyish people about their lead on the unregistered, Romanian tugboat and his disappointing dealings with the police. The Greek guests groaned and hailed curses at the absent authorities. It was a tough lead-in to Derek's part of the program. Brendan gestured to Derek, and he stepped forward and spoke about his sighting of the tugboat and then, in a pained and tearful voice, what he had done to instigate the fight between Brendan and Cal.

Three of Cal's brothers shot up to their feet with their chests puffed out, and they hurled threatening expletives at Derek. He had dishonored their baby brother and sent him off on his fateful, solitary trek down the beach. Mr. Panagopoulos, who had heard Derek's confession previously, was a moderate man, and he reined in his sons by shouting them down at the necessary decibel level. Derek had been beloved by Cal's family. He'd been Cal's best friend for five years. After his confession, he'd no doubt become persona non grata to all of them, though Mr. Panagopoulos appeared to be generous in his understanding of the follies of young men.

Brendan gave Derek a nod of respect and retook the floor. "I'm sure everyone is shocked by what Derek did, but that's a small part of why we called everyone together. Cal's been gone now for thirty-six hours. We suspect foul play. The police have put out some kind of all-points bulletin to their departments across the country, but we can't just wait around for something to turn up. We're going to need everyone's help to find Cal."

Cal's oldest brother, Sandy, spoke first. "We'll storm the goddamn parliament in Athens." That brought out a favorable commotion.

Riley jumped in. "We'll Facebook, Tweet, and Instagram it." Cal's local family stared at her. She tried to explain. "The FBI does it. That's how you find people these days." She passed a wrathful glance at her father who held her phone.

Any and all ideas were welcome to Brendan. Derek had volunteered for the task of taking down notes, and he was scribbling everything onto a pad of hotel stationery.

Grandad stepped forward, in his element at the fore of the convocation. "I have assurances from the U.S. Secretary of State. He is holding the Greek Prime Minister to the grindstone until Cal is found. The Secretary has also sent a directive to our military forces to do their own surveillance on the Romanian vessel of interest."

Genie stood up. "In thirty-six hours, they could be anywhere. Europe, Africa, the Middle East." Cal's mother moaned and broke into tears. Genie reseated herself at her side and took her hand.

A hollow ache grew in Brendan's stomach from the sight of Cal's mother. He drew a steadying breath. He needed to be a man of action.

"You're right, Genie," he said. "We have no idea where they went. All we have is some conjecture from the fuel attendant at the harbor. He thought he heard the kidnappers say they were headed to Psara, and the local police there are checking it out. But they could have stopped along the way or changed plans entirely. That's why I'm proposing we spread out in a circumference around Hydra to conduct our own search. We'll need teams of people. Some to canvas Athens. Some to the big islands like Rhodes and Crete to the south and west, and Andros and Mykonos to the north. We'll use my grandfather's jet, and we'll book tickets for others on commercial airlines. I also looked into chartering a private boat to trace a likely route through the Aegean. We'll need some people to stay in Hydra in case new information turns up here."

Cal's family muttered to each other in what sounded like agreeable discussions. Brendan's father gazed at him in admiration, and then he crumpled into tears, garnering a strained brushing of his back from his girlfriend, Gabriela.

Then Lieutenant Constantinides strolled into the dining hall en route to the dais, as smooth and debonair as ever in a tailored suit and tie. People jeered at him. Incapable of governing herself any longer, Riley wrestled her phone out of her father's hands and started snapping photos like an investigative reporter. Brendan's mother slid her sunglasses down her face for a looksee.

Brendan grudgingly ceded his spot on the dais to Constantinides. The lieutenant smiled at him, and then he spoke out to the hall. "My name is Lieutenant Giannis Constantinides. Forgive me for my lateness. I was told by Mr. Thackeray-Prentiss the meeting was to start at half past eight."

People booed him. Brendan glared at the man indignantly. Even if there had been a miscommunication, which there hadn't, he was fifteen minutes late.

Constantinides spoke over the commotion. "Family, friends—I know you are upset about the disappearance of Mr. Panagopoulos. Allow me to assure you his safe return is a top priority for the Hellenic Police. We have officers in all twelve of our jurisdictions searching for your loved one." He raised a finger in the air. "I have no doubt he will be found."

Sandy stood up again with steam rising from his ears. "You did nothing. You sent us away when we came to you. You told us Cal's disappearance was a domestic dispute."

The Panagopoulos clan rose up in a clamor to support him. Constantinides appealed to their patriotism by speaking to them in Greek.

Cal's brother Yannis took him on. "Screw your Hellenic Police. We're going to do our own investigation. We'll get more done in one night than you've done in thirty-six hours." The thirty-something Greek construction worker looked to Brendan, and people broke out in clapping and cries of support.

Constantinides glanced at Brendan with acrimony—the ringleader of the hostile audience in front of him. When the commotion trailed off somewhat, the lieutenant tried again. "It is my duty to advise you that any efforts to usurp the Hellenic Police's investigation will be both counterproductive and actionable by our courts of law."

They shouted him down. Constantinides forced a grin at their angry faces. Then he waved his hand dismissively and nudged past Brendan with some parting words. "This is what you want, Mr. Thackeray-Prentiss? A ragtag militia to find your fiancé? I wish you the best of luck." He stepped down from the dais, avoiding gazes. When he had left, the room erupted in a rousing cry.

Brendan looked over the hall. It *was* a ragtag militia: Blue-collar Greek-American husbands. Their equally feisty wives. Cal's Old World family—the men in moustaches and weathered shirts and trousers, the women in smock dresses and shawls. His well-clad college friends, who were strangers to pounding the pavement for any cause beyond a shopping jag in Manhattan, though they had taken to their feet in solidarity. Brendan's spirited but flighty father. His teenage sisters, already absorbed in organizing an Arab Spring–style media campaign. And Grandmum, clapping a steady beat for justice in a dignified display. They all believed they could do the impossible. They all believed in him. Intoxicated by the collective energy, Brendan launched his fist into the air.

THE NEXT MORNING, Brendan set out from Hydra in a chartered yacht with a captain and a below-deck crew. Some of Cal's relatives had ferried to Athens. They were organized in teams to overturn the city, alert the media, and placard the streets with posters, and others would go on to board planes to strategic points across the Aegean. Grandad, Grandmum, Brendan's mother, and his sisters had taken the private jet to Istanbul where they might head off Cal's Romanian captors at the Bosporus Strait, en route to the Black Sea. Betsy Schoonover, her husband, and Brendan's college friends had been assigned surveillance of westward routes through Italy. Genie was leading a team of her cousins and uncles to Bodrum on the Turkish coast of the Mediterranean. Brendan's father and his girlfriend had volunteered to fly south to Cypress where he knew some locals who'd been on a film crew for one of his documentaries. They would proceed to Cairo if necessary. Mrs. Panagopoulos and Cal's sisters Ana and Lucy were staying back in Hydra in case any information turned up there.

That left a team of the campaign's most strident supporters to accompany Brendan on his sea voyage to attempt to retrace the criminals' route from Hydra to the island of Psara. Naturally, Mr. Panagopoulos and the brothers Sandy, Yannis, George, and Demetri insisted on being at the forefront of the action. Louis Jeffries had offered to come, and Brendan was glad for it. He could use his lifelong pal's moral support. The brothers jeered at Derek coming along, but Derek had pleaded, and Brendan's heart had thawed to him. The kid had been through a trial of contrition, which wasn't to say Brendan trusted him completely, but it had earned his respect.

The plan was to follow a trade route through the Cyclades Islands and onward to the Northern Aegean Sea. Consulting with the harbor fuel attendant, they'd arrived at the disappointing conclusion that the rickety, little tugboat could likely make a trip of at least three days without stopping for fuel. Their modern, expedition yacht could gain on the Romanians' progress in half the time, and they could hope the outlaws had anchored at some port in the Aegean en route to Psara. The strategy was to radio every passing boat along the way in hopes of sightings. The crooks could not have fled Hydra entirely unnoticed.

Cal's father and brothers settled into the shaded, lower aft deck for rounds of rummy and bottles of Mythos from the yacht's well-stocked bar. They had the right idea to get involved in something distracting, but Brendan was so pent up with anxiety, he couldn't stop from planting himself at very pulpit of the bow, searching the seascape with a pair of binoculars like Captain Ahab. He pestered the crew in the above-deck wheelhouse at regular intervals just in case some news had come over the radio. Mere hours had passed since they motored out of the port of Hydra that morning, and they were deep in open sea, an everlasting plain of undulating, midnight blue seawater. Louis emerged from the cabin to join him on his lookout, carefully balancing in one hand his first tumbler of scotch on the rocks of the day.

"You're really handling this like a champ," Louis told him.

"Thanks," Brendan said. "And thanks for coming along."

"I'd follow you to the ends of the earth, my dearest bud." Louis looked out to the blank seascape. "Which may just be where we're headed."

Brendan took up his binoculars. He thought he'd seen something on the northern horizon, though he couldn't make out anything with his binoculars but open sea.

Louis sipped his scotch. "We've got a long trip ahead of us. What say we check out the main salon? They've got a billiard table and satellite TV." Brendan stepped down from the pulpit, but he quickly looked out from the bow and shook his head. "Xbox?" Louis tried. "Take you back to college when I used to kick your butt in *Street Fighter*?" Still, Brendan resisted. Louis clamped a hand on his shoulder. "I heard they have a collection of 1,000 movies. I'll even suffer through one of those subtitled, tragic, French, gay love stories you like so much." He retreated from the suggestion. "Something lighter? A Seth Rogen film?"

"I can't." Brendan sighed. "I know it's totally irrational, but I feel like if I miss something out here, I'll never forgive myself." He winced. A swoon of emotions was coming on. It didn't help that he hadn't slept more than an hour or two the past few nights, and he'd barely eaten.

Louis brought out carefully, "You know it's not your fault."

"I don't know that. Derek set up the fight, but I was the one who overreacted. If I hadn't done that, Cal wouldn't have run away."

"And he would have come right back." Louis shifted a bit in his houndstooth Bermuda shorts and crew neck pullover. "It's not like me to get all mushy. But I was wrong about you two when you first told me you were getting married. I've seen what you guys have together. The way you look at one another. It's the real deal, Brendan. I was a douche for not believing you. And whatever fight you had, Cal would have come around, just like you did. You don't give up that easily when you have something that strong."

Brendan dropped his head. The corners of his eyes burned. Louis's big hand rubbed his back.

"I keep trying to believe that," Brendan said through the tears. "But how can I know for sure? Maybe this is what Cal wanted. Maybe he wanted a way off Hydra, and he just disappeared. All because of me."

"That's your inner guilt monster talking," Louis said. "You've got to send that guy packing. And it doesn't help that you're running on fumes." He massaged Brendan's neck. "Brendan, you need some sleep. You need to eat something. You're the captain of this mission, buddy, and you won't be any help to us if you don't take care of yourself. You certainly won't be any help to Cal." He glanced at his watch. "Take a break. We only set sail from Hydra three hours ago."

Brendan sniffed back his tears, collecting himself. He gazed out to the water. The rushing sea breeze braced him a little. "I'll get some rest and something to eat. In a little while. Right now, I just need to be out here."

Louis patted his back. "Whatever you need, bud. But make sure it really is just 'a little while.'" He glanced to one side. "Looks like you've got another visitor. You want me to scare him back into his rat hole?"

Turning that way, Brendan saw Derek. He was slumped and forlorn, wearing a black T-shirt and jeans, staring at the two of them from the railing near the yacht's cabin. Brendan had the impression he'd been there awhile. Derek had his arms crossed over himself for warmth, and he reminded Brendan of a gecko, watching from the borders, expressionless, waiting for an opening to insert himself in the conversation.

"No. It's all right."

"Okay," Louis said. "I'll give you guys some privacy." He went to the cabin, giving Derek a dubious glare along the way.

Derek crept over to Brendan's side. Like Brendan, he looked wasted and delirious from the past few days, his black hair spiky and clumped, his beard-stubbled face drawn. Strangely, that brought Brendan some comfort.

"The captain thought he had a lead after radioing a freighter. It passed by some ship with a Romanian flag," Derek said. "Turns out it was just a recreational sailboat. Totally legit."

Brendan frowned. "It's going to be a long day." His empty stomach cramped, and he couldn't stop himself from yawning.

"I know nobody wants me to be here," Derek said. "When I pass by Cal's brothers, they look at me like they're sizing up how to chop me into cutlets."

"Yeah, well—"

"Means a lot to me that you let me come along."

Brendan glanced at the little guy. Derek's skinny arms were goose bumped, and he was trembling and probably didn't even realize it. It was pretty brisk out on the deck, and they were both underdressed. Brendan had come out in an untucked Oxford shirt and shorts.

"You really loved Cal, all this time," he said.

Derek nodded. "I did. I never told him though. At least not the way I meant it."

"He loves you too," Brendan said and added, pointedly, "as a friend."

"You think he'll ever forgive me?"

Brendan mulled it over. Cal would be mad. For days. Weeks even. But of course he'd eventually forgive Derek. Cal's heart was big and generous.

"Yeah." Brendan stared out to the water. They were approaching a minor island. It was all brown cliffs, shaved of vegetation by the wind and sun. It looked like it was uninhabited.

"Can I tell you something?" Derek said.

Brendan nodded.

"Here's the weird thing," Derek began. "I was in love with Cal all this time, keeping it a secret, like it was something too sacred to even speak about. Like it would disappear if I ever shared it with another person." He struggled to find the words. "Now that it's out in the open, it's like I'm free. Like it doesn't control me anymore. I don't know. Maybe it wasn't love. Maybe it was an obsession. You think there's a difference?"

Brendan remembered having a similar conversation with himself when he realized how his feelings for Thiago had fallen away. Though he had no idea if that was the same thing Derek was going through.

"It's not that I don't care about Cal anymore," Derek went on. "Believe me, I do. But maybe it wasn't him I was in love with. It was more the idea of him. That I had someone to love, and he would love me back. And that would make me a worthwhile person." Derek shook his head. "I don't know if I'm making any sense."

"No, you are," Brendan said. "I mean, you can't go for years being in love with someone you can never have. That's just...crazy."

"Well, I never said I wasn't crazy."

Brendan grinned. Derek grinned back.

"Cal's the nicest and sweetest and most honorable guy in the world," Derek said. "But I think I'm coming around to seeing he's not for me. And I'd never do anything to stand between the two of you. Never again, I mean. You believe me, don't you?"

Brendan put his arm around Derek's shoulder. "I do."

Derek leaned into his embrace. "I just pray to god we'll find him."

Brendan squeezed him tighter. So did he. "Hey, you want to go up and see if we missed any news in the past thirty seconds?"

"Sure."

They went into the cabin and climbed the stairs to the wheelhouse on the upper deck where the captain and the first officer navigated the vessel. It had a high-tech console and a big swiveling leather chair and a panoramic view of the sea. Brendan immediately tuned in to the sound and sight of the captain talking on the radio. He was a thirty-something South African dude named Wes, and he was conversing with someone in Greek. The first officer, a young Turk named Ahmed, stood close by. Brendan and Derek halted at the landing, waiting out the radio parlay.

Captain Wes glanced at Brendan while a staticky Greek voice came over the radio. Brendan didn't like his grim look.

The captain finished up the conversation and directed nautical instructions to Ahmed, who made some adjustments at the console. The captain then turned his attention to Brendan.

"We just received a transmission from the Greek Navy. They found a tugboat that fits your description in the Icarian Pelagos."

Brendan's lungs froze over. He could sense by the captain's tone it was not good news.

"We've set a course to get there straightaway," Captain Wes continued. "Should be five, six hours at the most. Now I don't want you to get too alarmed, Mr. Thackeray-Prentiss. The navy is still sorting things out. Nothing has been confirmed yet."

"What is it?" Brendan said.

Captain Wes hesitated for a breath. "The boat collided with a beacon tower. Sometime last night. They found it capsized, nearly drawn under."

"Th-they found passengers?"

Captain Wes nodded. "Three men. All Romanian. All trapped in a cargo hatch. They were nearly dead from hypothermia, but they got them to a naval hospital in time. They're in stable condition and being held for questioning."

Brendan was confused. "They think it's the boat, that it's the guys who took Cal?"

No answer. Just a steady gaze from the Captain.

The wheelhouse blurred and spun in Brendan's vision. He brought out the words he had to ask. "Then what happened to Cal?"

Captain Wes bit his lip. "They're bringing divers over to search for other passengers." He caught Brendan's glance gravely. "But they found Mr. Panagopoulos's wallet, passport, and shorts aboard the ship."

Chapter Eighteen

CHRISTOS NICOLAOU GATHERED the mooring lines to tie his fishing boat to the jetty of his seaside cabin. The American boy nearly tripped over himself trying to help him. Christos mildly shooed him away. Greek-Americans, they had the brass balls to call themselves. The only Greek thing about the boy was his proper, straight nose and his thick, curled hair. He spoke the language in a sloppy jabber and chattered on like all of his kind—happy as a lark in June from the opportunity to show off his credentials to a native of the Old Country.

This was why Christos made his home in the remote countryside of northwestern Samos. It was far enough away from town to rarely have to trouble with the *touristas*, or the locals for that matter, but it was a short enough drive when he couldn't avoid having to travel there for goods. He was a seventy-year-old widower, and his wife of forty years had been the one person he'd ever tolerated, and even then not without some effort, may Petrina's soul rest in heaven. As far as Christos was concerned, Greeks belonged in Greece and Americans in America, and he didn't hold well with either.

Still, there was respect owed to a young man fished out of the sea when he had expected to bring home a grouper or a mullet like every other morning he'd motored his boat out for a catch. The boy glowed like a Cherubim fallen from the sky. He tempted superstition.

Many nights, sitting alone in his whitewashed *spiti*, Christos had wondered what was left for him in this world. He had outlived his wife by three years now, and how quickly those years went by. They had never had a son or a daughter, and Christos never blamed Petrina for that, barren as she was. He lived on his meager government pension and sold whatever fish he didn't need to a market in town. It was not much of a life. He had no friends to care about him, just a fellow fisherman or two with whom he exchanged a nod when their boats crossed paths on the open sea. Christos had to admit a hermit's life came with a price. Some days it was hard to dredge up the spirit to get out of bed.

Now, he had found this boy. Bothersome as he was with his constant blabber, he made for a pretty sight for the eyes. That radiant hair, as though spun from gold. Those bright, aquamarine eyes. He brought a grin to Christos's face, which hadn't happened in a long while, maybe not since Petrina had fallen sick with cancer.

The right thing to do would be to take the boy to the police station in town to let them sort out getting him back to where he belonged. Christos's chin trembled as he wound one of the boat lines to its bollard. Thinking about giving up the boy made his heart cave in. *He* had found him. The boy was *his* treasure.

These feelings were a strange torment. Like his heart had been caught on a barbed hook and was getting tugged by a reel. Maybe it was an intuition. The boy had been blessed, a good luck charm. How else had he survived a shipwreck as he had said? He might bring some of that good luck to Christos.

Or maybe it was the tempting belief Christos's prayers had been answered. How many times had he lain down to sleep, hoping he might wake the next day to some sign his life had purpose, some possibility of happiness? He had never been a devout man, only allowing Petrina to drag him to church four or five times in their forty-year marriage. Though lord knew, he had been through trials that were owed some form of redemption. Orphaned by the death of his parents, so young he couldn't put to mind a picture of either of them. Cheated out of his inheritance by the scheming aunt who had taken him in. Never knowing the pride of raising a son. Exploited by the cruel boss of the fishing company where he had worked for fifty years. His one joy in life, Petrina, taken from him.

Accidents happened for a reason. This, Christos had always held to, from losing Petrina—a punishment for not being the good husband she deserved—to his treacherous aunt's *taverna* burning down to cinders in an electrical fire—her comeuppance. And that meant good accidents happened for a reason too.

The boy could make for a companion in Christos's gray years. He seemed a bit dainty and dim-witted, but maybe he could be taught to fish, like a son. Christos wasn't long for the world, and a man needed to have something to leave behind, didn't he? He hadn't much, but the idea of his home and pension being turned over to the government was pitiable. He would rest much better knowing he had left his little bit of wealth and his modest trade to someone who could prosper from them.

It would make for a scandal around town—the handsome lad living with curmudgeonly, old Christos. He could say his guest was a relation, a nephew's son. Otherwise, it would set people's minds to wonder if Christos was keeping the boy for deviant relations, like the old, fancy vineyard owner, Theodorus Michelakakis, who was known to take a grope and a slurp of his young grape pickers from time to time. Christos hadn't thought about that sort of recreation with anyone, woman or man, for quite some time. But glancing at the young man, who had introduced himself as Callisthenes, "vigor and beauty personified," certainly brought back familiar aches and curiosities. He was grubby and drowning in his oversized trousers. Imagine what he would look like fresh from a bath! They could be discreet about their private business. Christos had never cared for the kind of men who poofed around, flaunting their bedroom preferences, and he knew that sort of thing was a sin in the eyes of God. But God had to grant an old man some dispensation, didn't he? Hadn't he earned a little taste of sin after seventy years of hardship and toil?

Christos shook free from those dirty thoughts and wound up the last of the boat lines. What he needed to do was cobble together some way to delay the boy until he could figure out how to present him with his proposal. He had asked repeatedly about radioing the authorities to report his rescue. Christos had pretended he didn't understand what he was saying, but now that they were on land, the boy would be nipping at him to use a phone or to go into town to talk to the police.

He stepped off the boat, turned to Callisthenes, stretched his hand, and helped him climb up onto the jetty.

"Thank you," Callisthenes said. He looked around at the house and its grounds with wonder, like he had never seen a *spiti* built up on a coastal ledge, one of many thousands across the Aegean. "Wow. Your house is...a catapult."

Christos chuckled. He meant *katapliktikos*: amazing, not *katapeltis*: catapult. He thanked him for the compliment and shrugged his shoulder toward the house. "We go in. I make you coffee. Somewhat to eat."

"Oh, I do not wish to prosecute you. Throwing me from the sea satisfies me tender. I will only abuse your telephone to telephone my family. If such abuse is pleasing to you."

Christos sorted through the gibberish. He nodded his head and started toward the house. The boy followed. It was time to cobble. Christos tried to piece together some kind of story.

They climbed the steep steps to the house's terrace, and he held the back door open for his companion. They went through the larder, which led into the kitchen. A single old man didn't stir up much of a mess, but the girl who did his cleaning hadn't been by since last Thursday. Christos frowned at the cups and plates stacked in the sink. His guest took it all in as though he had entered a palace—Christos's ancient, humble abode with its peeling paint and warped wooden doors and shutters. Such a kind and generous creature. His poor, chapped lips. He had been exposed at sea for how long had he said?

Christos remembered the phone, which was in stark view, mounted on the far wall of the kitchen. He tramped over to it quickly and picked up the receiver. Holding the receiver close to his ear, he tapped repeatedly at the phone's clapper and put on a woeful grimace.

"No ring," he said. "This happens sometimes. The lines in Samos, they are very bad. Could be a strong wind and everything goes out." He replaced the phone. "This will only be for small time. I am sure of it."

The boy's face deflated. It hurt Christos's heart. He shuffled over to his coffee kettle. "I make you hot drink. And scones. I have very good scones."

"That is nice to you. But I truly do not wish to plunge your hospital. How do you say you transfer me to the most near village, at such a place I make my own telephone? You cannot imagine how sickening my family is."

Christos twitched. His Greek was terrible, but he could put together the gist of it. He needed to bide some time. "We go to town, yes," he said. "First, let me make you comfortable. You take bath. I bring you dry clothes. This will be much better for you, no?"

His heart hovered, waiting for the response. A grin lit up on the Cherubim's face.

"I conjecture I am incontinent to argue with that. Wow. A hot bath will be a tiny loaf of heaven."

Christos exhaled in relief. The boy wrestled his short-sleeved shirt over his head and smiled at him like a Hollywood movie star. A half-clothed, fully grown Cherubim standing in his tiny loaf of a kitchen. With a piercing through his nipple. Christos's blood pressure fluttered, and he reached out his hand to steady himself on the kitchen counter.

CAL SANK INTO the steaming bathtub. It made him feel like a little kid again, and he couldn't help sliding down and dunking his head completely underwater to blow up bubbles. The day was really turning out well. Just hours ago, he'd thought he was going to be shark fodder, and now he had a bath and a kind old man making him coffee and scones and then they would be going into town to call his parents to let them know he was safe and sound. What a sweetheart the old fisherman was! Cal couldn't imagine anyone in New York City treating a stranger so nicely. Not even people in Syracuse. That was the difference between Europeans and Americans. Europeans saw everyone as a potential friend, and Americans saw everyone as a potential enemy. Cal had to credit his command of Greek. That had to have helped some.

He found a cake of soap alongside the tub and lathered up his face, his arms, his legs, his feet, his torso, and all the nooks and crannies. Then he doused and splashed himself and used his hands like squeegees to wash the soap off.

He grabbed a bottle of Greek shampoo and got to work on washing his hair. The excitement of finally being able to speak to his parents made him want to rush through things a bit. After all, they'd been waiting to hear from him for three days. Did he ever have stories to tell everyone! He would see Brendan again. God, he longed for that. Cal was sure of it now—after everything that had happened, his fight with Brendan would be like a tiny blip in the past. He clopped his hands on the water in a tam-tam flourish. Everything would go back to normal. Everything would go back to perfect. He and Brendan were getting married!

"Callisthenes? Are you all right in there?"

It was the fisherman's voice at the other side of the door. Cal laughed. "Yes. Thank you. It's just me. Sorry about that. I'm a sloppy bather."

A moment's silence.

"I go out to get the rods and tackle from the boat."

"Okay."

He heard the man's footsteps creak away from the door. Cal ducked under the water to rinse his hair. Then he pulled out the stopper, grabbed a towel, and stepped out of the tub to sop up the water he'd splashed onto the floor. What a spaz he was, making such a mess. Cal made sure he cleaned up every drop of water from the nice man's bathroom.

He toweled off and stepped into the clothes the fisherman had given him. Briefs that actually fit. Faded dungarees that were fine around his waist, but they ended a good two inches short of his ankles. A blue-and-white striped, long-sleeved, button-down shirt that similarly rode up his arms a bit. Cal giggled. He'd been doomed to dress up like a clown ever since he'd left Hydra.

He had no right to complain. The clothes smelled fresh from the laundry, and he was sparkling clean. The fisherman had even given him a comfy pair of sheepskin slippers. Cal went to the sink, found a tube of toothpaste, squirted a generous gob onto his finger and used it to brush his teeth. An actual toothbrush would have been heavenly, but he couldn't trouble the fisherman for that. He'd passed by a single bedroom in the cottage and gathered the man lived alone. Maybe he was a widower, and his grown children had long since left town. That would explain why he was so happy to have a guest. Cal cranked on the faucet, cupped water into his mouth and took a long gargle. After spitting it out, he cleaned up the sink so it was just as tidy as when he'd stepped into the bathroom.

Looking in the cabinet mirror above the sink, Cal picked through his damp mop of hair to see if anything could be done to make himself more presentable. His gaze wandered to the golden, red-flecked beard sprouting from his cheeks and chin. Cal hadn't gone three days without a shave since college. He looked like he should be on that gay dating site, *Scruff*. He was a bear cub! Or was it an otter? Cal grinned. He didn't mind the look. Maybe he'd give facial hair a try. He folded up his towel neatly on the rack and ventured out into the house.

It was a cozy, rustic cabin, like something right out of a travel guide for Greece. The kitchen was just down the hall, and he could smell the rich aroma of fresh-brewed coffee. He padded over to the room in his slippers. The dishes that had been in the sink were washed and dried and lined up on a rack on the counter. Such a courteous old man, cleaning up the room on his account. He must have still been down by his boat. Did he need a hand? Before Cal went to do that, his glance passed over the telephone on the wall. Maybe it was a little presumptuous, but he was dying to see if service had come back.

Cal picked up the receiver. The funny, two-ring European dial tone hummed in his ear. What luck! The phone was back in order. Now, how to make a call? Before their trip, he and Brendan had set up international service on their cell phones, but the instructions for making calls in Greece were fuzzy in Cal's head. There was a number to punch in for an outgoing call and then a code to enter before dialing Brendan's cell phone number. Cal tried a combination of numbers. He got a canned message in a Greek woman's voice. He tried a second combination. The same mildly scolding voice came back to him.

Footsteps traveled up the stairs, and the door pushed open before Cal could react.

The fisherman, with his arms full with a rod and tackle case, froze up at the sight of him. Cal felt like a jerk for using the man's phone without asking. He replaced the receiver. "The line came back. Like you said it would." Caught in the man's fearful stare, Cal felt like he'd done something terrible.

The fisherman propped his rod against the wall and dropped his tackle case on the kitchen table. Some of its paraphernalia tumbled out of its lid. He rushed at Cal. "No, no, no." He flushed Cal away from the phone, badgering him in English. "I tell you— We go to town. I make you nice coffee. Give you something to eat." He pulled Cal by the elbow toward the table.

A wave of vertigo hit Cal. Had the fisherman lied about the phone? Why would he do that? Only if he never intended to help Cal get back to Hydra.

"You sit," the man told him, gesturing to a chair. "I bring you coffee, and we make breakfast."

Cal didn't budge. The old man wiped his face. He was shifty, troubled. Icy tentacles spread through Cal's body.

"Did you lie to me about the phone?" he asked.

"No, no, no. This is not supposed to be like this." The fisherman glanced at Cal piteously, a man caught red-handed, desperate for forgiveness. How desperate was he? Cal noticed a short, serrated fishing knife had dropped out of the tackle box. It was in arm's reach from either of them.

"I save you," the man said. "I bring you to my home. Make you a bath. Give you clothes to wear."

"I need to call my family," Cal said. "I was kidnapped. I need to get back to Hydra."

The man's eyes trembled. "Why can you not stay here with me? Just a little while. I make you nice home. I treat you well."

Cal felt like he had plunged back into a nightmare. Though the man was small and unintimidating, Cal was suddenly terrified of him. What schemes had been brewing in his head? He'd been trying to gain Cal's trust. Would he drug him and tie him up like the Romanian brutes?

Cal sprang down the hall, farther into the house. The fisherman called after him. He had to find a way out. The man could come after him with his knife. Cal stumbled into a living space. Dead, lacquered fish were mounted on one wall. He spotted a door. Cal ran to it and threw it open. He fled down a cobbled walkway, past a driveway and out to a single-lane country highway.

HE WAS ON the bluffs of a strange island. A highway wound along the coast, and the inland was a desolate expanse of grassy brush. Cal had seen a mini-truck in the driveway of the fisherman's house. The demented man could come after him in that vehicle. Cal looked up and down the road. Wagering a guess, Cal took off in the direction where the highway sloped downward, hopefully leading to a seaside village where he could find a phone and people to protect him from the fisherman.

Staggering down the middle of the declining highway in his undersized, sheepskin slippers, Cal tripped and caught his fall with his hands, scraping them bloody on the asphalt. Up the hill behind him, a car engine coughed and revved. The fisherman had gotten into his truck. Cal righted himself, shook off the pain in his hands, and looked around for somewhere to hide.

He saw no cover anywhere. His only option was to duck down the steep escarpment along the road. If he slipped, he would tumble down the cliff and be crippled on the rocky shore.

He grabbed the slippers off his feet, threw them over the side of the highway, and climbed over the railing. It was a near vertical drop, forty, maybe fifty feet above the shore. Cal sorted out hand and footholds, climbing down the rocky ledge where he would be unseen from the road. Ocean surf echoed below him. He didn't dare look down. Cal had never been crazy about heights, and his present debacle had him hanging from a cliff. He heard the fisherman's truck rumble down the road at a slow, deliberate pace. Cal stifled a whimper. The deranged old man would look for him high and low. The world had gone batshit crazy. Was he safe anywhere?

Cal stayed put until he couldn't hear the truck, and then he climbed back up to the road. He hobbled up the hill on his bare feet, praying the fisherman wouldn't come back in his direction.

Past the cabin, he saw nothing but barren countryside. Cal broke into a run. What was he to do? Hope to find a house along the road and try his luck with another stranger? What if that person tried to bring him back to the fisherman? Cal was wearing the man's clothes. He had no money and no identification. People might think he was a criminal. They might try to trick him like the fisherman had. In the terror state of Cal's imagination, he wondered if he had landed on an island of maniacs, disguised as kind old men, who lured strangers to their homes and mounted them on their walls like fishing trophies.

He shuffled along to a bend in the highway, after which the road descended to a cove with a minor harbor. A big gray navy vessel was anchored there, and men in military uniforms milled around the pier. They weren't Greek or American. Cal saw a flag on the bow of the ship—red, black, white and green—nothing he recognized. Who knew what the foreigners would make of him?

A car droned through the countryside behind him. Cal picked up his pace to reach the harbor. He would take his chances blending in. It was the only place to hide from the fisherman. He kept to the shoulder of the road, searching the seaport ahead for cover. Storehouses and market stalls faced the pier. Could he risk asking someone for help? Cal decided against it. He didn't trust anyone besides a policeman or, if he should be so lucky, an official from the American embassy. The hum of the fisherman's truck gained on him. This was a situation where it would help if he could make himself invisible, like an X-Men superhero, or if some god from Mount Olympus took pity on him and turned him into a juniper tree, just temporarily.

Cal rushed down to the pier, locked his gaze on a wooden platform loaded with crates, and snuck into a tight space within the cargo. He heard the fisherman's truck roll by and caught a glimpse of the vehicle. He sank down in his hiding spot. A few yards away, the truck stopped, the door opened, and the man climbed out. Jesus, this was a nightmare. Was the man going to search through the seaport for him?

He heard the bleep of an industrial vehicle, and then his platform lifted in the air. Cal put it all together too late. A forklift truck was carrying him down the pier to be loaded in the navy ship. Cal couldn't poke out from the crates and jump down to the ground. The fisherman might see him. Not far away, the guy was toddling around, questioning passersby for information. Then, as the truck carted him farther down the pier, he was faced with the dilemma of leaping down amid foreign seamen, announcing his folly and creating a commotion that would draw the fisherman's attention. Cal made himself small and buried his face in his hands, debrained again by the new predicament he'd created for himself. He was stowing away in a military vessel headed to who knew where?

Chapter Nineteen

BRENDAN'S YACHT MET the Greek Navy at a marine station on the island of Icaria. The navy had hauled the Romanian tugboat into the boatyard, and the commander of the unit called Brendan, Cal's father, and the rest of their party to the station house and briefed them with gut-wrenching news. Cal had clearly been on board. Besides his wallet and his passport, they found the cargo shorts he'd been wearing on the morning he disappeared. The absence of Cal's body had provided a sliver of hope until the commander explained some further findings of their investigation.

They had recovered the vessel's lifeboat a few dozen nautical miles away from the wreck. All of its supplies had been used, and the passenger was gone. The only explanation was admirable, though ultimately bleak. Cal must have somehow broken free from his captors, locked them in the ship's cargo hatch, and gotten away in the lifeboat. The facts pointed to a tragic conclusion. The boat's motor had run out of fuel, leaving Cal stranded many miles from land. Excepting the unlikely event he had been rescued by a passing ship, which inexplicably had made no report, he must have gone overboard. The navy had surveillance aircraft searching the surrounding waters. The commander told Brendan that recovering Cal's body could take weeks.

Afterward, Brendan wandered out to the naval pier, stunned by the surreality of the situation. He should call people to let them know the news. That was what a person did when something like this happened, wasn't it? In a flat and stunted voice, he phoned his grandad in Istanbul, Cal's sister Genie in Bodrum, Betsy Schoonover in Kalamata, and his father in Crete. When his phone battery died, he walked out to the end of the pier, staring out at the enormous Aegean seascape. Pregnant storm clouds cast a dark shadow over everything.

He was stricken by a wave of agony, picturing Cal bound and gagged by criminals, frightened beyond belief, and then making a desperate attempt to gain his freedom, all alone, trapped on the open sea. How was it possible for the world to turn so cruel, so tragic, in the blink of an eye? Cal was such a good guy. He'd never done anything to deserve being hurt in the slightest way. Nothing would ever explain his life ending like this. No loving god would have let it happen.

Instead of a wedding and a honeymoon, Brendan would be overseeing his fiancé's funeral.

Two figures encroached in his peripheral vision. Louis and Derek. Brendan wiped his eyes and awakened to his surroundings. Drops of rain were falling. He was suddenly freezing cold.

"Come in out of the rain, buddy," Louis said.

Brendan said nothing. Louis's able arm surrounded him, and he kissed him on the side of the head.

"Everyone's in the mess hall. They've got coffee. Some lousy food. What do you say? They say there's a big storm coming ashore."

Brendan shook his head and looked to the wave-capped horizon. "No. I want to go out there. I can't leave him out there in a storm."

Louis brought out carefully, "They called back the surveillance units. Soon as there's a break in the weather, they'll head out again."

"I want to go out myself." Brendan caught a glimmer of interest from Derek, who had drawn up beside him.

Louis gave him a squeeze. "Brendan, I can't imagine what you're feeling." He looked out to the water. "You're probably ready to dive in there yourself. I'd do it, too, if it would help. But you've got to listen to me, bud. Right now, we go inside, get a warm drink and warm food into your body, and wait it out for a bit. These navy guys told me there's a nice hotel in town where we can stay overnight. The yacht crew is already heading over there."

"Who told them to do that?"

Louis looked at him gently. "The boat's been chained to a storm slip. There's nothing for them to do. The search is in the navy's hands now, Brendan."

"No. Cal's out there somewhere. I'll talk to Captain Wes. I'm paying that motherfucker to help us."

Derek broke in, "He's waiting for a taxi to take him into town. We can catch him if we hurry."

Louis glanced at both men. "Guys, the charter's over. There's no boats headed out to sea until the storm passes. There's nothing they could do anyway."

"That's bullshit," Brendan said. He brushed past his friend and charged down the pier. He wasn't going to sit around any longer to wait for the navy to bring him information. He wasn't going to believe Cal was dead until he saw his body himself. And if he wasn't dead, he needed help. The storm wasn't so bad. Just some wind and a trickle of rain.

Brendan reached the foot of the pier where he spotted Captain Wes and his crew standing under umbrellas. Derek and Louis hurried after him.

He called out to Wes, and the captain turned to him.

"I want to go out there. Where they found the lifeboat."

The blond-bearded South African looked at his crew, and they stepped away to give them some privacy. Louis and Derek looked on from beneath the eave of the marine station house.

"I'm very sorry about your friend," Wes said. "But I'm afraid the navy commander has grounded us until the weather clears."

"He's not my friend. He's my husband," Brendan corrected him.

"Of course. Your husband," Wes said. "I wish there was better news."

"The navy called off their search. That means no one is looking for Cal." Brendan looked to the cloud-clogged sky. "The storm's not so bad. They take these precautions to cover their asses on the one in a million chance some recreational vessel gets in trouble. I need to get out there. Even if it's just to make a couple passes around the area."

He could see he was straining the captain's professional demeanor.

"I understand your concern," Wes said. "But ships are ordered to harbor for a reason. The weather report is pretty serious."

"What if it was your husband? Or wife?" Brendan said. "Would you give up now? Every minute we wait, the odds of finding Cal are turning to shit."

Wes drew a breath. Brendan came at him again.

"You've traveled around the world. I'm not asking you to sail into the eye of a hurricane. Just motor me out there while it's still pretty calm."

"The conditions can change quickly," Wes said. "I'm sorry, Mr. Thackeray-Prentiss, but I can't do it. I would be putting my crew in danger. I would be putting my livelihood in danger if the boat is damaged."

"I'll double your pay," Brendan said. "It'll just be for a couple of hours." Wes shook his head. Brendan didn't break his gaze. "Name your price for the yacht. I'll buy it off you and figure out how to work it myself. Wes, you've got to help me. I'll die back here. I'd spend every cent to my name, steal my own motorboat to get out there if there's even the tiniest chance it could help Cal."

The captain shifted his weight. He glanced around. The boatyard was deserted except for the little congregation in front of the station house. Breaking the silence, a taxi whirred down the coastal roadway in their direction.

"All right, Mr. Thackeray-Prentiss," Wes said. "I will take you out. But only you and my first officer, Ahmed. I will not put anyone else in danger."

Brendan gave him a grim nod of appreciation. The captain called over his first officer, and after a brief discussion, the three men traveled briskly to the slip where the yacht was moored.

ONCE THEY WERE out on the open sea, Brendan began to appreciate the weather warning. Standing in the wheelhouse with Captain Wes and First Officer Ahmed, he had to hold onto the back of the captain's chair to keep his balance while the yacht rocked back and forth. Rain pelted the windows, and a howling wind lashed at them. Though it was only six o'clock in the evening, they had every indoor and sidelight operating as well as a searchlight above the wheelhouse tower.

Ahmed was monitoring the navigational screens while Wes manned the engine and the wheel through increasingly taller swells. Brendan had grown to admire both of the guys. Wes was proudly and immaculately professional, but

Brendan could sense the spirit of a thrill-seeker in him as he helmed his vessel. He was the kind of guy who'd probably been to beaches around the world with his surfboard and went skydiving for fun. Ahmed was a more quiet type, locked into his job at the navigational controls with proficiency. Neither of them gave off a hint of wanting to turn back, and Brendan was grateful for it.

The navy commander had told them Cal's dinghy had been recovered about ten nautical miles northwest of the island of Samos. At a moderate cruising speed, it would take a good hour and a half for them to reach that location from their departure point at the Icaria marine station. They had set out only forty-five minutes ago, and Captain Wes had the engine at low throttle.

Brendan hadn't tried using his binoculars to look out on the water since it was hard enough to keep up with the motion of the boat with one hand free, let alone two. Besides, they probably hadn't ventured far enough for it to be worth a look. He checked out the nautical atlas on the side of the console. The notations and the map of curvy, ring-shaped lines were inscrutable to him, but he was able to locate the islands of Icaria and nearby Samos by name. They were two of the biggest islands in the Northeastern Aegean, not far from the coast of Turkey.

He fixed in on Ahmed and raised his voice to be heard above the wind whipping against their cabin. "Let's say he fell out of the lifeboat with a life preserver. Can you project which way he'd drift based on the currents?"

"Hard to say," Ahmed said. "Current is based on many factors. Tides, winds, air temperature, and water temperature. Generally, the North Aegean has a tendency to flow toward the Cyclades." He pointed out on the map a scattering of islands between Icaria and the coast of Greece.

"That means we're best off searching westward from where they recovered the lifeboat?" Brendan asked.

"Normally, yes," Ahmed said. "But the storm is another factor." He pointed out a weather map on one of the console's monitors. "You see this area of low barometric pressure to the north, near Lesbos. It's making its way along the coast of Turkey and drawing up a fierce northwesterly wind. You can feel it on the port."

Brendan noticed the surge of wind battering the left side of the ship. Waves were also spraying up onto the deck from that direction.

Brendan glanced at the map. "It would push him toward Samos, then?"

Ahmed nodded. "It's possible. The north-central coast of Samos would be your husband's best chance to reach land. I'm monitoring police channels from there. The navy has notified them. They haven't turned up anything, but it's possible a recreational boat picked up your husband, and they have yet to report it. Otherwise, I don't see why he'd abandon the lifeboat. Unless he was injured and disoriented, it doesn't make sense. He wouldn't have encountered any weather. The seas have been calm all this week. Besides, he was in good enough shape to motor a distance away from the tugboat. He couldn't have been out on the water for more than twelve hours, based on the time the tugboat collided with the beacon tower, and most of that time was overnight. Sun exposure should not have been a problem for him."

This was a much more encouraging attitude than Brendan had gotten from the navy commander. Their next trip should be to Samos to turn over the island themselves. Brendan gazed out of the starboard windows, squinting through a blur of rain. The searchlight oscillated, throwing light on the surrounding gray waves for brief moments, but it was hard to make out anything.

The ship shuddered, taking a high wave head-on. The interior and exterior lights flickered, and when Brendan could see out of the window again, he saw the lower deck had been doused by seawater. He looked to Captain Wes to get a read on his thoughts.

"This is starting to feel like an Atlantic event more than an inland sea event," the captain said. "I can take us another few knots eastward. Then I'm afraid we have to turn back, Mr. Thackeray-Prentiss. Otherwise, our return trip is going to be difficult."

Brendan nodded. The yacht, which was a solid, double-deck craft of 117 feet, felt unstable. Not a good thing. As they veered starboard, another big swell battered the vessel from the portside. This time, Brendan lost his footing and swung into the wall of the wheelhouse.

After rubbing off the hard hit to his shoulder, he carefully stepped back to the dashboard windows to gaze out at the violent sea. God help Cal if he was out there. Brendan tried looking out with his binoculars. It was impossible to penetrate the many troughs of the sea. He wished they had a better way to illuminate the water.

Ahmed put on his radio headset, drawn to something on his radar screen. Brendan listened to him talking to Captain Wes.

"This ship I picked up a little while ago has crossed into a mile radius."

Wes glanced at the radar screen with some alarm.

"Looks like a fishing pontoon," Ahmed said. "It's moving erratically and pretty fast. We better alter course a few degrees. Looks like they haven't picked us up."

"What's a fishing boat doing out in these conditions?" Wes said.

"I'll try radioing them."

Brendan edged closer to the men. He didn't need to know much about fishing boats or sea travel to understand it was an odd situation. Their deck heaved up and down from the storm. Unless the other vessel was taping an episode for some extreme fishing show, they couldn't have ventured out for everyday business. Maybe they'd been caught off guard by the storm.

Ahmed tried a series of channels, trying to gain the ship's attention with dispatches in English, Greek, and Turkish. Nothing but static returned to him. Meanwhile, though Captain Wes had steered them southward, the outlined vessel on the green radar screen appeared to be following their trajectory. Brendan was startled by how quickly the strange ship had gained on their position.

"I don't like this," Wes said. "Radio Icaria, and let's fire up the wakeboard tower lights."

Ahmed flipped some switches, and lights flooded out from above the wheelhouse. That had to make their yacht starkly visible, even in the storm. Ahmed radioed in a choppy dispatch to the navy base, hampered by the rail of the wind and surf. He read off their coordinates and tried to ascertain if they had any report of a naval vessel making a crossing in the vicinity. Before he could get an answer, all three men stared in awe at the sight of a gray, rusted long-liner emerging from the misty squall of rain on the port side of the yacht.

It was no more than a boat's length away. No flag. No signal lights. As the yacht's tower lights beamed onto its jutting bow, Brendan thought he glimpsed a team of men on its deck.

"What the hell are they doing?" Wes cursed. He reached to the console and activated the yacht's siren. That did nothing to deter the boat's approach. Wes steered hard to starboard. The sea swells tossed the hull, and the yacht careened in helter-skelter waves.

The long-liner rumbled toward them, and all three men braced themselves. The foreign ship's bow plowed into the side of the yacht with a violent clatter that threw the hull to one side at an extreme angle. The impact rattled Brendan's insides and sent him into a bracing squat while he clung to the captain's chair. The lights flickered again. Ahmed managed to recover his headset and call out Mayday to Icaria. Captain Wes brought out a pistol from a compartment beneath the console.

Men's voices shouted from the ship that had rammed them. Brendan stumbled to the port windows and looked out at an inconceivable scene. The long-liner's crew was tossing grappling lines onto the deck to catch its rails. Wes tried to maneuver with the wheel but didn't make much progress. The attack ship, which was no larger than the yacht, wallowed about and then pulled fast to their vessel, hull to hull.

Wes and Ahmed drew up at the port window. "Fucking pirates in the Aegean?" Wes said. Brendan stared at the men on the attack ship reining in their grappling lines. They wore headscarves and armbands. An Arab militia? One of them held what looked like a machine gun.

"Who are they?" he asked.

"North African pirates?" Ahmed guessed. "Awfully far from their usual territory. I can't see any flag or markings on their ship."

Wes cocked his handgun and looked to the door to the upper deck. He turned to Brendan. "Stay here." He glanced at Ahmed. "Both of you."

Brendan had no problem doing that. But where would they go if the militants came aboard? What would they do if they intended to sabotage their ship?

Wes pushed open the wheelhouse door and stepped out into the storm. Brendan and Ahmed watched in tense silence. The captain called out to the ship's crew, asking them what they wanted, promising no reprisal, though he had his gun tucked into the back of his belt. Brendan counted a dozen men holding the grappling lines, and several others were on the deck behind those men. Squinting through the blur of rain, he guessed there were other members of the crew he couldn't see. One of the pirates shouted at Wes, an indistinct dialect, maybe Arabic. Two of the guys managed to climb over the rails of their vessel and onto the yacht's deck.

Wes whipped out his pistol, braced it on his forearm, and fired at the guys who had come aboard. Brendan's heart caught in his throat. It looked like the shots had missed. With all the wind and surf, the vessel was unsteady. Then: machine-gun fire. Brendan ducked from a terrifying sound. He heard a gasp from Captain Wes, and shrapnel riveted the cabin, shattering glass. A soaking wind wailed into the wheelhouse. Brendan looked to Ahmed, who had taken cover beside him. The young Turk's eyes were wide with terror.

Neither man moved. More angry shouts traveled from the pirate ship, and Brendan listened to the horrifying sound of men clopping onto the lower deck, cries piercing the storm, movement on the cabin below them.

He stuttered to Ahmed, "What do we do?"

Ahmed shook his head. He had to be thinking the same thing as Brendan. Wes had been shot. Did they go out into the crossfire to bring him into the cabin? They had no weapons to defend themselves, and neither of them was much of a fighter. Particularly against a squad of men who rammed boats and came armed with machine guns.

A decision was made for them when a troop of men tramped up the stairs to the wheelhouse. Peeking out from behind the captain's chair, Brendan saw a wild-eyed, rain-soaked Arab in a headscarf and fatigues casing the cabin through the crosshair scope of his assault rifle. Three men came up behind him. From their position, low on the floor, Brendan and Ahmed were unseen at first. Brendan tried to steady the trembles of his body.

A cry hailed, and the rifleman edged around the captain's chair with his weapon pointed at Ahmed. Both Brendan and Ahmed threw up their hands. The gunslinger shouted at them in a foreign language. His companions joined in. It sounded like angry, curse-filled accusations.

Ahmed answered them in their language, assuring, pleading. Brendan winced as the pirate's rifle pointed at him. Ahmed's voice rose up, and words went back and forth between him and one of the guys standing behind the rifleman.

The one word Brendan caught from the foreigners as they looked him up and down: "American?"

The pirates gestured for the two of them to stand, and one of the guys came around and bound their hands behind their backs with cords.

Ahmed spoke quietly to Brendan, "They're some kind of political dissidents. They're taking us prisoner."

Chapter Twenty

CAL WAS BACK in a freight hold headed out to sea. It was a situation that put to mind the incredible variations of absurdity in the world, like taking the wrong exit on an interstate highway and doubling back to the interstate only to take the same wrong exit from the opposite direction. He was grateful to have escaped from the demented fisherman. Though it sank in quickly he had a whole new host of troubles.

He was a stowaway on a military cruiser manned by seamen from a foreign nation. He had nothing to show his identity nor a particularly compelling explanation as to how he'd come to be aboard. From the conversations he'd heard among the uniformed men overseeing his platform of crates being loaded into the boat, it sounded like they spoke Arabic. Peeking out from a slender gap between the crates, he hadn't recognized their tan camouflage uniforms. Their flag patches were not from any country with which he was familiar. They were dark-skinned Arabs wearing black berets. Were they friendly allies of the United States, or from some rogue nation in the Middle East?

The hold was vast, and it was starved of light since they'd lowered him into it with a crane and sealed its overhead hatch. Cal was safe from detection for the moment, and he longed to stretch out from his cramped position. He was also thirsty, hungry, and shivering from the cold. He figured he had time to bide until the ship reached its next port, and he would have to figure out how to sneak off, or to somehow present himself on sympathetic terms.

Could he have been so lucky as to have stowed away with bottled water and something to eat? Cal groped around the top of one of the wooden crates, feeling for grooves where he could wrench one open. He found a place to dig in his fingers, and he pried and jostled the nailed-down lid. With a mighty effort, he uprooted nails on one side and then the other. He lifted the lid open just enough to dig his hand inside the box and feel around, displacing the packing shred. And discovered a familiar texture and shape. The neck of a glass bottle.

Cal brought the bottle out. By its size and weight, he judged it to be wine. Not exactly the quenching drink or nourishment he was hoping for. But for Christ's sake, after everything he'd been through, a guzzle of wine was a marvelous idea.

How to open it? He felt a wrapper around the top, where presumably it was corked. Naturally, it couldn't have been a twist-off cap, the way his luck had been going lately. Cal carefully snuck out of the crates with the wine in hand. Feeling along the steel deck of the hull, he decided on a spot to crack it open. He knelt down on the deck. In a swift motion, he bashed the neck of the bottle on the deck at a slanting angle, creating a sharp and echoing shatter. Cool liquid spattered on his pants and spilled onto the floor. Fortunately, the crew was above deck, too far away to hear Cal's act of desperation.

Cal righted the wine to preserve its contents and felt around the jagged neck. Bringing it close to his lips, he tested out the shattered glass rim very carefully with his tongue. Cal tipped the bottle back to spill some of its contents into his mouth, sloshing the rich, fermented liquid around to make sure he wasn't about to swallow slivers of glass.

He drank it down. It was delicious and velvety like liquid black cherries. The military seamen had gotten the shipment from Samos. Everyone knew the Greeks had invented wine and their hearty soil produced the best in the world, so Cal's uncle had always said. Cal took another cautious drink, and then another and another until there was no more. He'd never been so gluttonous, but his thirst and frayed nerves demanded it.

Desperate situations taught new knowledge about oneself. In this case, locked up on a foreign military cruiser—perhaps to be trapped for many days, with the possibility of being tied up and blindfolded as a political hostage when he was discovered—Cal learned he was not opposed to drinking away his sorrows. He fished out another bottle from the crate, cracked open its neck on the deck, and sat, propped against the cargo platform, to empty it in judicious glugs.

He was soon light-headed and merry. When this ordeal was all over, he would do a circuit of talk shows to tell his story. He could write a book about it. Maybe Brendan's father could adapt it into a biopic like *Captain Phillips* with Tom Hanks or *Wild* with Reese Witherspoon.

Cal giggled. Who would they cast as him? He would insist on someone Greek, and hot, with gravitas, like Criss Angel, if he dyed his hair blond and could act. Brendan would have to be played by someone handsome and a little quirky and endearing. Maybe they could find real gay actors to play real gay people for a change. It was about time for

Hollywood to do a big budget movie like that. Cal imagined movie premieres, red carpets, and award shows, until he started feeling sluggish and numb. He fell asleep in the pitch-black cargo hold.

CAL STIRRED AWAKE to the sound of a heavy door shrieking open in the void above him. Lights blinked on in the hold, and he heard voices from a distance. Cal propped himself up on his elbows, catching sight of himself in the light for the first time. He looked like he'd lost badly in a game of paintball as a result of his messy binge. He scurried back into the cover of the crates.

Spying out from his nook, he spotted two military officers descending into the hold from a towering, industrial staircase. He hadn't noticed that way in before. He hadn't noticed much of anything about the hold while he'd hidden in the crates. It was the size of an Olympic swimming pool and three or four stories high. Some dozen beds of crates were lined up in rows in the middle of the deck.

The two officers looked and sounded like they were out for a casual excursion. They had moustaches and beards, tan uniforms with medals, and decorated caps. Stepping down to the landing, they headed straight for the stacks of cargo. One of them held a crowbar and the other a pair of goblets.

They'd come to sample the wine? Cal made himself as small as he could, wedged between the crates.

The clack of their shoes against the metal deck traveled toward him, and then he heard a startled mutter. An animated conversation broke out. Dreadfully, that had to be about their discovery of the broken bottles and the puddle of wine Cal had left behind. Brisk steps drew closer, and the officers barked back and forth in Arabic, now standing at the site of his wine-pilfering vandalism. The crate with the pried-open lid was right above Cal's head. A pair of shiny, black oxford shoes appeared at the edge of the platform. In favor of being dragged out from hiding, Cal stood and showed himself.

The two men backed up on their heels in alarm.

Cal raised his hands above his head. "I'm really sorry. I can explain." That was promising a lot more than he could deliver, but what could he say?

One of the officers shouted halting words in Arabic. The other gauged Cal warily, clasping a crowbar at his side like a weapon.

"Really, this is all the biggest mix-up," Cal said. "I didn't intend to come on board. I was a fugitive. And before that, I was being held hostage by Romanians." He glanced at the mess he'd created on the deck. "I don't normally do this sort of thing. I mean, I've never done this sort of thing. I'll clean it up. As soon as I get back to my husband, we'll pay you back for all the damage. It was just two bottles." Cal's cheeks burned. He looked to the men with a hapless grin. "Looks worse than that, doesn't it?"

The officer with the crowbar narrowed his eyes at Cal. "You, American?"

"Yes. Well, Greek originally. Part German and Polish on my mother's side."

The two men deliberated in their native language. The guy with the crowbar stepped closer. He had more medals on his cap and his epaulets than his partner. His eyes lit up with a touch of humor. "How do you come aboard?"

"It was an accident," Cal said, relieved the tension appeared to have thawed. "I was running away from this crazy, Greek fisherman. He found me in a lifeboat. I thought for sure I was saved. But he wanted to keep me captive. He followed me to your pier, and I thought I could duck into these crates, just until he lost my trail." Cal shrugged his shoulders with a smile. "Bad idea, huh?"

The guys went back and forth with conversation, disbelieving, chuckling, and pointing out Cal's wine-stained, ill-fitting clothes. It might have been humiliating in other circumstances, but Cal found himself nodding and laughing along with them nervously.

The head officer confronted Cal soberly. "You come with us."

"I'm all yours. Hey, if you have a phone on board, I can call my husband, and he'll explain everything to you."

The man waved for Cal to step out from the platform. Cal squeezed his way through the crates and clopped down on the deck.

"We make investigation of this," the officer said. "Meanwhile, you are prisoner."

That put things into harsher focus, though Cal supposed he couldn't blame them for being concerned about security. "I'm getting used to that," he said. "You know, you might just try the U.S. embassy. I'm pretty sure this has all been reported to them."

The officers said nothing. They flanked Cal and walked him toward the stairwell.

"I really appreciate you guys taking this so well," Cal said. "Where's the boat headed anyway?"

The officers exchanged a glance. The lead man told him, "This is the Abbas Barundi of the Royal Navy of the Sultanate of Maritime Kindah. We are returning home. When we reach port, His Majesty, the King, will make judgment of you."

Cal's eyeballs widened. This did not sound good.

ALL THINGS CONSIDERED, it was not so bad being a prisoner on the Abbas Barundi of the Sultanate of Maritime Kindah. The officers escorted Cal to the ship's brig, which he had entirely to himself. His cell room had a cot with freshly laundered linens and a clean toilet and a sink. The young sailor who came by to watch over him spoke some English. His manner was friendly, and he had a pleasant face, with a trim beard and moustache, and curled, jet-black hair poked out from beneath his naval beret. He brought Cal a clean change of clothes, albeit a gray-and-white striped prisoner's jumpsuit. But the drawstring trousers and the roomy, short-sleeved shirt were comfy, and the uniformed young man even gave him a pair of pedi-foam slippers, like the kind they gave to patients in hospitals.

Passing a glance over Cal's wine-stained lips and sodden feet, the sailor offered to escort him to the bathhouse. There, Cal stripped down and washed up as modestly as the situation permitted, in a communal shower room, with his very accommodating warden staring at him the entire time. Maybe he hadn't encountered many Caucasians in his young seafaring life.

The sailor brought him a towel and asked if he would like something to eat. Cal took him up on that offer enthusiastically. They went back to his cell, where he locked Cal up. The young man returned in short order with a tray loaded with plates of food—chicken kabobs, rice with vegetables and lentils, flatbread, yogurt and cheese, and an ice-cold can of Coca Cola.

It was such a big meal that Cal asked his guard if he would like some. The sailor's face darkened, and he politely declined. Taking a peek up and down the gray-painted corridor, he waved for Cal to come out and sit on the floor to eat, and then he brought out a transistor radio from a cargo pocket in his fatigues. The sailor turned it on and tuned into an Arabian pop music station. He sat down cross-legged in front of Cal, shrugging his thick, dark eyebrows at his clever contrivance of some entertainment for the two of them.

Cal dug into the food with a plastic fork and smiled at his companion. It was far more fresh and tasty than he'd have expected from a military galley.

"My name's Callisthenes, but everyone calls me Cal," he said. He looked at the badge above the sailor's shirt pocket, but it was written in Arabic. "What's your name? Or should I call you by your military title?"

The sailor fingered his badge, grinning bashfully. He may have been Cal's age or younger. "I am only ensign," he said. "You say Faraj bin Abdullah Al-Moghadam." He emphasized, patting his chest, "For you, I am Faraj."

"Faraj," Cal repeated. He scarfed down some more food and wiped his mouth with the paper napkin Faraj had brought him. "This is really delicious. I haven't had a real meal since the rehearsal dinner. For my wedding. I don't even remember how long ago that was." His face went slack. "I don't even know what day it is."

"This is Friday," Faraj told him, looking pleased with himself at his fluency in English. "This is twenty-seventh day of September."

Cal's mouth hung open for a moment. "I've been gone for five days. My family probably thinks I'm dead. My husband—"

He halted for a moment. It was Cal's first chance to unburden himself of the facts to anyone, and even though Faraj was a stranger, he looked like the kind of person who might understand. "We had a fight. Right before I was kidnapped by the Romanians."

He told Faraj the whole story, from the condom and tie appearing out of nowhere on the morning of his wedding to the fisherman from Samos who wanted to hold him hostage in his cliffside cabin. "I miss Brendan so much. He's my soul mate. We were supposed to have our honeymoon in Mauritius. Then I was going to get my master's degree in classical studies, and he was going to take a course in nonprofit management. He's going to start his own charity for homeless gay youth. How amazing is that?"

Faraj smiled at him, in a general sort of way. "You like Arabian music?" He looked to the transistor radio. "This is very famous singer from Lebanon. Make beautiful melody."

"Yes. I like it," Cal said. "It's kind of like Bollywood. But I don't mind the shrieking as much."

Faraj's brow narrowed. "How you make life in America? They say everyone is criminal there. Only very rich survive. And very rich is hating Muslims. And fat. How you are not fat?"

"Oh. I guess I'm just lucky. It must be genetics. I eat whatever I want." Cal shoveled in another forkful of chicken and rice and chewed it down. "And I work out sometimes, but honestly, I don't really enjoy it. Especially the cardio machines. My husband, Brendan, he works out all the time."

"You have beautiful body," Faraj said. "Like rich, American movie star."

"Thanks," Cal said. "But believe me, I'm nobody famous back in America. I'm just a broke, college grad. We're basically a dime a dozen. I've never even met a rich American movie star." Cal thought on it. "I once saw Kevin Bacon on the street in the West Village, but that doesn't really count. Everyone in America has run into Kevin Bacon. And he's a lot shorter than he looks on TV. "

"Why you pierce nipple?" Faraj asked. "This is punishment for crime?"

"Oh no," Cal said. He hiked up his shirt to show Faraj the piercing. "I did that willingly. On my twenty-first birthday. It was my best friend Derek's idea. We were both supposed to get our nipples pierced, and I went first and he chickened out."

Faraj stared at the little stainless steel barbell ring bisecting Cal's nipple. "This is for making sex games?"

"Oh, not with Derek." Cal let his shirt fall down. "I just liked the way it looked." He blushed a little. "It does make your nipple a lot more sensitive, which can be fun." Cal looked at Faraj instructively. "American men get all kinds of piercings. I know a guy who has a Prince Albert, and his scrotum pierced in a dozen places. He looks like an underwater sea creature. Do you know what a Prince Albert is?"

Faraj's face screwed up. "This is obese black man with voice of pervert, Bill Cosby?"

Cal giggled. "That's Fat Albert. Prince Albert is British."

Faraj fell back on his thoughts. "Is it true American men make shameless lust together in light of day, in middle of street?"

Cal pshawed. "I hope you don't mind me saying it, but that sounds like propaganda to me. It's true, things get a bit raunchy at Pride parades, but that's only once a year. Or maybe your government only broadcasts footage from Palm Springs. I've never been, but I've heard that clothing-optional resorts are very popular there."

"You have very beautiful, how you say, penis."

"Wow. Look at that. A little warming up, and your English is really good."

Faraj gazed at him earnestly. "I have big penis." He rustled with his belt buckle. "I show you, and we touch each other with mouths like dogs."

"Oh, I don't think that's necessary, Faraj." Cal said. "I mean, I'm flattered. But I'm engaged now, and we don't have that kind of relationship. Don't get me wrong—I think sexual liberation is wonderful. But in my opinion, most open relationships are doomed to fail."

Faraj reaffixed his belt, looking crestfallen. Cal glanced kindly at his young admirer.

"Faraj, how old are you?"

His companion glanced up at him with a lachrymose face. "I make twenty-one years in December month."

Cal fixed in on him. It was time for a gay-to-gay chat. "You're really young. Do you do this pulling-out-your-junk thing with strangers a lot?"

"Why you not like me? You stamp on my heart like American imperialist army."

"Faraj, I'm taken," Cal said. "And even if I wasn't, that's no way to go about finding a boyfriend. You know nothing about me. I could be some kind of serial killer. Not to mention, you could get an STD or even AIDS."

"No one can know my secret passion," Faraj said, with a steady eye on Cal. "This is forbidden in my country. My life is ruined when people speak of it."

Cal made a gesture, sealing his lips. "I won't say a word. That's got to be a huge burden for you, though. Things are really strict in the Sultanate, huh? I thought, when I saw all the wine in the cargo hold, maybe your people were more westernized. Isn't alcohol forbidden by Islamic law?"

"The cargo is property of His Majesty King Abdullah bin Salib Al-Moghadam," Faraj said. "Allah permits him special indulgence in private residence."

This sounded a bit hypocritical to Cal, but he kept that thought to himself, not wanting to be disrespectful. Instead, he asked, "Faraj, the officers told me I'll be brought before the king. What do you think will happen to me?"

"His Majesty King Abdullah bin Salib Al-Moghadam is Supreme Leader of the Faithful. He alone decides justice for criminals."

"But I've done nothing wrong," Cal said. "I was fleeing for my life, and I ended up on board by mistake. I guess I should start thinking about defending myself. Have you ever met the king?"

"He is my father."

Cal's eyes bugged. "Really?"

"The king makes twenty-nine sons with five wives. I am ninth. My mother is third wife."

"Wow. That's amazing. I thought *I* had a big family. So, what's your father like?"

"For eighteenth birthday, he give me eighty lashes for eating cake before my older brothers eat."

"Jesus... That's...seriously effed up. I guess it wouldn't help then to ask you to put in a good word for me."

"The king must always be brutal tyrant. He is one true sovereign of the Sultanate. Praise Allah." Faraj gave Cal a musing look. "For you, maybe he will cut off hand or foot."

"That's sounds terrible. Does he choose which one, or do I? How would I even decide?"

"I pray for you," Faraj said. He glanced at his watch. "In fact, it is time for Asr prayer." He stood. "Now I put you back in cell."

Cal got up. "Thanks again for the food."

Faraj glanced at Cal confidentially. "After prayers, I go to bathroom stall where I abuse myself with hand in thinking of you defiling my virgin buttocks."

"Oh! Well. Gosh." Cal's glance drifted away. Boy, the little guy was really open about his habits. Cal stepped into his cell and sat on the cot while the door clanged shut. He looked at his hands and feet, wondering what it would be like to live as an amputee.

Chapter Twenty-One

IT WAS THE most hellish night of Brendan's life. After he and Ahmed had their hands bound behind their backs, the Arab pirates turned them over, grabbing their wallets and passports, Ahmed's gold link necklace, Brendan's European wristwatch, and his platinum engagement band. They shoved the two men down to the deck with a rifle pointed at their heads, while the world rocked from the roiling sea, and rain beat down on them. Two others dragged along Captain Wes, who was hunched over himself, wincing, with a bleeding gunshot to his shoulder. Brendan glimpsed pirates scouring the yacht for anything of worth they could steal. Then, a team of head-scarved raiders pulled and wrangled the three of them from the yacht to their commercial long-liner.

Brendan considered many times he might die, whether falling overboard with his hands bound while the tethered vessels creased apart amid the storm, or from being strangled by the pirates' rough handling. Eventually, they wrestled him, Ahmed, and Wes to the metal deck of their ship. They were harassed into the cabin where they were blindfolded and gagged and shoved into some sort of locker with very thin air.

Brendan tucked his knees into his chest while he lay jumbled with the guys. Nearest, Ahmed's frightened breaths snorted and whistled near his ear. Wes groaned, which was a good sign, though with their mouths choked, he couldn't answer questions about how he was doing. Brendan tried to plead for medical help crying out against whatever rag the criminals had muzzled him with. No one answered. He couldn't even tell if anyone was in the vicinity of their lockup.

His head spun and his stomach wrenched while the boat rocked back and forth for an interminable span of time. He fought to get into an upright position, worried about choking on his own vomit. Finally, the vessel's engine churned into higher gear, and that seasick movement gave way to bumpy progress over the storm-tossed sea. They must have released the yacht. Celebratory cheers hailed from the deck. They were off to claim spoils elsewhere, or who knew what?

From the kidnapping ordeal, his body throbbed in pain in many places. He could feel blood oozing from his temple. He'd landed headfirst on the deck when the pirates threw him aboard. Brendan grasped onto the hope they'd have been killed if the raiders intended to do away with them. And if the bastards wanted ransom, he could pray his grandfather would arrange to pay a hefty sum to release them.

After drifting in and out of a shallow sleep for what seemed like a never-ending night, he hearkened to the sound of the boat being brought to port. The engine droned down low and sputtered off. Men scrambled around the deck, calling to one another, hitching lines. A heavy footfall traveled toward the locker, and the door squeaked open. Ahmed's body trembled against his. Hands yanked the two of them up to their feet. Arabic curses lashed at them, and Brendan was wrangled out of the locker into fresher air.

They pushed him and Ahmed through the cabin, out to the sunny warmth of the deck, and onto the sturdy surface of a wooden pier. He was wrestled along on a blind, stumbling path, down the pier, across a paved road, up a gravel footpath, and into a damp house that smelled of mildew. Ahmed's gasps and steps traveled behind him, providing a slim measure of reassurance that at least Brendan wasn't facing the next horror alone. Into a backroom of the house, he was shoved down to a seat on a hard, wooden bench. Ahmed's body came slamming down next to his.

Their captors ungagged Ahmed, and hyped-up demands and accusations in Arabic assaulted him. The first officer's voice was brittle and pleading, making Brendan sink deeper into terror. He winced from the expectation of being beaten or shot. Maybe it was less messy for their captors to do it now that they were on land, at some headquarters of their criminal operations. Maybe they had taken them away while others were putting Wes out of his misery.

A man stepped around him and hands roughly pulled out his gag and unknotted his blindfold. Indoor lighting throbbed and faded in Brendan's oxygen-deprived vision. He blurrily took in that he was in a cramped room, some compartment of a seaside cabin. A single window, opaque from grime and the salty sea air, glowed with daylight. Three men lorded over him and Ahmed, including the Arab tough with the rifle. They untangled Ahmed's blindfold, and the two men looked at one another fearfully. Ahmed's face was ashy and clammy. They had both sweated through their shirts.

One of their captors stared at Brendan with a strange fascination. He wore a black *keffiyeh* like the others, but his military fatigues were dry and less worn. He must not have been aboard the pirate vessel. Brendan guessed he had a role of authority, though he looked no older than the others in his well-groomed black moustache and beard—maybe in his early thirties.

"Brendan Thackeray-Prentiss." The man's accent was faint and more British than Arab. "American millionaire," he said, with a wry grin. "How fortuitous that you crossed paths with one of my ships."

Brendan stared at the young criminal ringleader. "What do you want from us?"

The mercenary didn't answer him. His bearing was amiable, but like a schoolyard bully, that seemed to be only because he had the upper hand. How much information had he retrieved about Brendan since his thieves had stolen his passport?

"What were you doing in the Icarian Sea in the middle of a storm?"

"We were looking for my husband." Brendan's voice cracked, wrought with both his fear and his indignity. "The Greek Navy found his lifeboat. He escaped from a wreck. We thought we might find him, or his body, in the sea."

The man looked to his companions, hinting mildly at his disappointment with them. "I had heard something of this. We received radio dispatches on the disappearance of an American believed to be held by the Romanian mafia." His gaze held Brendan's, strangely kind, no doubt disguising other motives. "I am sorry about your husband. We are not barbarians. Or terrorists. If my men had known, we could have avoided this unpleasant business altogether."

"They shot our captain," Brendan spat at him angrily.

His tormentor stepped to one side, portraying contemplation. "A regrettable accident. This is the price of raising funds for our righteous cause. Your family operates an international corporation. I suspect you understand the inevitability of collateral damage."

That wasn't a fair comparison, but Brendan thought better of arguing the point.

Taking in Brendan's distress, the fellow added in a semblance of brotherly compassion, "We have a medic tending to your captain as we speak. His injury is not extreme. I assure you he will be fine."

Brendan had no idea what to believe. Though he was well aware he had no leverage to confirm that Wes was being treated. "What's this all about? Your 'righteous cause?'" he asked.

"We are the New Arab Democracy League," the man said. "We stand for the people oppressed by King Abdullah bin Salib Al-Moghadam's regime. Our mission is to depose the tyrant and bring democracy to the people."

His accomplices stood straighter with a salute and an oath in Arabic.

Freedom fighters? Brendan didn't know what to make of the pirates who had attacked his yacht, but the man who spoke for them was more refined than he would have pictured for a leader of a militant group. He spoke in fluent, foreign-schooled English, and his hands were tidily manicured, hardly those of a soldier.

Brendan knew something of Middle Eastern politics. He'd met the queen of Jordan and members of the Saudi royal family at charity events. The name Al-Moghadam did not register to him.

"What king are you talking about?" he asked.

"I would not expect you to be familiar with him," the man said. "He is not a spectacle of the tabloids like the House of Saud in Saudi Arabia and the House of Sabah in Kuwait, though like those other families, his political and economic ties to your country run deep. And so it has been easy enough for your politicians and your media to turn a blind eye to his crimes against his people."

He gestured to his unarmed companion while the rifleman stood at attention. The man left the room and returned with a bottle of water. He twisted off its cap and brought it to Brendan's lips, tipping it back for a merciful, quenching drink, and then he fed the water to Ahmed.

The leader's gaze returned to Brendan. "Equally, we have not enjoyed the same international profile of our neighbors, though our history of sovereignty predates the modern Arab states. We are an island nation off the coast of the southern Arabian Peninsula in the Arabian Sea. The Sultanate of Maritime Kindah. We have maintained our independence all the way back to the Ottoman Empire." His expression hardened. "And the dynasty of Al-Moghadam has maintained its greed throughout the centuries. Offshore oil wells, shark fishing, tax-free banking for the foreign wealthy—all exploited by the House of Al-Moghadam to preserve its serfdom."

Revitalized from his drink, Brendan ventured to speak more boldly. "So you're financing a rebellion by pirating boats on the Aegean Sea? Seems like a desperate strategy, but that's your business, not ours. What's your plan now? Extort money from my family? I can make a call if that's what you want. But Ahmed here, and Wes, why don't you just let them go?"

The rebel leader smiled, brandishing his perfectly straight and perfectly white teeth. "Mr. Thackeray-Prentiss, with your Ivy League education, I would think you would be a clever enough man to understand that ransom is an unpredictable venture. Besides, we have no need of your family's money. My ship was returning from the Black Sea with everything we require to accomplish the insurrection." He passed a disgruntled glance at his rifleman. "If my men had not been so paranoid as to imagine your ship was a military vessel monitoring their course, they would have left you to go about your business. Sadly, by the time they could confirm they were intercepting a private yacht, their mercenary instincts overtook them. Your yacht returned meager spoils. Perhaps sufficient to bribe the Egyptian military at the Suez Canal, but not much else."

"So you'll release us then?"

A taunting grin came back at Brendan. The young revolutionary translated in Arabic to his companions, and the two men laughed.

"We could hold you and release you at a proper time," he said in a supposing tone. "We have safe houses across the Arabian peninsula. When the revolution is accomplished, we would have no need to keep you prisoner. You could be sent out to the desert to find your way back home."

Brendan remembered something. "We radioed the Greek Navy before our ship was attacked. They'll notify the U.S. military. They've already been called into the region to help search for my husband. They're probably tracking your progress as we speak."

His captor sneered at him. "You have the arrogance to threaten me, Mr. Thackeray-Prentiss? You overestimate your own importance, and the capability of your American friends. It will take weeks, perhaps months, for the United States to organize a reconnaissance mission. Their resources are devoted to the faraway Persian Gulf and Iraq and Afghanistan. By the time they mobilize resources on your behalf, our ship will have vanished. More importantly, the Sultanate of Maritime Kindah will be liberated."

Brendan imagined he spoke the truth. Grandad was well connected, but surely Brendan was small fry among U.S. military concerns in the Middle East. He was trapped, unable to search for Cal. His captivity could go on for weeks.

If Cal's body was found, he wouldn't even be able to see him and pay his last respects. It was so cruel, so unnecessary. Was there any point in pleading for the man's sympathy? It was the only thing Brendan could do.

"We won't interfere with your revolution," Brendan said. "Can't you release us and go on your way? Holding us will only slow you down." A swoon of emotion made his eyes tear up. He swallowed it down and forced his gaze at his captor. "I need to find my husband. Please. You have to understand that."

"Release you? On your word of honor you won't inform international authorities of anything you heard?" He looked down at Brendan. "Mr. Thackeray-Prentiss, I am afraid I am not that stupid. But as I told you, we are not barbarians. I will offer you a choice. We can imprison you in a safe house until our mission is accomplished, or you can join us."

"Join you?"

"Yes." The rebel leader stepped back and massaged his well-trimmed, bearded chin. "Do not look upon me with such disgust from the suggestion. It seems that fate has entwined our paths with all of its ironic mystery. We are destined to liberate the people of the Sultanate of Maritime Kindah, which is precisely the location where you will find your husband. An operative in His Majesty's Navy has reported to us that Mr. Callisthenes Panagopoulos is being held prisoner aboard a cruiser en route to the capital city of Abbas Barundi."

FOR SOME TIME, Brendan could not utter a word while his desperation to believe and a wave of prudent doubt fought inside him. He bowed his head and clenched his eyes shut, the only form of privacy the circumstances allowed. Two men rustled Ahmed out of the room. Brendan opened his eyes to see what was going on. They closed the door behind them, and he was alone with the mysterious captain of their party. The smooth fellow said nothing, though Brendan perceived a mild air of amusement in his face.

"You can't be fucking with me."

"I understand this is hard for you to believe." He brought out a smart phone, tapped open one of its apps, and scrolled through some things. Then he brought the small screen in front of Brendan at eye level.

The photo was slightly blurred and taken from some distance, but he recognized Cal's side profile, unshaven for days, and his thick, wavy blond hair. He was wearing a striped jumpsuit. His head was downcast. It looked like he was being escorted through some below-deck corridor of a military vessel. Tears welled in Brendan's eyes. His captor swiped to a second photo taken at a closer range. Half of Cal's face was disguised, but it was unmistakably the man Brendan loved with all his heart. Reflexively, he tried to grasp the phone in his own hands, to bring Cal's image nearer. A moan escaped his throat. He couldn't move his arms from behind his back.

Brendan's voice was hoarse and strained. "When were these taken?"

"Three hours ago. Upon the Abbas Barundi as it approached the Suez Canal."

"How?"

"How did Mr. Panagopoulos come to be taken into custody?"

Brendan nodded vigorously.

"Our operative reports he was discovered as a stowaway. A remarkable story, if it can be believed. Our spy is a junior officer with limited information. The cruiser was on a routine maneuver in the Aegean Sea to assist the Turkish military with the surveillance of Syrian refugees. They made port in Samos to receive a shipment for the king. It was only half a day before your yacht encountered our ship returning from the Black Sea. That appears to be the location where Mr. Panagopoulos came aboard. He was discovered by my operative the next morning. The navy commander seems to be keeping him quite comfortable in the brig."

Many things blew up in Brendan's head. Half a day. He was half a day too late to find Cal. How far behind him were they now? Yesterday was Thursday, he thought, though he was so rattled by all of the recent events, his orientation to time was unreliable.

"Why would they take him prisoner? You said the Sultanate is friends with the U.S."

"I cannot say." The rebel leader returned his phone to his pocket. "It is possible the Royal Navy's prerogative to manage criminals aboard its own sovereign warships supersedes their diplomatic concerns. They are headed straightaway to the Sultanate."

"Cal's not a criminal," Brendan said. "You've got to let me call a U.S. embassy. They need to release him and let him return to his family."

The fellow stood in front of Brendan. "I think you know that is not going to happen, Mr. Thackeray-Prentiss. Nothing can interfere with our operation."

Brendan heaved an exasperated breath. "What'll they do to Cal?"

His companion shrugged. "Death at the extreme. An amputation. Flogging. If he is lucky, a term of confinement. The Sultanate dispenses justice based on King Al-

Moghadam's unique interpretation of Sharia law." He squatted down, eye to eye with Brendan. "You see now that our agendas are aligned."

Brendan shivered. He was suddenly aware he was drenched in cold sweat. "I don't understand. You want me to join your military operation against the Sultanate?"

"Yes." He studied Brendan's face. "Do not look so appalled. I don't intend to put you in charge of sea-to-land artillery. I have skilled men for that purpose. In fact, we procured a decisive advantage from arms dealers in Georgia. A Russian Scud missile launcher. It will easily destroy the modest coastal defenses surrounding Abbas Barundi."

"What use do you have for me?" Brendan asked.

The man grinned briefly. "A squad of men will storm the beach while we attack the city's naval base. Every man we can enlist will help ensure our success. You will be part of that team. To take out any soldiers who are activated to protect the city on land. We have a clandestine force in Abbas Barundi and many peasant sympathizers who will join our cause. They will take out the military police within the city. Once the beach force secures the port, our ships will enter, and a second round of troops will disembark. We will assemble to surround the King's palace and force his surrender."

Brendan's mind reeled. It was a stunning amount of confidence to place in him, or a suicide mission about which the young fanatic did not care. And how was he going to rescue Cal amid missile strikes and rioting in the streets?

"This sounds like there'll be many casualties," he said. "What makes all that bloodshed worth it to you?"

"You would not know what it is like to live in tyranny, would you, Mr. Thackeray-Prentiss? To be afraid of having your house stormed by the military based on rumors someone spoke against the king. To see your loved ones stoned to death in a public square. To have everything you own seized by a corrupt government."

He stopped there. Brendan's eyes must have betrayed his dubious appraisal of the man. Though he wore the attire of a revolutionary, he spoke and looked, with a quick change of clothes, like he would fit perfectly fine in a members-only club in London's Soho.

"Is there something you wish to say?" he said.

"I was just wondering what your part is in this?"

"The people need a leader. They have been disenfranchised for so long, they do not have the freedom or the means to organize for themselves. The great Che Guevara of the Americas was born into a privileged family. Like him, I have matured with an affection for the masses who have been exploited by the ruling class. I can also supply them with information they would otherwise not have access to."

"How so?"

Brendan's companion hesitated. His gaze returned fiercely, brooking no disdain. "King Abdullah bin Salib Al-Moghadam is my father. I was sent away for a British education at a young age, and our relationship has always been strained. With the benefit of living abroad, I came to see my family's treatment of its subjects through an objective lens. Perhaps you know something of this phenomenon. My brief research turned up that your involvement in Thackeray Worldwide Enterprises has been, how shall I say, ceremonial?"

Nothing the guy said inspired a sense of kinship, but Brendan thought it wise to play along. He shrugged. That brought a smirk to his companion's lips. Brendan told him, "I don't even know your name. I suppose I should call you Prince?"

"Bassam bin Abdullah Al-Moghadam. I am my father's firstborn son. But I have forsworn my family name, which has been held by dictators since the 17th century. I have abdicated my title. I am now Bassam El-Amin. You may call me Bassam." A clever grin crept on his face. "And now that you have extracted that information, you see there is no way I could set you free."

"Why would you trust me to help with your operation?" Brendan said.

Bassam frowned. "I see I have not succeeded in converting you to our cause. No matter. You have no choice but to help me. If you wish to see your husband again."

"How is he supposed to survive while you're blasting the city with missiles?"

"He will be held in the naval prison," Bassam said. "Our strategic targets are a distance away. Abbas Barundi has two missile silos to defend its port. Our attack will take them by surprise, and once they are immobilized, we will destroy the city's airfield and naval base. After that, it will be a simple matter of overpowering the few surviving soldiers with rifles."

Did Bassam overestimate his strategy? Truly, Brendan would have no idea, though it sounded a lot more complicated than he seemed to believe, and with a whole lot of ways things could go wrong.

"How can I be sure Cal will be set free once you've taken the palace?"

"Indeed, you cannot," Bassam said. "But you will have earned my gratitude by helping to support the revolution. I believe in honoring my promises."

Brendan was not so sure. They meant nothing to one another, mere strangers whose paths had crossed by unlucky circumstances.

"So you'll free Cal and let us both go safely home."

"Unless you decide to stay on to enjoy the celebration of the Sultanate's liberation. You may find revolution to your liking, Mr. Thackeray-Prentiss."

Brendan was quite sure he wouldn't. It was insanity to be drafted into a bloody takeover of an Arab state. He didn't trust Bassam. But what could he do? If there was a remote chance he could find Cal in the carnage and get him safely out, he had to do it.

Chapter Twenty-Two

THEY REACHED ABBAS Barundi, and Cal was cuffed and brought on deck where he had his first glimpse of the Sultanate of Maritime Kindah's island capital. The ship was anchored at a naval base that stretched across a long peninsula to one side of the city center. The city was a treeless plain, dominated by a coastal thatch of glass and chrome skyscrapers. Beyond, a grid of streets disappeared into a hazy, desert horizon. The crystal blue Arabian Sea surrounded the city on three sides, and Cal saw white sand beaches and a harbor with boat yards for luxury yachts. It was grand but desolate, and the metallic landscape glared and steamed beneath the equatorial sun.

Faraj ushered him along behind scores of sailors who were disembarking from the warship. Cal had successfully skirted the young man's repeated offers to show him his penis during their two-day sail, and notwithstanding that bit of awkwardness, Cal was going to miss Faraj's company. They had talked all about his adventure, and Cal had given Faraj lots of tips on gay clubs and beaches on Mykonos if he ever had leave to visit the Greek isles. Faraj, in turn, had coached him on the protocol for when he was brought before the king, and he'd helped Cal shave and trim his hair. Cal had even discovered a new appreciation for Arabian pop music.

He was a mess of nerves now that they were on land, and he was headed inevitably to answer to King Abdullah bin Salib Al-Moghadam. After crossing the gangplank, he spotted a group of military Humvees at the end of the pier, one of which would be conveying him to a detention center.

They followed the sailors in that direction, and Faraj walked him to a utility vehicle where a naval officer stood waiting to take custody of him. Both men let their pace drag.

"I guess this is goodbye, Faraj," Cal said.

Faraj halted. "In my country, men say goodbye with holding each other and kissing faces."

Cal couldn't move his hands to give Faraj a hug, but the young man's arms soon enough surrounded him, and he kissed Cal's cheeks. As the embrace went on, Cal's hands were in the unfortunate position to feel the ardor between Faraj's legs.

Faraj sniffled. "I never forget you."

Cal nodded his head. "I never forget you either."

Faraj released him, and an older, sterner naval officer showed Cal to the back seat of the Humvee.

Cal gazed out of his window while they drove through the base, feeling like it was all surreal. Kidnapped by Romanian mobsters, lost at sea in a lifeboat, and now a prisoner in a foreign nation. What was next? Would the earth cleave open and a black hole suck him into another dimension? Cal wondered how Brendan was holding up. He'd now been gone a whole week. The possibility had to be sinking in that he was dead. Who knew how long he'd be kept in detention, and after weeks, maybe months, the search for him would go cold. Brendan and his family would have to come to terms with that and return to their lives in the States. Cal was beginning to believe in fate. Unbeknownst to him, all his life had been leading up to this: his disappearance from the world. He wished there had been time to say goodbye, to tell Brendan it wasn't his fault; it wasn't anybody's fault. He had just reached his expiration date.

They drove him to a gated barracks with a high, barbed-wire fence, and the naval officer escorted him into the facility. Cal had liked the ship's brig a whole lot more. The detention center was cold and cordoned off by many locked gates. It smelled like ammonia and, if Cal had to describe it, suffering. The officer brought him to a barred counter where he spoke with a uniformed man on the other side. The conversation was in Arabic, so Cal couldn't tell what was being said. The detention clerk wrote something down on a clipboard and pushed it back through a slot for the officer to sign. Then he buzzed open a door, and the officer took Cal by the arm to bring him into the lockup.

SOMETIME THE NEXT morning, the door to Cal's cell rattled open, and a detention officer grumbled at him in Arabic, waving a pair of handcuffs and gesturing for him to come over. Cal shook out of his cot, offered his hands for shackling, and followed the man out of his cell. With all of the dreadful anticipation that had been coursing through him, he'd barely slept overnight and barely eaten his navy-issued tray of colorless and tasteless food. Now he wished he'd been given more time to enjoy his privacy. He had no idea what was going on, but the possibilities—interrogation and torture—were not encouraging.

He was led to the far end of the cellblock and buzzed out to another corridor. After passing through a hydraulic gate, the detention officer put him into the custody of a pair of soldiers. Cal tried out a smile, but neither man smiled back and their eyes were hidden behind sunglasses. They brought him out to a blinding, sunbaked lot and into the barred backseat of another Humvee. They drove out of the detention center, through the naval base, out of the gated security booth, and onto a highway through the sterile cityscape of Abbas Barundi. Neither of the soldiers in the front of the military vehicle told Cal where they were going. Cal's throat was too dry to ask.

They took a ramp off the highway and onto a boulevard lined with palm trees and a green, landscaped median. It looked to be a municipal district with its many flagpoles and grand office buildings. Cal noticed a pair of police cars surrounding a van on the opposite side of the street. Passengers had been drawn out of the vehicle, and it looked like men with rifles were questioning them. Cal's gaze locked in on a man in a headscarf who had been pulled out of the vehicle. His face was bloodied, as from being jabbed by the butt end of a rifle.

They whirred by that scene, and farther along, Cal saw a group of workers washing a wall that had been defaced with graffiti in bloodred Arabic script. All along the boulevard, billboards and posters showed the portrait of a politician in a banded, white *keffiyeh*. That had to be King Abdullah bin Salib Al-Moghadam. He held a quiet smile on his full face, and he had a neatly groomed moustache and goatee and wore a golden collarless jacket. He was a man in his fifties perhaps. The father of twenty-nine sons.

The Humvee stopped at a military checkpoint and drove onward to a neoclassical-style building, draped with flags, with a grand, arched staircase to its columned entrance. Soldiers stood around in various posts, and Cal saw Arabian gentlemen here and there in white robes and *keffiyehs*—businessmen or ministers, he supposed. The Humvee traveled around to the back of the building where there was a fenced-in entryway that looked like it was the place where they delivered prisoners. A courthouse? Cal was appearing in front of the king already? His hands were suddenly as cold as ice blocks.

The soldiers took him into the building where there was a processing station, and then a gloomy waiting area where two dozen other prisoners sat on benches, wearing handcuffs. Some of them glanced his way when he entered, his skin color a minor curiosity. They were all Arab men and mostly young. Some had cuts and bruises on their faces, and they all looked like they'd been detained much longer than Cal had. The moment of curiosity passed, and the prisoners returned to their whispered exchanges, skyward gazes, and mumbled prayers. Cal seated himself in a quiet corner of the holding pen.

He hoped to maintain a low profile. Cal had always sympathized with the criminal justice reform movement—the problems of racial profiling, mandatory sentencing, and the like—but now he'd been thrust into the company of men who could be murderers and rapists. A bedraggled young man with a moustache was eying him with a gap-toothed grin. Cal looked the other way, not wanting to encourage any sort of friendly interaction at all. He had seen enough TV prison dramas to know what happened to the new kid in town. At least in American prisons. He sprouted sweat when the guy shuffled over to sit down next to him. In addition to his busted teeth, he had a jagged scar across his chin.

"Where you from?" he asked.

Cal didn't answer him. He could be lured into some seedy dealings in the prisoners' economy, or entrapped into sexual favors. Furthermore, he had no idea what prejudices the desperado might harbor, or what any of the other prisoners might make of a nominally Greek Orthodox, gay American in their midst. An armed soldier watched over the room from some distance. Cal's knee bounced. What if his companion got angry at him for not responding to his question?

In the end, the gracious opportunity to speak to someone in English wore down Cal's defenses.

"I'm from Syracuse. That's Upstate New York." He glanced at the man's dumbfounded face. "I know. It's unreal. I was supposed to be getting married in Hydra and going on a honeymoon in the Mauritius."

"You are American?"

"Yes, sir."

His companion's face lit up. "I went to college in Southern California. Pepperdine University."

Cal did a double take. "You're kidding! What are the chances? Pepperdine! That's a really great school. I majored in Classical Studies at Syracuse University. I graduated in 2016. What about you?"

"Business administration. I graduated in 2014. I took the MCATs, and I plan to go on for my master's degree."

"That's really smart. Who can do anything with a bachelor's degree these days? Hey, my name's Cal. I'd shake your hand if I could." He rolled his eyes grievously. "Looks like we somehow ended up in the same situation."

"My name is Hakim."

"Nice to meet you, Hakim. Boy, have I got a story for you. But I can be such a chatterbox. How did you end up in this place?"

"When I came home to renew my visa, the military police imprisoned me for bringing blasphemous Western ideology to the Sultanate."

"That's terrible. I mean, I met someone from here who was telling me how strict the government is, but I didn't realize it was *that* bad. If you don't mind me asking, why did your family let you go to an American university in the first place?"

"All wealthy families send their sons to schools in Europe or America," Hakim said. "The king's own sons have their education in Great Britain. My father was accused of insulting the king's first wife, and so the king cut out his tongue and punished him by imprisoning his family. I spent two years in jail. This makes the first time the king will see me to appeal my sentence."

Cal gaped at him. "Holy hell. That's an awful story. I hope the king is lenient with you."

Hakim nodded somberly.

Just then, the door to the courtroom flew open, and two soldiers dragged a prisoner into the room. The man screamed, beseeching mercy, though Cal could not be sure exactly what was going on because all of his commotion was in Arabic. The soldiers harassed him onward and through the waiting room's other locked door. Prisoners around the pen shook their heads and spoke *sotto voce* oaths of disbelief.

After a moment, Cal gathered the courage to ask Hakim about it. "What happened to him?"

"The king has sentenced him to beheading."

Cal took a dry gulp. "What did he do?"

"He was the king's manicurist. He was accused of trimming His Majesty's nails too short."

"Holy Moley. Talk about capricious justice."

Hakim muttered quietly. "It is all a farce. The king is paranoid. He sees enemies everywhere. We are all doomed. Until the revolution comes." He knelt on the floor and bowed down, calling out some prayer to Allah. The other prisoners around the room got down on their knees and joined him in his prostration. Overwhelmed by his vulnerability, and feeling starkly left out, Cal knelt down with Hakim and imitated his movements. Cal had been raised Greek Orthodox, but he really only kept up with religion for the sake of family tradition. Given the circumstances, how could praying to a Muslim god hurt?

A voice cried out: "Callisthenes Panagopoulos?"

Cal felt as though he'd been stricken to stone. He glimpsed a court officer looking around the room. Timid glances fell on Cal. He was the only Greek in the prisoner's pen; that was for sure.

He stood and answered the officer.

"Wish me luck," Cal told Hakim.

The young Arab gazed at him in solidarity, and the whole room watched Cal as he met the court officer and followed him into the courthouse.

Chapter Twenty-Three

KING ABDULLAH BIN Salib Al-Moghadam sat on his throne with his hands on its upholstered arm rests, trying to ignore the blight and sting of the hangnail on his left ring finger. He had told his miserable manicurist Jafar to be careful with his instruments. He had foreseen this inevitable misfortune. Jafar had always been too jumpy to do a proper job.

One could say a sentencing of beheading had been a bit extreme, but managing a kingdom was a tiresome occupation. A certain, authoritarian moodiness was *de rigueur*. Besides, the nervous lackey was just the kind of man whose weak character could be exploited by political upstarts, bullying him into sharing compromising information. Abdullah had met the man's wife and sons. They were a far more handsome and capable family than the imbecile deserved. Abdullah doubted anyone would miss Jafar's head.

Out in his courthouse, his Minister of Justice, Abdullah's son Ghalib, was conferring with his Commander of the Navy, Abdullah's son Karif. The king had lost track of the day's docket, but he had no doubt there would be the usual tedium of listening to the pleas of an endless succession of deviants and political agitators. He would have left such tasks to Ghalib if his second-born son could be trusted to handle any responsibility without sending the kingdom into chaos and destruction. Ghalib, a full-grown man, was known to lose his way traveling back from a visit to the courthouse bathroom, and he still slept with stuffed animals. Twenty-nine sons, without a brain among them. His third-born son, Karif, was a dipsomaniac. He had probably drunk his entire shipment of Samosan wine already. Youssef, his fourth-born son and his Minister of Economics, was a loafer who spent all his time betting on losing bulls at the camel races. The flaws continued all the way to little Rashad, born just last spring, who had the narrow-set eyes of a simpleton.

It was a curse to father such a sorry lot of ne'er-do-wells. Only his first-born, Bassam, had possessed the hardiness and intelligence of a leader, but Bassam had reviled him ever since he was a little boy. Now, Bassam had abandoned him completely, living abroad, renouncing the family name, no doubt wallowing in his juvenile sense of moral superiority with some ridiculous entourage of European friends who were delighted to show off their worldliness by hanging around an exotic Arab expatriate.

If Abdullah kept thinking about it, he would be headed to a dismal place. He looked to his sons impatiently. He could save some time and declare death sentences for all of the men awaiting trial. He could return to the palace and salvage part of the day, catching up on his favorite Persian soap operas. Ghalib stepped to the foot of the dais, and the courthouse bailiff brought another prisoner into the hall.

Ghalib called the room to order. "All hail His Majesty King Abdullah bin Salib Al-Moghadam, Commander of the Faithful, Emir of Emirs, Sovereign and Most Holy Lord of the Sultanate of Maritime Kindah. Praise his wisdom and his justice as the court hears the case of—" He looked down at his clipboard. "—Callisthenes Panagopoulos, detained by His Majesty's Royal Navy for the crimes of—" He glanced again at his notes. "—trespassing, theft, and public drunkenness."

The dozen or so ministers and clerks in the hall knelt on the floor respectfully. Abdullah gave the call for them to take their seats. He looked upon the young prisoner who remained kneeling with a bowed head before his dais. A Greek? This was a prickly matter. His sop-headed son Karif had stirred up an international incident? No one particularly cared for the Greeks, with their whiny little dependency, some two millennia past its heyday, but they had leeched onto a powerful Euro-American alliance.

Karif stood beside the prisoner and addressed his father. "Your Majesty, we discovered this man hidden in the cargo hold of the Abbas Barundi after we made port in Samos. He claims to be an American who took flight from kidnappers, though he bears no identification, nor personal belongings for that matter."

Abdullah stared at the golden-haired prisoner. The young man lifted his head timidly. Abdullah's breath halted. What vision was this before his eyes? A ghost from his past? That face, as clear and bright as the full moon. That vigorous, boyish mop of hair. He was the reincarnation of Abdullah's most cherished friend from boarding school, Basil Cuttingsworth, who had a touch of Greek ancestry, Abdullah recalled as the blessed memory returned to him.

Words nearly escaped his lips—*Basil, my beloved.*

They had met in third form at Winchester College. Basil was the son of a British parliamentarian. They were inseparable all that year—study partners, cricket teammates, running off for private confidences to secluded spots on the pastoral grounds. In fourth form, they arranged to room together.

Basil had been Abdullah's earth and heaven. Physically, the boy was perfection. Abdullah had shyly glanced at him at dressing and showering times, envying the lithe and rangy contours of his body, his easy masculinity. Beyond that fascination, Basil was a kind and faithful friend, and he was unmatched in popularity both for his athleticism and his generous, comradely nature. One blissful, wintry night, while they shared a blanket, warming themselves before the fireplace in the fourth form residence hall after all the other boys had gone to bed, they confessed their love for one another and sealed their vow in a tender kiss.

The king's cheeks burned, remembering. No one had ever loved him so, nor had he ever loved anyone so completely. Their beautiful affair lasted another year. They visited each other's families between terms. Basil was to be his lifetime companion. Then cruelly, horribly, Abdullah's father intervened. His father had detected the unmanly nature of their attachment. He removed Abdullah from Winchester College and sent him off to a school in New Zealand. Abdullah was forbidden from seeing Basil again. Letters were intercepted. His father threatened to expose him as a deviant if he tried to make contact with Basil.

By Sharia law, men were put to death for such behavior. It was the 1970s in Great Britain, with its grotesquerie of sexual liberation, but it remained the Middle Ages in Maritime Kindah. Not that Abdullah ever considered himself a homosexual. What he had with Basil was too right and pure for such an ugly label, just as it was above accusation of sin.

Abdullah had thought he would die from their separation. He tried to kill himself while away in New Zealand, and only managed to dislocate his shoulder, throwing himself from a horse. Time healed that injury and hardened Abdullah's heart to iron. He managed to continue through his lonely college years, a hemisphere away from his beloved, never knowing if Basil yearned for him equally, hated him for leaving, had forgotten him or, worse yet, found another special friend.

Years later, graduated from college and law school, Abdullah had his freedom to travel to London and learned Basil had been killed in an automobile accident while a student at University College. His life had ended at the tender age of twenty. Abdullah's heart was broken a second time. He and Basil would never be reunited. If he hadn't been taken away from Basil, he might have been able to stop him on the fateful night when he had boarded a car with a drunken friend. The world offered no sympathy for his heartbreak. To speak of it would have destroyed his career and brought scandal to the House of Al-Moghadam. Abdullah had no choice but to bury his memory of Basil and accept what was expected of him as his father's heir—arranged marriages, siring children, surrounded by people who flattered him for their self-serving uses, an island of solitude.

Yet now, by Allah's grace, the exquisite replica of the man he had loved knelt before him in his courthouse. To look upon him, Abdullah felt young again, a fourth form student reunited with his best mate, with a lifetime of joys ahead of them.

He was not a fool. He knew it could not be Basil, reanimated from the grave, miraculously preserved from nearly three decades ago. But how was a man to reckon the resemblance, to understand the unlikelihood of the circumstances without superstition? That this young Greek, who shone as handsome and virtuous as his beloved, had been brought to face his judgment after smuggling aboard one of his navy's ships? It could not have happened without a purpose, without the intercession of fate. Abdullah shifted in his seat, aware that his ministers and clerks awaited his bearing on the prisoner.

He cleared his throat. "The King shall allow this man to speak." His son Karif stooped down and translated to the prisoner.

The young man looked up. "Thank you, Your Majesty. This has all been a big mistake. I've never even rolled through a stop sign, let alone trespassed on a military vessel before. Not that I don't understand what I did was wrong. I mean, I really should have asked someone before helping myself to the wine. That's totally not like me. I swear. I'd call character witnesses to my defense, but everyone's back in Hydra."

Abdullah gazed at him in delight. The voice of a stoned, American teenager, but a smile so charming it would calve ice from a glacier. He was Abdullah's second chance at love. Where he had failed dear Basil, he would redeem himself with this young man. He could start by getting him out of his dingy prisoner gear and into proper clothes. Good god, his mouth was watering just imagining the stripping. He waved over his son Ghalib for a whispered exchange.

"Mr. Panagopoulos shall be brought to the palace. A diplomatic guest. Call ahead and have my valet make preparations for his arrival. We'll need the best suite cleared out. The one that looks out on the cricket field."

Ghalib's voice rose up petulantly. "That's my room."

"Right. Find somewhere to go for the next few days. Take your brothers with you. You'll offend our guest."

Abdullah glanced at Callisthenes with a grin and a helpless shrug. Such a bother to put him through this tiresome formality. Was it possible his mother had held onto one of his old Winchester uniforms? The young man would fill out a kit of cricket whites divinely. If Abdullah couldn't find them in the house, he would have them ordered for next-day delivery.

"What would His Majesty like to say about his judgment for the court record?" Ghalib pressed.

"The prisoner is released," Abdullah spoke out to the court. To his son: "Send for my driver. We'll go on recess for the rest of the day."

"Shall we notify the American embassy?"

Abdullah fretted. What a horrible notion. Yet one that could be delayed. "I'll see to it myself. Now have Mr. Panagopoulos taken around the back. My bodyguard will convey him to the palace in your limousine."

"Where will I go?"

"I don't care. Stop breathing on me. What did you have for breakfast? You're suffocating me with garlic and chickpeas."

Chapter Twenty-Four

THE NEW ARAB Democracy League reached the maritime border of Abbas Barundi late in the day on their fifth day at sea. Brendan had been ushered back aboard the pirate long-liner, which delivered him to Bassam at his remote Aegean byway station. He was relieved to see Captain Wes being brought to land in a stretcher. It looked like he'd been bandaged, and though he was pale and feeble, the captain's eyes were open, signaling he had life in him. Wes and Ahmed would stay back to be kept as prisoners. Brendan prayed Bassam would be true to his word about releasing the men after they'd accomplished their revolt.

The long-liner carried some three dozen men along with Bassam's missile launcher. It had been a crowded and sluggish journey. Bassam had carefully navigated a route through the Mediterranean, the Suez Canal, and across the Red Sea to the Arabian Sea. They needed to evade detection by military vessels, and they also needed to time their rendezvous with five other rebel ships making their way from Turkey, Egypt, and Pakistan—or so Brendan had overheard. He'd fallen into a peaceable camaraderie with a group of Kindahnese insurgents who spoke English and had been educated abroad. Like Bassam, they'd all forsaken their families to fight for democracy in their homeland. Listening to their stories of political persecution, Brendan had grown to respect their cause.

He kept to himself, however, his only objective was to find Cal once they reached the shores of Abbas Barundi. With each passing day, he worried ever more he would be too late. Cal was being held prisoner. Thoughts of him being lashed for punishment, or worse, had Brendan in an island of turmoil. He had no way to speed their course and no way to contact anyone for help. He wondered if by some miracle, Captain Wes's distress call near Samos had somehow led to American intelligence tracking him. Despite Bassam laughing at that possibility, Brendan held onto the hope. He knew his grandfather would move mountains to find him and Cal. Grandad had a reputation for making victory out of losses to reclaim his ego, both in and out of the office.

From the deck of the long-liner, Brendan looked across the murky sea at the distant lights of the Kindahnese capital. Like the wealthy, coastal metropolises of the Persian Gulf he'd seen in photos, Abbas Burundi was a surreal outcropping of skyscrapers amid a desert landscape. It had to contain many thousands of people.

The rebels' plan was thus: Their boat would take up a position to shell the naval base and the nearby airfield while motorboats from their craft and the other vessels ferried soldiers to the shores of the coastal city at two strategic points. One team of ground troops would secure the naval base. The other would lock down the city's municipal district with help from civilian rebels who would be activated to arms at the sound of the first missile strike. According to Bassam's comrades, the city's defenses were not especially sophisticated or extensive. Abbas Barundi had not seen combat since the 18th century, when they fought off an armada from the Ottoman Empire. The country's navy was a token force in the region's peacekeeping alliance led by the Americans and the British. Still, Bassam had to be precise with his strikes. If they didn't quickly take out their targets, the naval base could launch missiles from its silos and send out maritime patrol bombers from the airfields.

They motored closer toward the city. Brendan startled as the deck enlivened with cheers. The missile launcher was being raised from the ship's cargo hold. Meanwhile, a pair of dinghies was lowered to the water. Brendan breathed in deep, trying to control his rapidly palpitating heart. He turned to the sound of footsteps approaching him.

Bassam had come out from the cabin with a pair of guerrillas who were handing out rifles. The Arab Che Guevara gazed at Brendan with his unflappable grin. "The time has come, Mr. Thackeray-Prentiss. Are you ready to storm the naval base in the name of the people's revolution?"

Brendan looked at him grimly. "You promised not to strike the detention center."

"Naturally. Beyond your interest in freeing Mr. Panagopoulos, the navy's detainees could be useful allies to our cause. Our targets are around the perimeter of the base and the airfield control tower. Your team will find, at the most, two dozen sailors holding the base. Once you secure the base, you will be free to release any prisoners from detention. You will find the lockup barracks in the center of the armory, near its administrative headquarters."

Brendan snorted in a breath through his nose. He was already perspiring from his brow and armpits. The clothes he wore felt like a bizarre costume—brown camouflage fatigues, combat boots, and a hard hat.

One of the lieutenants handed him a service rifle. He'd only ever used a firearm once, back in boarding school when his house prefect had taken him and his friends to a firing range on a weekend excursion. Brendan had been a terrible aim with a hunting rifle. The semiautomatic weapon in his hands was much more powerful, with a rotating bolt for machine gun–style fusillade. He'd been coached a little in how to use it. The thought of firing on anonymous strangers sickened him. Dodging enemy fire was equally terrifying to imagine.

Bassam turned to the deck and hailed a call to arms. Men raised their rifles in the air and cried back to him. Brendan shuffled over to the side of the ship where the ground force was climbing down into the dinghies.

THE MISSILE STRIKE began when Brendan's dinghy was about halfway to the harbor of the naval base. A terrifying screech sailed overhead, and then a thunderous blast erupted, lighting up the base for a breath. The dozen men around Brendan cheered while he held onto his helmet, which felt like it could blow off from the rocketing and explosion of missiles. Kazi, the steersman at the outboard motor in the back, revved up the engine, and the boat clapped over the waves toward the boatyard.

This was fucking insanity. More missiles screeched overhead and exploded on the coastline of the peninsular station. A navy alarm blared on, and from the streets of the high-rise city center farther away, sirens lit up. Police vehicles were scrambling toward the strike zone. Brendan was headed into a fiery storm of scud missiles and who knew how many men with guns. Those men would be willing to lay down their lives to protect the base. He didn't want to die in an errant missile explosion, or riddled with bullets. His mission to rescue Cal steadied him while the boat cruised inevitably forward and into a smog of dust and smoke from the shelling.

Kazi slowed the outboard motor, carefully navigating the vessel through the smog and to the far end of a minor jetty in the boatyard. The lead man of their team, Benny, radioed back to Bassam. Hopefully, that meant he'd hold off with his missiles while they fought through the perimeter of the base.

Men secured the boat to the jetty, and they climbed off one by one, goading each other forward, hyped up on adrenalin like Navy Seals. Brendan attached himself to a university student named Ibrahim who he'd become friendly with during their journey. They'd talked about the pub scene in London's Camden Town, where Brendan had spent some time in a semester abroad, and they both had an affinity for British punk. Now, keeping up with the kid signified something much more urgent since he looked far more comfortable than Brendan holding a rifle.

Once everyone was on the jetty, Benny led them stalking toward the naval esplanade. They were the vanguard of the operation, which was a nice way of saying sitting ducks. Rebels from a second dinghy would be joining them from another landing point, but it would be up to Brendan's team to take out however many sailors survived the shelling of the base.

When the smog drifted, Brendan made out scant silhouettes of freight containers and barracks around the esplanade. Benny pointed out the damage to the shipyard's main piers nearby. The navy's biggest craft, a warship that looked like it was at least fifty yards in length, had drifted from the decimated wharf and was listing in the water. Far to the right, Benny pointed out a smoldering sight, and Ibrahim translated to Brendan that it was the airfield control tower. It looked like Bassam had done well striking his targets.

Brendan heard the clop of soldiers bustling out to the esplanade. His company halted, spread out, and crouched down to various positions at the end of the jetty. Most of the concrete yard ahead of them was cloaked in darkness and a ponderous bank of smoke. The only light was from the barracks farther inland. Stooped down behind Ibrahim at the back of their party, Brendan couldn't spot the squad he'd heard, and it seemed like no one else in his company could either. Meanwhile, they had no cover at their position. If they didn't surprise the approaching sailors, they were sitting ducks.

Frantic voices traveled nearer. Benny stood and rifled off a round of ammunition that scalded Brendan's ears and rattled his bones. The lead men of the team skulked into the esplanade. Ibrahim clipped Brendan on the shoulder, and Brendan followed in a hunched down, jittery stumble. He dreaded the sightless, open zone ahead of him.

Bullets burst and ricocheted on the asphalt field. Brendan dropped down flat on the jetty. They'd been spotted. Benny and his lead men fixed in on targets and fired into the smog-filled night. A flurry of agonized cries and collapsing bodies traveled from some distance away.

His squad was heading farther into the esplanade. Brendan couldn't lose them, especially Ibrahim, who he was counting on helping him find the detention center. He got up and hurried to the back of their formation.

Another round of gunfire rang out, this time from a higher vantage. A bullet whizzed overhead and burst open from its casing no more than a foot away from Brendan's leg. Sharpshooters from towers? Before Brendan could get a handle on anything, Benny and his team sprayed bullets toward one side of the esplanade. A hail of gunshots returned to them, and Brendan watched in disbelief as Benny's body twisted and collapsed onto the concrete basin.

A round of crossfire blasted, sending Brendan back down on all fours, ducking his head, praying this would not be his last memory of the world. The exchange tapered off, and two men from the team dragged Benny behind a nearby freight bin. Everyone was heading to that sheltered position. Brendan scrambled over.

Benny was shadowed on the ground, but Brendan could hear his anguished moans. Kazi took possession of his radio and called in a report to Bassam's long-liner. Brendan listened for sounds, wondering how long they could hole up in their position, how many sailors with guns they'd have to fight off, and how the hell he'd ended up in this situation. The esplanade was quiet for the moment. He drew up beside Ibrahim.

"What do we do now?"

The kid looked like he was receiving Brendan's voice on a time delay. Like everyone, he was dazed from the crossfire exchange and seeing Benny go down. "We need to take out the towers," Ibrahim told him. "Otherwise, we'll never make it to the command center."

Police sirens shrieked through the night, from a distance, but growing louder.

"We also need to take out the bridge from the highway so those reinforcements don't get across. There'll be a riot squad here in minutes."

Brendan cursed to himself. They were eleven men now with Benny incapacitated, possibly dying from his wounds. Where was the second round of troops?

"What can we do?"

"Kazi's radioing in locations for a missile strike."

Brendan looked at their new lead man. He was speaking into the radio handset while glancing at some GPS device on his cell phone. Brendan's chest shrunk up tight. "They're going to shell the base again?"

Ibrahim nodded.

"What happens to us? We'll be in the middle of the fallout," Brendan said. "Bassam said he wouldn't strike too far inland. He can't hit the detention center."

The other men worked quickly to push the steel freight container over on one side so its lid faced opposite from the esplanade. The bin toppled down with a giant, hollow thud, and they pried off the lid. They pulled Benny's body inside and did their best to make him comfortable. Then they cached themselves in the hollow of the freight bin. Brendan stole inside with them.

A scud missile screamed through the sky on a trajectory that felt like it was no more than an arm's reach above their heads. An earsplitting explosion of metal and concrete shook the ground like an earthquake. Three more missiles bombarded the base. Brendan tucked into himself, trying to draw in breaths through the foul air. His eyes burned. He coughed out grit and shrapnel fumes.

Kazi shouted orders. Brendan rubbed his eyes with the inside of his shirt. He watched his team move out from the freight bin. He guessed they'd come back for Benny when they had a chance to get him medical attention. Ibrahim gave Brendan a look and a nudge, but he couldn't move for a moment. Some primal panic switch inside him had been activated. It was supposed to be fight or flight, but his instinct was telling him to play dead. Ibrahim disappeared around the side of the freight bin. The terror of being left alone finally pushed Brendan to get up and join his team.

A thicker haze of smoke and dust smothered the esplanade. Brendan pulled up the collar of his shirt to mask his mouth and nose. In two locations, he could see a glow of flames from the missile strikes, but everything else was murky. Maybe the smog would make for better cover, though even with his mouth and nose covered, he was trying desperately not to cough in the foul air and draw attention. Besides the crackling of burning metal, everything was dead still. Kazi led the team into what looked like the barracks area of the base.

Brendan nearly tripped over a body on the ground. The man was burned and bloody. No gunshot wounds. He looked like he'd been thrown by one of the explosions. Brendan came upon another body, another naval officer, charred, with his limbs twisted in disturbing angles. Nausea welled inside him. Luckily, he'd eaten very little over the past day. Before he could dry heave, a round of bullets sent a shock to his system and buried that impulse. He jumped behind Ibrahim who'd taken cover at the side of one of the barracks.

Three of the guys rifled shots back at their attackers. Brendan and Ibrahim were safe from the crossfire, but who knew how long their teammates would hold up? Sailors with guns could emerge from another direction. Brendan sank down to his knees, fidgeting with his gun—stricken with amnesia over how to use it. Bullets thudded and pinged against the aluminum wall of the house. He heard a pop and a gasp, and then a guy from their party collapsed to the ground nearby.

Ibrahim squatted down by Brendan and yanked the gun out of his hands to show him how to pull back the bolt and place his hand on the trigger.

More rounds of ammunition rat-tat-ted in the night. They were coming from at least two other directions. Behind them, from the boatyard? Brendan couldn't tell for sure. But the guys around the corner seemed to be taking on less fire. One of them cried out in Arabic. Ibrahim stood and nudged Brendan with his hand. Then the kid went around the side of the house.

Brendan stood and welded his hands to his rifle in firing position. His internal compass was still telling him to play dead, but he couldn't be a fink and bail on the other guys who were risking their lives. He'd cast his lot with the freedom fighters, even if he had no stake in their cause. Lord knew, he wasn't going to be much help, but if by luck, he could do something to spare some bloodshed on his team, he had to do his part.

Mercifully, the crossfire had ceased when he walked into the alley. Through the shadows, he spotted the backs of two men from his team who were surveying the way ahead. Three others were holding positions against the side of one house, and three more against the house on the other side of the alley. With himself and Ibrahim, that made ten. Only one man had gone down.

Ammunition rifled from spots farther into the base. Kazi cried out and waved the team forward. He was leading them in the direction of the rifle fire. Brendan drew up behind Ibrahim at the rear of the pack.

As they closed in on the barrage, Brendan heard gut-wrenching cries of men going down. Then, voices in Arabic, shouting to one another, hopped-up on mutiny, gradually familiar.

Light shone from a building ahead. A short distance away, the alley opened up to a yard. A half dozen bodies littered the ground. All in tan naval uniforms. Kazi took their approach cautiously, directing men to either side of the alley, creeping up on that big opening ahead of them. Sidling forward against the wall of a barracks, Brendan squinted toward the yard. The building on the far side looked like a stone-walled construction, two stories high, topped with a mansard roof and a lookout tower. That had the markings of an administrative building, if not the control center they were looking for.

Shots rang out from the tower. They were aimed away from the team, though it still made Brendan seal himself to the wall. A single rifleman, he deciphered. A battery of rounds scoured the lookout gallery. In its wake, the tower was silent. The stone house was still. A cheer hailed from a group of men some distance away.

Kazi called out in Arabic. Boisterous voices returned to him. It was the second team of ground troops. Kazi looked back at his company and waved them on. As they stepped into the yard in front of the building, their rebel brothers emerged from the surrounding alleys.

The men grasped each other and shouted out in victory. Kazi held a conversation with one of his comrades as they eyed the stone house.

Brendan gained up on Ibrahim. "It's over?"

Ibrahim smiled. "Around the front of the building, they put out the flag of surrender across the door. They're taking the people inside prisoners." He clasped Brendan's shoulder. "We won."

Brendan decompressed for a moment. In an odd way, he felt proud. It was a stretch to say he'd done much of anything to accomplish the victory, but like a benchwarmer, he'd been there for moral support and to take the field if the situation turned desperate. He caught Ibrahim before the kid wandered off to chat with the others.

"I have to find the detention center. Will you help me?"

Ibrahim glanced at the guys congratulating each other around the yard.

"Please. Just to take a quick look," Brendan said. "I have to find Cal." He had told Ibrahim and his friends about Cal's situation. Now he prayed he wouldn't have to go looking for it himself. The men were acting like the base was secure, but who knew what he would encounter searching around blindly? Even meeting a surrendered sailor was dangerous since he didn't speak Arabic.

"Okay," Ibrahim said. "But we have to be quick. As soon as the wounded men are settled in the infirmary, the team's heading out to rendezvous at the king's palace."

He stepped over to Kazi to let him know they were going, and then Brendan ran after him to thread the byways of the base in search of the detention house.

BASSAM HAD SAID the detention barracks would be near the administrative center. That didn't help much, in the dark, trying to keep up with Ibrahim who'd taken off in a brisk jog around a naval base neither one of them had ever set foot in before. They circled around the stone tower building, and then they followed a paved road through rows of shadowy prefab houses. None of them had the familiar characteristics of a lockup facility, though Brendan wondered if they should venture off the road to take a closer look. Ibrahim didn't break from his jog. Maybe he knew better what to look for. Maybe he was just going through the motions to help Brendan out. Brendan couldn't tell, though really, anything was possible. They traveled a good distance away from the rest of the team. He worried Ibrahim would try to lead him back.

At a crossroad, Brendan spotted a facility with a tall barbed-wire fence. He called out to Ibrahim, and they headed over to it. A gate by a scaffold watchtower was open. The rectangular house inside was dark except for a single barred window in the front—perhaps some administrative foyer. The place was eerily still. Brendan followed Ibrahim's lead, raising his rifle to eye level, anticipating enemy targets, and they crept up to the door, minding the lighted window.

It was a heavy-duty, steel-frame door that had an intercom on the side. The two men glanced at one another, listening for activity inside. The navy certainly hadn't put much effort into keeping detainees in lockup during the siege. Could they be so lucky as to be able to waltz right in? Brendan grasped the lever-latch door handle and tried pressing it down and pulling the door open. It wouldn't give.

Bullets pounded against the side of the door. Brendan and Ibrahim jumped away from it and got down low. It took a minute or two for Brendan to regain his bearings. Warning shots from someone inside? How were they going to get in with an armed guard waiting for them at the entry to the house?

The little time hanging out with gun-toting insurgents inspired a newfound boldness. He looked to the barred window, set up his gun, and blasted a round into the thick polyurethane glass. The gun's action made him stumble backward and sent a stinging pain into his shoulder. Brendan shook it off and fired another round. They had to get into the house. Cal was locked up in there. The glass didn't shatter, but it was cracked enough to be pounded through with the stock end of his rifle. Then he could fire right into the guard's station and hopefully scare him away.

Ibrahim meanwhile sprayed rounds at the lock in the door. They kept at that racket until Brendan heard Ibrahim calling out to him. His partner had eased up to the door. Brendan heard a frantic voice inside. It sounded like some guy might be talking on a radio. He heard a rustle of movement fading farther into the house.

Brendan kicked at the door, hoping it was wobbly from the damage to the lock. Ibrahim helped him pry it open, and they went guns-first into the lobby.

The lobby was barren—an unattended counter window next to a locked gate—but rustling sounds gave away someone fumbling beyond that window. Ibrahim swung over to the window, poked his gun into the station, and pointed the muzzle firmly at a target. A man's pleading voice called out to him in Arabic.

Brendan scurried over. A man in a naval uniform and cap was curled up on the floor, against a door into the facility. He was just short of opening it up with his ring of keys but now held up his hands. His face was wildly frightened. Ibrahim shouted at him, and he kept repeating back the same words.

"He says there's no one in detention," Ibrahim told Brendan.

"Tell him to open up."

Ibrahim worked on that with a threatening conversation and the threatening pointing of his rifle. The guy got up off the floor and cowered over to the counter where he pressed a switch, releasing the lobby gate.

Brendan stepped through the gate into the facility and found the back door of the guard's station. He pounded on it. Keys jangled and scraped against the lock on the other side, and the door swung open. The guard drew back from Brendan as he entered, shifting his glance back and forth between the two men—Ibrahim with his gun pointed at him from the counter, Brendan with his gun readied in his hands. The guard's rifle lay on the floor, presumably thrown aside because he was out of ammunition.

The guy shook his head and pleaded with Brendan.

Ibrahim told him, "He says they haven't had anyone in detention since yesterday morning."

"Would he tell the truth?"

Ibrahim shrugged. "I think so. He's really shaken up. The only guard on duty. You see the place is deserted."

"Tell him to give me the keys."

Ibrahim conversed with the guard, and the guy spoke back, shaking his head. He told Ibrahim something and very gingerly drifted to his desk. The guard picked up a clipboard and showed it to Ibrahim, pointing at what looked like a sign-in sheet. Then he followed Ibrahim's instructions to get back down on the floor with his hands held up.

Brendan stepped over to take a look. Just one line was filled out on the page with several columns. Numbers, names maybe, nothing he could read. Could Ibrahim make sense of it?

His partner looked at him soberly. "One entry. Callisthenes Panagopoulos. Brought in October 2nd, released October 3rd."

Brendan's heart plunged. Then he slammed his hand into the cabinet above the desk. "What the fuck?" He paced around. He felt like an angel of fate had swooped down from the heavens and pissed on him. One day too late. How could he be so goddamn unlucky?

He shouted at the guard, "Where did he go?" Brendan didn't wait for an answer. "What did they do with him? Where is he now?"

The guard backed away from him, shaking his head. Ibrahim translated some questions. The guy's response didn't sound encouraging. Brendan wiped his face. He was ready to throw his fist into the wall.

"He says he doesn't know," Ibrahim said. "He was taken to the courthouse." The kid gazed at Brendan steadily. "We've got to get back to the others. They'll be leaving soon."

"You don't understand. The only reason I came was to find my husband. Tell this guy he's got to give us information. Where's the courthouse? Where would they have taken him after that?"

"He could be in a dozen places. A police station. A prison in the city. They could have transported him to a facility out of town."

"I'll check every one of them."

Ibrahim's eyes flashed. His hands tightened around his rifle. "If you run off, you'll be a deserter and an enemy of the revolution."

Brendan stared helplessly at his companion. So much for brotherhood over warm ale and Joe Strummer's howling vocals. Ibrahim had no investment in finding Cal. The college student was sworn to Bassam's insurgency, and he would shoot Brendan right then and there if he declared he was leaving. For a crazy moment, Brendan imagined hiking up his rifle on the chance he would be quicker than the young militant. There was a radio and a landline telephone on the guard's desk. If he got rid of Ibrahim, he could figure out a way to call the U.S. authorities or his grandfather. They would come to help him.

The guard at his feet whimpered out a plea. Brendan looked down at him, and then he jumped away from a rifle blare. Bullets riddled the guard's body, pinning him to the floor, drawing up wisps of smoke. Brendan shrank down to the floor in a corner of the guard's station and covered his face.

Gasping, he peeked out to the counter window. Ibrahim's rifle was pointed at him.

"Let's go," Ibrahim told him.

Chapter Twenty-Five

CAL SAT IN the recessed salon of his luxurious suite, picking at an abundance of *mezze* laid out on silver platters on a low, ebony dining table, as he waited for King Abdullah to join him. If this adventure was to be made into a movie, it was turning out to be like *Pretty Woman.* Lord knew, he'd never been in a palace before.

The enormous, white-domed estate had taken his breath away when the limousine had driven him through its gates. A man-made lake dominated the front of the grounds, kind of like pictures Cal had seen of the Taj Mahal. The main house had a two-story, arched window above its grand roofed porch, and it rivaled a museum in scale. Verdant palm trees surrounded it, and its grassy lawns looked like they went on into infinity. Cal glimpsed gardens that were bigger than a botanical park, and a golf course and horse stables. His rooms even looked out on a cricket field.

Inside, everything was immaculate—ornate carpets, crystal chandeliers, gleaming, oiled wood furniture, and painted portraits in gilded frames. Cal had been ushered to his upstairs room by Irfan, a well-groomed valet in a fine, quilted jacket. The friendly manservant provided him with a plush bathrobe and took away his embarrassing jumpsuit. Cal's "room" was, in fact, an apartment bigger than the house he'd grown up in. He didn't plan on mentioning it to Brendan, but the furnishings made his fiancé's penthouse apartment seem austere in comparison. The best part was the bathroom, all done up in blue mosaic tiles, and with a glass-paneled, walk-in shower and its own fireplace. Cal had already soaked in the sunken bathtub that had whirlpool settings and a big-screen TV that raised up from the floor.

His only complaint was the clothes that had been laid out for him by Irfan were an undersized outfit meant to be worn by a boy half his age. He'd barely managed to get the shorts up and around his butt, and they were obscenely snug in the crotch. The red-striped, jersey-style shirt, which bore a prep-school insignia, rode up his sides, exposing a lot of midriff. The only thing that fit was a pair of knee-high socks and cleats, which were unworn, fresh from the store. Cal had covered up in his robe and tried asking Irfan if he might try on something else. The suave attendant just raised his eyebrows and left the room, onto other important business apparently.

For all its walk-in closets, fancy cabinets, and ornate chests, the suite had no other clothes Cal could find. It was absent a phone as well, which Cal really desperately needed to use to call Brendan and his mom and dad. When Irfan finally returned, he'd come to throw open the double doors for a squad of male domestics carting in a feast of food and drink. Irfan said His Majesty would be joining him directly.

That really threw Cal for a loop. He'd be dining with the king? A man who had sentenced his own son to be whipped on his birthday for bad table manners, not to mention ordering the beheading of his manicurist earlier that day? Where was the estate's stuffy British governess to give him a briefing on etiquette? Cal's nerves overtook his concern about reaching Brendan and his family. He decided he'd better ask Irfan about using a phone later, after dinner. Meanwhile, he dispensed with his robe to make the best of the clothes that had been given to him since, really, how could he wear a bathrobe to dinner with a king?

When the king arrived, Cal stood, wiped off his hands, and froze in place, not knowing what to say to the ruler of a sovereign nation who had miraculously exonerated him from stowing away on his navy ship and breaking into his shipment of wine. The king smiled at him warmly and graciously, and he seated himself across the table on a matching velvet-upholstered divan. For a man who made his subjects cower and beg their god for mercy, he was much more easygoing than Cal had expected. Stupidly, Cal thanked him for his hospitality a half dozen times, and the king insisted he was the one who owed Cal thanks and an apology for being mistreated by his navy. That was awfully generous and helped put Cal at ease. The king was dressed down in a night-blue, silken robe. A white *keffiyeh* framed his mustached and goateed face. He was distinguished and a little flashy with all of his gold and gem-laid rings. He insisted that Cal go ahead and eat even though he seemed disinterested in the food himself.

Cal finished off his third stuffed grape leaf. The king lifted a platter of oval-shaped meatballs from the table and pushed it toward Cal.

"You must try the *kibbeh*. It is the very best in the Middle East."

"Oh. I don't know if I have room for it," Cal said, realizing he was being quite literal based on his clothes nearly bursting at their seams. He'd tried just about everything at the table, and the spread was big enough for the defense lineup of a college football team. Still, he opted not to refuse His Majesty and picked out one of the fried brown meatballs and took a great big bite of it.

"It's delicious," he mumbled through chews. Cal wiped his mouth with his cloth napkin. He grinned at the king bashfully. "I'm sorry. My manners must seem terrible. My mom always used to tell me not to speak with my mouth full, but it never caught on. If you ever had dinner with my family, you'd probably think we were all cavemen."

The king tutted. "Nonsense. It is a great compliment to show one's host you are enjoying his meal."

"That's what I always thought," Cal said. "I heard, in some cultures, it's even considered a compliment to burp and fart." He caught himself getting loopy. "Not that I intend to do that. I'm just grateful to be treated to all of this, Your Majesty. That's what I should call you, isn't it? I feel like a total doofus having to ask."

The king shook his head. "We are friends. You may call me Abdullah."

Cal's eyes grew wide. He'd never been on a first name basis with a man of Abdullah's stature. The guy had posters of himself emblazoned all over the city, and he employed more people to take care of his home than a Las Vegas casino hotel.

"Well, you can call me Cal," he offered companionably. "Everybody does. Except my grandparents. And my dentist. Though I think Dr. Rosenstern only calls me Callisthenes because he thinks it makes him sound cultured. I'm pretty sure I'm the only Greek patient in his practice. In Upstate New York, we barely count as Caucasians."

Abdullah took a quiet account of Cal while he finished off his *kibbeh*. "There are many famous Greeks," he said.

"Not on *my* dad's side of the family."

"Alexander the Great. Plato. Aristotle. Sophocles."

"You should talk to my Uncle Theo. He'd keep you busy all night with a list of every famous Greek who ever lived."

"This is a very celebrated and honorable culture."

"I like to think so." Cal added, "I majored in classical studies."

Abdullah's eyes brightened. "You are a college student?"

Cal nodded. "I graduated with my bachelor's from Syracuse University. I'm going back for my masters' degree."

"This must make your family proud."

Cal shrugged. "I think they'd actually be happier if I learned a trade like my older brothers. They don't really understand what I'm doing with my life. To be honest with you, Abdullah, most of the time, *I* don't understand what I'm doing with my life. I mean, if we're being honest—there's not a lot you can do with a classical studies degree."

Abdullah took up defending him again. "Nothing is more important than education. We must understand our history, and the origins of philosophy and the arts and sciences." He sat up a bit straighter. "I studied all the world cultures when I was a student. From antiquity and from around the globe."

"Really? That's, like, amazing. I guess you'd have to. I mean, it probably helps, doesn't it? Being an international leader."

His companion waved his hand. "I did it for the sake of knowledge. This is what keeps us vital. Every man should have a traditional education. How else does he understand his place in the world?"

Cal wasn't sure what to say to that. He had a feeling if the conversation turned philosophical, he'd be quickly outwitted and disappoint Abdullah. Cal's interest in classical studies was more on the archeology and art history side, so if the king wanted to have a conversation about the work of Phidias, he had a lot to say. But who, outside of classical studies majors, wanted to talk about ancient Greek sculptors?

He noticed the king's glance passing over his outfit and his lap. Cal would have crossed his legs for modesty, but he was afraid he'd rip the seams of his shorts. They were straining even more after having put away so much food.

"Did you play American football?" Abdullah said.

"Gosh no. I'm totally uncoordinated."

"Soccer?"

"Nope."

"Track and field?"

Cal shook his head.

"Tennis?"

Now Cal's face was really burning. "I'm telling you— I have absolutely zero athletic ability. For my two semesters of mandatory PE, I chose ping-pong and bowling. My older brother Demetri used to give me his lunch money to pretend to be sick so I didn't have to play on our little league baseball team."

Abdullah snorted in disbelief. "You are very fit." He fixed in on Cal decisively. "Tomorrow, I will teach you cricket."

Cal glanced around. "This sure would be the place to learn. I saw you have a field right on the grounds." He grasped his gold-rimmed goblet and took a sip of the Samosan wine. "That's really nice of you, Abdullah. But tomorrow, I have to be getting back to my husband and my family." Cal felt like a jerk. He knew that Middle Easterners, like Europeans, took great pride in their hospitality, and they thought Americans were too uptight. But Abdullah had to understand people were worried about him. He'd been gone now for over a week.

Abdullah snapped his fingers to direct their male attendant to refresh Cal's goblet of wine. The young servant did so, and then the king waved him from the room. Cal sank a little in his seat. He was certain he was about to be on the receiving end of a sharp lesson on etiquette. The king stood and walked around the table to Cal's divan, looking at him for a gesture of invitation. Cal opened his mouth, but no sound came out. He managed to gather the sense to scoot over to make room. They were alone in the recessed salon, in the flickering light of a single hanging lantern.

A billow of *oud* and musk surrounded Cal as the king seated himself. "I must make my apologies, Cal. You must miss your family terribly."

"I do," Cal said. "I mean, I can't thank you enough for putting me up like this. But everyone back in Hydra, they probably think I'm dead. If they knew I was lounging around in a palace while they were worrying, they'd kill me themselves."

Abdullah leaned in close with a grave look on his face. "A young man like you must have many people who care for him."

Cal was nearly wearing the man's robe. He leaned away from his companion, trying not to be rude about it. "You know Greeks. Big families," he said, hoping to lighten the mood.

"Naturally, they must be assured you are safe and sound."

Cal nodded nervously. "They'd really appreciate it."

"I will call them in the morning. I will explain to them that I insist you stay here as my guest. It will be a great pleasure to show you the wonders of Maritime Kindah."

Cal's stomach knotted up. He didn't dare to look, but he had the distinct impression the king was sniffing him.

"Do you believe in destiny, Cal?"

"Oh. Well, I guess I believe in destiny with a little 'd.' There has to be a balance, don't you think? Destiny and free will, I mean."

"I like your face."

"You do? Well—"

"I like your legs."

"Ha!"

"Would you mind if I called you Basil?"

"Oh. Well, that would be a first. I guess if you really want to. Gosh, it's hot in here. Maybe I'll just get up and crack open the balcony door a little."

Abdullah's hand closed firmly on Cal's arm. "Don't."

Cal sat back down.

"I enjoy your company so much," Abdullah said. "Let's not ruin the moment. I can feel the sultry heat from your body. If you would like to take off your shirt, I wouldn't mind."

"'The moment'? Right. I'm just fine keeping the shirt on. I'm used to hand-me-down clothes. I'll admit it— I was a little skeptical about the shirt at first, but I'm actually starting to like it. Does it belong to one of your sons?"

"Basil, would you do me the favor of speaking to me in a British accent?"

Cal whinnied a nervous laugh. "I think I'm starting to understand the kind of moment you're driving for. I don't think you really want to hear me do a British accent, Abdullah. I haven't tried that since I was in sixth grade. I had a part in my elementary school's production of *A Christmas Carol*, and the music teacher, Mr. Benson, took away my lines because I couldn't get my tongue tips right."

Abdullah's hand gently closed on Cal's thigh. "Try, Basil. Please."

Cal croaked out a weak attempt. "Awms four tha pour, Govenah? Wood ye like to play a game ov Quidditch? Pleez sir, kin I half so' more?"

His companion gazed at him, wounded. "Do not mock me, Basil. To be so near to you, I feel as though my heart is bleeding."

"Wow. That's intense. I'm actually having a bit of indigestion. Y'know, so many spices I'm not used to." Cal squirmed out from under Abdullah's hand. "I'll just make a quick trip to the bathroom."

Abdullah looked up at him. "What can I do to make you stay?"

Cal inferred he meant more than delaying him from using the bathroom. He looked upon the man. "It's not you, Abdullah. It's me. I'm not 'Basil.'" He glanced down at his outfit. "That's what all of this is about, isn't it? You're trying to make me into some London schoolboy, and I'm sure you have your reasons for it. Really sincere and private reasons you don't even have to share with me. But Abdullah, I'm not that boy. I'm twenty-four years old. I'm getting married. To the guy of my dreams."

Abdullah stood. "I will speak to your fiancé. I will pay him to release you."

That raised Cal's hackles. "It doesn't work like that. "

"I will pay him one million U.S. dollars."

"You can't just buy people. At least not in America." He ventured a firm look at Abdullah. "It's actually insulting."

Abdullah stepped closer. "Of course. You are worth more than that. I will pay your fiancé two million dollars."

"Listen, Abdullah. I think it would be best for both of us if we called it a night."

A glare sprang from the Arabian king's face. "You would dismiss me from your room?"

Cal backed out of the salon and into the front hall of the suite. "Maybe that came out harsh. But yes, that's exactly what I mean. I'm afraid that's the way it's got to be."

Abdullah followed him out of the salon. "No man has ever spoken to me that way."

Cal held his ground. "I'm sorry, Abdullah, but I can see where this is leading. I've tried to be polite. I don't mean to be ungrateful. You're looking at a man pushed to his breaking point. I've been kidnapped by mobsters. I've been lost at sea in a lifeboat. I've had to fight off pervy guys like you all week, and I hope you don't take that the wrong way. Do you know what I'd do for a pair of pants that fit and a little peace and quiet?"

Abdullah looked stricken. For a blink. Then he trotted toward Cal, newly inspired. "You arouse me with your brash ways. Your youthful impertinence."

Cal held his hands in front of himself as though tempering a charging bull. "Back off, Sultan. I may look dainty, but for your information, I took out a Romanian Mob-Daddy twice your size."

The king persisted, rounding Cal while he held him back. "Give me a chance, Cal. I can be a very generous lover. And discreet. Your fiancé doesn't have to know about anything."

Cal shook his head.

"A kiss?" Abdullah suggested. "What's a kiss?"

"Not happening."

Abdullah retreated. Cal kept a sharp eye on him. Beneath the sleeve of his robe, the king was doing something with his watch.

"I see you will not allow me to take you gently," Abdullah said. "I'm afraid you leave me no choice. I will have to use other methods to persuade you."

The door to the hall flew open. Two hulking bodyguards swaggered into the room. The king must have called them from a device on his watch.

Cal backed slowly away from the thugs. Holy Jesus. He was going to get the crap beaten out of him. One of the goons had a gag and a length of rope for tying him up.

"Take him," the king commanded.

Just as the bodyguards lurched toward Cal, a distant boom rumbled through the house, and the lights flickered on and off. Everybody froze. It sounded like they were under attack.

A staticky voice came over the bodyguards' earbuds. The king drifted over to them to see what was the matter.

Cal had an opportunity while they were all confused, though he had to be lightning quick. He bolted farther into the apartment to find the balcony. He would shimmy down the side of the house or even take his chances with a leap down to the grounds. Otherwise, his biopic was about to turn into *The Jeffrey Dahmer Story*.

He heard the king shout after him and a fluster of movement from the front hall. Then, as Cal raced for his life, he heard a dreadful noise, even worse than the explosion somewhere on the property. The seat of his shorts had ripped open.

Chapter Twenty-Six

BACK AT THE navy base, Brendan had followed Ibrahim and boarded a Humvee that a group of rebels had commandeered from the sailors. Their mission now was to rendezvous at the king's palace with the other foreign insurgents and their local counterparts and storm the estate. They'd left the base on an off-road route since the raised highway from the peninsula to the mainland had been demolished by one of Bassam's missiles. Across a bumpy, treeless plain, they refound paved streets. Ibrahim had told Brendan they'd have to traverse the city to get to the king's compound on the outskirts of town.

Inside the military vehicle, Brendan glanced out of the windows from a safe distance in the middle of the backseat. It was now deep in the night, but from what he could see and hear, Abbas Barundi had become a warzone. His shoulders clenched from the sound of rifle fire, traveling to them from places nearby. Hordes of people swarmed police vehicles, overturning them and setting them ablaze. Molotov cocktails burst and blazed at barricaded checkpoints, and the country's soldiers desperately tried to defend themselves by blasting rounds of bullets into the crowds. Stray rocks and ammunition pelted the Humvee as they rolled through the chaos.

All of this inspired very bleak feelings about finding Cal. Their Humvee wouldn't stop until they reached the king's compound, and even if he figured out a way to wrestle his way out the door of the moving vehicle, he would have to swim through rioting mobs with absolutely no idea where to look for his husband. He had no idea what the natives would make of him, a dazed American plunked down in the middle of their bloodthirsty revolt. The police stations they passed by were under siege. Would officers loyal to the king kill their prisoners out of spite?

A choppy radio dispatch fizzed on from the front of the vehicle. Kazi, who was in the passenger's seat, picked up the receiver and held a conversation while the other guys in the artillery truck hollered about what had to be good news. Brendan looked to Ibrahim for a translation.

"Bassam's ship made landing in the harbor. They're loading the missile launcher onto a truck. We'll need the heavy artillery. The palace will be defended. As soon as they break down the walls, we've been ordered to secure the compound."

Brendan hadn't known what to expect, though Bassam had made it sound like taking the palace would be easier. He had no interest in attacking the king's palace. He didn't want to kill anyone. He just needed to get Cal and get out of this country that had gone berserk.

He leaned over the front seat and spoke to Kazi. "Is that Bassam on the radio? Can I speak to him?" He was desperate to believe the revolutionary leader had some advice on where to find his husband.

Kazi didn't answer him. The rest of the troop ignored Brendan as well.

Ibrahim told Brendan, "Relax, cowboy. We follow orders until the mission is complete. After the surrender, Bassam will organize teams to investigate the detention centers."

"When?"

"Could be a couple of days."

Brendan couldn't wait that long. He'd frickin' die.

"Let me talk to Bassam. We had a deal. I did what I was supposed to do, helping secure the navy base. I've got to find Cal."

He could feel the attitude of his companions shifting. Comments flew around in Arabic, and more than one suspicious glare dug into him.

"You did nothing at the navy base," Ibrahim told him. "Now you want to desert the revolution?"

Brendan said nothing. After the scene at the detention center, the college student clearly had his doubts about him, as had every other guy in the vehicle.

"Watch yourself," Ibrahim said. "When we get to the palace, you follow the team. If you lag behind or run off, you will be considered an open target." His hand was fixed on the handle of his rifle.

They swerved through the streets and onto sidewalks to avoid immobilized police cars and throngs of people declaiming the king's regime. Past the rioting in the city center, they arrived on an open boulevard that led into the suburbs. Brendan still saw signs of anarchy. Storefronts and gas stations had been ransacked by looters. Everywhere, posters of King Al-Moghadam were defaced with graffiti. Some of the king's billboards had been set ablaze.

A missile scraped through the sky and exploded at a distant point on the horizon.

The SUV erupted with cheers while Brendan gripped his seat. Ibrahim drew his attention to what was up ahead. "The palace. Bassam is targeting the gates."

Brendan stared through the night. Missiles screamed overhead. Explosions flared and thundered on the horizon and sent sparks into the air. A phantom chorus of "The Star-Spangled Banner" resounded in his head.

And the rockets' red glare, the bombs bursting in air,
Gave proof through the night that our flag was still there…

While they gained on the compound, that refrain stayed with him like a movie soundtrack, lifting him to some out-of-body place where his frightening reality seemed muted, as if he were watching it instead of living it. The Humvee rumbled to a halt some yards from a smoldering crater that looked like it had once been the walled compound's main gate. Brendan's companions filed out of the vehicle with their rifles, and he kept up with them as they crept up on what was left of the gates.

Machine gun fire erupted from soldiers hidden behind the wreckage. Men from the team went down. Brendan dodged and ducked the onslaught of bullets, sidestepping his fallen comrades, trying to stay near Ibrahim and the rest of their party. He still felt disembodied from the physical danger.

O say does that star-spangled banner yet wave
O'er the land of the free and the home of the brave?

Kazi and some others found targets and blasted the men guarding the compound. Brendan propped his rifle into firing position though he was helplessly confused about where to aim. He couldn't see any of the men defending the gates, which was merely a ditch between two piles of boulders. There could have been two or two hundred soldiers on the other side.

Another Humvee rolled onto the scene, and a team of rebels scrambled out of the vehicle. The camouflaged freedom fighters took up positions and pelted the murky entrance to the estate with rifle fire. One man tossed a hand grenade into that barrier. The blast brought Brendan down to his knees.

Smoke coughed out of the opening to the compound. Rifle fire from the other side ceased. Kazi cried out a call to attack, and the two teams marauded forward through the smog and into the compound.

Brendan jogged after them. Past the smoking crater, he flinched from a rat-a-tat of gunshots in many directions. The only thing he could discern was some soldiers must have been waiting for them. He got down low and tried to take things in. Guys cried out in agony. Their voices were less familiar, suggesting possibly the compound guards were taking the brunt of the bullets. He glimpsed Ibrahim picking off a guy in a military uniform at close range. Some guy in civilian attire had come onto the scene with a handgun. Past the murky zone of combat, lights from an estate house glowed in the distance. The vast grounds were veiled in darkness.

Brendan awakened from his daze of shock and seized on his slim chance to escape the fray. He tore into an empty field, away from the rifle fire, praying by his speed and by some higher power he would make it out unseen. His revolutionary teammates would shoot him for deserting. Anyone guarding the palace would shoot him too. His legs carried him ever farther from the hail of bullets, though he could hardly be sure he was headed to safety. The way was shadowed, but the only escape from his team was toward the lighted house.

Chapter Twenty-Seven

CAL HOP STEPPED out to the balcony with one hand trying to hold together the rip in the seat of his shorts, while the guards clopped through the suite, searching for him, not far behind. He hustled to the edge of the balcony.

A glance at the grounds revealed a befuddling scene. House guards burst out from the front of the estate. They piled into black sedans parked around the circular driveway and tore off down the road toward the gates. Beyond the man-made lake, Cal glimpsed the glow of flames. None of this made sense to him at the time. He just needed to get away from Abdullah's guards before they roughed him up and bound him for whatever kinky torture Abdullah had in mind.

It was a good fifteen-foot drop to the lawn below outside the cricket field. He had a better chance of not breaking any bones if he climbed over the railing and hung off the balcony floor for his descent. Throwing one leg over, he heard and felt the split in the seat of his shorts tear wider. A guard swept open the curtain to the balcony door, and his gaze found Cal.

Cal pulled his other leg over the railing. He looked down at the steep drop below him, whimpered, and took the plunge.

Anticipating crushing pain, he hit the ground on stiffened legs, lost his balance, and tucked into a somersaulting tumble with his ass flying free in the night air.

The tumble knocked the breath out of him, but as he gathered himself on all fours, he realized his limbs were all intact. Besides a little brush burn on his knees and elbows, it really hadn't been that bad. Maybe he had some athletic ability after all. Not that Cal cared to try it again.

The guard shouted at him from above. Cal got up and booked onto the cricket field. The palace had to be teeming with men from the king's security team who would come after him. Though they all seemed to be drawn to that fiery disturbance by the gates. Cal prayed that was the case and he could disappear into the night-shrouded grounds.

He bolted across the field and onward to a rolling lawn, now assured the seat of his shorts was a gaping hole, ripped open even wider as he ran. When he found the perimeter of the estate, he'd climb the wall and beg someone to lend him a phone. Though he didn't speak Arabic, and he had to look ridiculously sketchy, dressed up in a boy's cricket outfit with his butt hanging out the back. Cal raced on, thinking: one step at a time. At least the cleats had come in handy. They really gave good traction on the lawn, which was wet with evening dew. He envisioned himself as a star soccer player, charging to the goal line.

Gunfire erupted in the distance. Cal seized up and nearly wiped out. It was nowhere near him, but what the heck was going on? A siege on the palace? That danger fueled him forward, and Cal remembered the young man, Hakim, who he had met in the courthouse waiting pen.

We are all doomed. Until the revolution comes.

Was "the revolution" underway? It sure sounded like it. In the distance, he heard heavy vehicles rounding the estate, rowdy voices, and the hail of machine gun fire. What would he find when he made it out of the palace compound and into the city streets?

Cal had ventured onto a shadowy golf course, where beneath the glow of a full moon he could make out the silhouettes of putting greens, patches of trees, and sand traps. His legs felt like they could carry him all the way back to Hydra, but his lungs weren't doing as well keeping up. He spotted a gazebo—some rest stop on the course. It was dark, secluded, a decent place to hole up for a moment while he gathered his breath and his thoughts. Cal stumbled into the enclosure, sucking in air, trying to be quiet about it. Good god, he'd wound up in a mess even worse than waking up in a tugboat chartered by Romanian mobsters.

BRENDAN CHARGED THROUGH the night, achieving a greater distance from the melee back at the compound gates. Cars sped down the road from the estate house, and he veered away from their headlights.

Mostly, the palace grounds were a sightless void. A narrow lake stretched along the road to a lighted house that looked like a government monument. The king's palace. Decorative lampposts lined the driveway. He could stay out of detection in the shadowy acres of the lawn, but how long until battalions of revolutionaries made their way into the estate, firing at any target, and locking down the compound? If he didn't find a way out, or at least a fail-safe hiding place, he was dead meat.

Military vehicles rumbled from the streets surrounding the walled estate. His only option was to venture closer to the house where it was quieter and farther away from the inevitable approach of Bassam's bloodthirsty militia.

He let his pace drag, wiping his face with his shirtsleeve, trying to sort out a route. Sweat rolled down his forehead, stinging his eyes, and his vision throbbed in and out while his lungs clenched for air. He had to skirt the main house, which was lit up by every outside fixture and every window of its front facade and its symmetrical wings. He spotted a copse of trees to one side and beyond that, what looked like steps down to a dimly lit topiary garden. With his rifle tucked under one arm, Brendan staggered in that direction.

Drawing nearer to the house, he heard men shouting to one another and sharp bursts of communication from radio headsets. Everyone was in a panic, and likely, the king would have bodyguards patrolling the grounds. He skulked his way into a garden with pebbled trails, which made some regrettable noise as he stepped tenderly through. Lighted fountains in the grand topiary also presented obstacles. It was a maze garden fit for a seventeenth-century French king. Brendan crept along a shadowed aisle with an eye on the side of the garden nearest the house.

From some balcony of the estate, he heard a noise, and then bullets from a handgun blasted and sniped in his direction. Brendan ducked behind some hedges, trying to control his frightened breaths. He heard hollering and curses from the house. Naturally, in his fatigues, someone had probably thought he was one of the insurgents staking out the grounds. When it sounded like the shooter had gone back inside, he didn't wait around to confirm it. He scurried through the gardens toward a clearing behind the house.

Brendan ran on to a vast lawn with only the cover of night. He imagined an alarm blaring on and a team of Rottweilers chasing after him, though mercifully none of that happened. The chaos of Bassam's insurgency was working to his advantage. Every man in the security force of the estate had to be hunkering down to defend the main house and protect the king. Brendan glanced at some commotion from a back bay to the house. People loaded into a car and drove across the grounds to a heliport. Doors creaked open and slammed shut as lights from a chopper blinked on, and its blades churned to life.

It looked like the king was making his escape. The helicopter lifted from the grounds and whirred off in the night. None too soon. From some distance behind Brendan, on the front side of the house, he heard the roar of an approaching mob. He hoofed it away from that. Did he stand a chance finding his way out of the estate and taking harbor somewhere that hopefully had a phone?

Blindly guessing on a direction for his flight, he arrived on a golf course. How fucking extensive was the palace estate? He must have run two miles already. It felt like he could be lost in the place until dawn.

A full moon glowed overhead. Brendan hadn't noticed that before. It made sense for a night when the world had gone insane, sucking him into the middle of a revolution. A grassy fairway glinted in the silvery light, and up a hill, he saw a teeing ground and a secluded gazebo. The peaceful rest stop called to him. He needed to rest his legs and pull himself together to finish off the disappearing act of a lifetime. The darkened hideaway was a good distance from the shouting and gunfire exchange at the main house.

He trudged toward the gazebo and halted at the sound of a faint noise. Was it possible someone was in there? It was too dark to see. It could have been his imagination, or droppings from a nearby tree when the wind passed through. On the other hand, someone from the estate might have smuggled into the hiding place to escape from the encroaching militia.

Brendan raised his rifle, slid open the bolt, and warily drew closer. Truly, he didn't want to hurt anyone, but whoever was in the gazebo was not likely to be friendly, and his only advantage was intimidation, just to flush the stranger out. His firing hand quivered. What if the stranger was also armed? He had only used his rifle once, back at the navy base, spraying bullets at the stationary window of the detention center, at close range.

He edged up to about a yard's length from the entrance to the enclosure. Moonlight traced a few steps inside, but the interior of the gazebo was almost entirely a hollow of shadow. He definitely heard a rustle and a gasp. The rifle trembled in his hands. He couldn't see a target. The stranger could rush out, catch him off guard, and knock the rifle right out of his hands. Brendan thought of calling out a warning. His throat was bone dry. Thinking he would just test the resistance on the trigger spring, his finger set it off, and the rifle discharged a round of bullets, throwing him back on his heels, riveting the roof of the gazebo.

A voice said, "I surrender. No need for excessive force. I'm an American. With no allegiance to the king. Believe me. I just broke out of the palace to get away from him. He wanted to hold me hostage to reenact some kinky scene from *Nicholas Nickleby.* "

A shadowed figure stood up in the gazebo, hands raised in the air.

"I've always believed in diplomatic solutions first, but in this situation, I'm totally nonjudgmental. I'll even help out, if you need me. KP duty? Keeping up morale in the medic's tent? I'm basically, totally unskilled, but I was a Cub Scout for a summer. I came pretty close to earning my Bobcat badge."

Brendan's heart hovered. Could it possibly be? He threw down his rifle and staggered toward his husband.

"Cal?"

"Brendan?"

Brendan scooped Cal up in his arms, and they clung to one another, both hiccupping with tears. Brendan swooned with waves of joy and waves of disbelief. It could not be a mirage. He could feel Cal's rapid heartbeat against his own, breathe in his familiar smell, and hear his tearful breaths. No matter how impossible it was that they'd ended up in the same gazebo, on the vast estate, in a foreign country that was under siege. And Brendan had almost killed him. He lightly broke their embrace to look at Cal.

"Are you hurt?"

Cal pulled him close again. "I'm fine. Thank god you're a lousy shot. Brendan, is it really you? Please tell me this isn't a dream. If it is, I never want to wake up again."

Brendan sank into his arms. After the week he'd had, it felt like the first comfort of his lifetime. He gripped Cal hard, moaned, kissed the side of his face.

"It's me. I found you, and I'm never going to let you go."

Cal's body quivered against his. Brendan thought they might both faint from shock, so he gently stooped down to the earthen floor of the gazebo with Cal. As Cal lay on his back, Brendan straddled his hips while holding his precious face. He choked out words that he'd feared he'd never have a chance to say.

"I'm sorry. I said horrible things. I was wrong. And I scared you away."

"It was my fault too," Cal said. "I shouldn't have run off on you." He gazed at Brendan in wonder. "You came to rescue me. My hero."

Brendan leaned down and kissed him deeply. He had found his Cal. He nuzzled against Cal's neck, tasting his sweat, nipping gently on his earlobe.

"God, I missed you so much. My baby."

Cal's quickening breaths fanned his cheek. "My darling. It is you." His hands slid beneath Brendan's shirt, discovering the sweat-slick skin of his back and gliding up his sides. "I thought I'd never see you again."

"I thought so too."

A primal need overwhelmed Brendan. He pinned Cal's hands behind his head, pulled his lover's undersized shirt up to his armpits and ravished every wondrous part of his chest and stomach. This was the homecoming Brendan had needed to claim, and for all he knew, with the violent clash all around them, it might be their last. He tugged open the button fly of Cal's shorts and slid them down to his knees. He made love to Cal with his mouth, there in the gazebo, transported for a moment from the gunfire, missile strikes, and the cries of revolutionaries.

Afterward, he lay beside his husband while they caught their breaths and entangled themselves in an embrace. An enormous smile grew on Cal's face.

"For this, it was almost worth being kidnapped."

Brendan combed through Cal's sweat-dampened, curly hair. "I'd fight through an army for you. Ford seas and deserts."

"And golf courses," Cal pointed out.

They both chuckled.

Just then, violent sounds echoed through the grounds. Rat-a-tat-tat rifle fire. Someone calling out on a megaphone. Cheers of victory. The rebels must have taken the king's home. The two men looked at each other, awakening to the danger of their situation.

"What do we do now?" Cal said.

Brendan grimaced. He pulled up his fatigues and stood to look out from the gazebo. He couldn't see the estate house from their location. A dark expanse of trees and hills led back that way. The golf course was still. Though it would be better for them to get a move on sooner than later.

He reached his hand to help Cal get up on his feet. "I wish I could say I had a plan. We need to find somewhere to hole up for the night until things calm down. When it's safe, we'll have to figure out a way to the U.S. embassy. If this crazy country even has one."

He just then took a full account of his husband's strange outfit.

"It's a long story," Cal said.

Brendan was curious to hear it. He had a hell of a story to share with Cal as well. But that would have to wait. Right now, they had to get to a safer place than the backyard of the king's besieged home. He pulled off his shirt so Cal could tie it around his waist and cover up in the back.

The menacing clamor of the revolution was coming from one direction, so Brendan led Cal to head off the opposite way. But they'd barely ventured out of the gazebo when a terrifying sound and sight froze them in their steps.

A military helicopter. Swooping down from the sky, practically on top of them within a span of seconds. Its searchlights caught the two men like a UFO on the hunt for human specimens. Cal tugged at Brendan's hand to make a break for it, but Brendan was strangely transfixed. Bassam didn't have aircraft in his militia. And if the helicopter belonged to the Sultanate's military, why would it bother with the two of them when all the action was happening acres away?

The helicopter whumped down on the golf course about thirty yards away from them. Brendan's jaw dropped. In the aircraft's blinking lights, the American flag was emblazoned on the side of its cabin. The rear door of the aircraft swung open, and a U.S. marine, holding a rifle, climbed out.

Grandad emerged behind him in what, Brendan supposed, was his most search-and-rescue-appropriate outfit—an Oxford shirt and sweater vest, khakis, and tennis shoes.

"Boys, get the hell over here," Grandad shouted. "There's a goddamn revolution going on."

They traipsed over to the helicopter hand in hand. Brendan stared at his grandfather in awe.

"You're lucky the CIA director is an old buddy of mine," Grandad explained. "A Yalie Sigma Chi. From back in the good old days before the liberal-fascists turned the university into a petting zoo for neutered, teetotalling weirdos." Grandad regained his train of thought. "The CIA was keeping tabs on this little coup in Maritime Kin-dah. When one of their agents, cached in the king's household, called in a sighting of Cal, my old pal rang me up, worked out some authorizations, and we took the jet down to the nearest air base pronto."

Cal ventured toward the cabin. Did he recognize someone in there? Brendan didn't understand much of what was going on, but he was mesmerized. An Arab man in a business suit waved out from the open helicopter door.

"Irfan!" Cal exclaimed.

The CIA agent smiled. "At your service, Mr. Panagopoulos."

"But how did you find us out here?" Cal said.

"I sewed a radio chip into your shorts," Irfan said.

Grandad took Brendan by the shoulder to lead him into the cabin. "And happily, Brendy, that tracking device bought us two for the price of one." He glanced at the two of them. They were both half-naked. Brendan's fatigues were worn down in the knees. Cal looked like he'd been set upon by nymphomaniac groupies, and they each had dirt and grass clinging to their skin.

A tick of understanding showed on Grandad's face, and he pushed them toward the door of the aircraft. "Let's burn ozone, lover boys. We've got a rendezvous with the *U.S.S. George W. Bush*, and then a sea voyage to the air base in Al Dhafra. With all due haste, we can be back in Hydra in three days." He added, dryly, "A shower and a change of clothes will spare us all some straits at the reunion with the children and the ladyfolk."

Brendan and Cal climbed into the cabin of the helicopter and belted themselves into seats across from Grandad, Irfan, and the uniformed marine. The rotor blades chirped into high gear, and they lifted off the ground.

Brendan exchanged a dumbfounded grin with Cal. They were soaring in the night sky, leaving behind scud missile attacks and machine-gun fire and every other terrifying detail of their visit to the Sultanate of Maritime Kindah. Their lives had fallen apart in the blink of an eye, and it seemed they'd been put back together just as quickly. Brendan gripped Cal's hand. After everything, they would have their happily-ever-after story.

Epilogue

SEVEN MONTHS LATER

The following April, on an unseasonably warm Sunday in New York City, Cal and Brendan hosted an Easter brunch on the roof deck of their penthouse apartment. It was their first time entertaining since making the place their home. They'd needed a break from the world after their near disastrous wedding vacation, and with all of the media attention after their return to the States, it had taken several months for life to begin to approach feeling routine again. Brendan played off their first home-warming get-together as a low-key affair, but Cal wanted everything to be perfect.

He ordered a marble-topped dining table with cushioned banquettes to seat the twenty guests, replacing Brendan's wooden booth set. He hired a contractor to install aisles of stone planters and filled them with red azaleas, and updated the space with rose bushes, spiral junipers, and billowing canopies. At his uncle's shop, Cal found a Valencia cherub fountain, which was perhaps too much, but its sentimentality overtook his doubts. A cherub cameo had brought him and Brendan together. His husband loved the idea.

Brendan was wonderfully supportive of all of Cal's ideas. Cal worked with the caterer to put together a menu that was a blend of Greek and New American sensibilities. Lamb chops, charred eggplant salad, *dolmadakia*, eggs benedict sliders, truffle fries, and Virginia ham with a spicy pineapple chutney. Cal was calling the theme "casual but classy." He wanted their guests to be comfortable while giving the occasion the touch of (called-for) refinement.

After everyone arrived, Cal drifted through the party, making stops to chat with each group of guests so everyone would feel welcomed and appreciated for coming, while he also kept an eye on the service by the chef, the cater waiter, and the bartender. He wore a candy-red, textured, Cuban-collared shirt that had caught his eye at Barney's, and fashionably baggy slacks and slip-on vintage sneakers.

That was a departure from his usual attire of mall-bought shirts and jeans. Cal had needed to update his wardrobe to fit into his husband's world. Though his brothers teased him that New York City had made him uppity, and his eldest brother, Sandy, called him a fashion whore, Cal hadn't given up his own sense of style. He still wore his wavy, golden hair in a barely tended mop, halfway covering his ears. He couldn't part with his woven bracelets. Marriage was about blending lives, and sharing new things, not giving up the old. Cal liked to think his earthy touches, like hand-knotted carpets and antique candelabras, had made Brendan's apartment homier. It belonged to both of them now, after all.

He made a stop to catch up with Genie and Louis Jeffries who were standing just outside the balcony's double doors, snuggled up together. Since the wedding in Hydra, the two had started dating, which was really fabulous and unexpected. Though Genie had always liked an alpha-dog kind of guy. Cal suspected there was actually a puppy dog beneath Louis's sardonic exterior. Genie still lived upstate, but they were spending nearly every weekend together. Louis had an arm around her waist, and they were grinning and whispering to one another in that flirty manner of a newly sexually acquainted couple. Cal left them to their PDAs and moved on to the next group of guests.

His dad and mom had taken over a shaded alcove with Brendan's grandad and grandmum. Millie was proudly wearing the cherub cameo Brendan had bought at the antiques shop, that morning when Cal and Brendan had met. They were all engaged in lively conversation. That foursome taking a liking to one another had been an even more surprising development. Grandmum had a knack for making everyone feel like an old friend, and it turned out the two patriarchs could talk for hours about politics and college football even though they came from entirely different worlds. Cal's dad was presently educating Brendan's grandfather on the discontents of the European Union. Though he hadn't gone to college, Mr. Panagopoulos never missed his daily *New York Times* and *To Vima* newspaper from Athens. The ladies meanwhile chatted about their gardens and the latest true crime miniseries on cable TV.

Cal moved on and gently sidestepped his three-year-old nephew Alex who came toddling after a beach ball thrown to him by his six-year-old brother, Manny. A beleaguered shout at the boys traveled across the deck from Cal's youngest brother, Demetri, who had driven his family down from Syracuse Friday night. His wife, Victoria, was admiring the rooftop's westward view of Central Park. She was eight months pregnant, yet far more cheerful than her sleep-deprived husband.

Brendan's half sisters, Daryl and Riley, corralled the restless brothers for an indoor game of *Just Dance* on the home theater. Their mother, Belinda, stood at the bar, twirling the sugar cane in her caipirinha while chatting up the handsome Puerto Rican bartender. Apparently,

Brendan's mother had not yet discovered Gustavo was gay. Cal waved to her and made a stop next to her husband, Roger, who stood holding the handbags of his wife and daughters. Cal called over the waiter to unburden Roger of the bags, and he tried to cheer the man up by talking about his and Brendan's visit to the Hamptons that summer. Roger had promised to take them windsurfing.

Cal was accosted out of nowhere by Brendan's hug-happy father, Donovan, who was in good spirits considering his girlfriend, Gabriela, had recently left him and moved back to Venezuela. Of all the things that had happened since the wedding, Cal was happiest about the fact that Brendan had thawed a bit to his father. This was Donovan's second visit to New York in as many months. Though Brendan had said, cynically, that his father was only interested in reconnecting because he was lonely after getting dumped, Cal thought Donovan was really trying to get to know his son.

Seeing Cal as an intermediary for that purpose, Donovan treated him like an old buddy. In semi-awkward, weepy moments, he had bared his soul and asked for advice on how to repair his relationship with his son. Brendan needed to come around at his own pace, so Cal didn't push the issue with his husband. Inviting his dad to the party showed he was getting there.

Meanwhile, Donovan was vetting TV and film studios to make a biopic of the whole Hydra ordeal. People at the Discovery channel were interested. Donovan also had encouraging meetings with a gay TV network, and even Angelina Jolie's production firm was considering going in on the project. The story had gotten a storm of press back in October. It had been exciting for a while to see his face on local and national news, and then Cal started receiving letters from fans, some of them on the creepy side.

As much as Cal had fantasized about his story becoming a bestselling book and movie, he decided he wasn't interested in being a celebrity. Too little privacy went with that, and his awful experiences with crazy admirers made him wary. Brendan agreed double on that score. They both needed some peace and quiet, a return to normalcy. Cal had started his online master's degree and had an eye on a position at the department of antiquities at the Metropolitan Museum. Brendan had finished an intensive course in nonprofit management and was meeting with potential board members to start a fund for homeless LGBTQIA youth.

Cal told Donovan again they preferred to put the incident behind them. Brendan's father had good intentions. He just needed to be reined in at times.

Cal spotted Derek behind the cherub fountain, texting on his phone, and he wandered over. Forgiving his best friend had not come easily. Derek had nearly ruined his marriage. His sabotage of the wedding had nearly gotten both him and Brendan killed. Cal hadn't wanted to hear Derek's apologies when he'd first returned to Hydra, and he hadn't returned his friend's calls all through the holidays.

Then the new year came with its promise of fresh starts. Cal had sent Derek a brief reply to his latest text, which led to him agreeing to a FaceTime call, and a tearful conversation, and a follow-up handwritten thank you letter. Derek then wore him down with texts with all of Cal's favorite emojis, and a link to his Instagram account where he had posted photos from their college days, and even some pics of their "gay tour" of New York City.

It helped that Brendan had put in a good word for Derek, explaining how he'd been instrumental in the search to find Cal. After much deliberation, Cal had agreed to meet

Derek for coffee while he was on campus in Syracuse for a monthly advisement meeting. Things turned a corner when Derek told him he was seeing a therapist to work on his issues with self-esteem and jealousy. He told Cal he'd learned he hadn't truly been in love with him. He'd clung to that idea because he was afraid no one else would ever love him.

It was still too soon for the two of them to go back to being besties. Maybe that would never happen. Cal believed in second chances, and Derek would always be part of his life. He'd written his place there with an indelible magic marker. But that mark he made still felt like it had threatening edges at times. Cal wasn't sure that feeling would ever go away. He was happy for Derek though. His friend was presently sending cutesy texts to a graduate assistant he'd started dating. It was the first guy Derek had shown interest in since freshman year.

A lot of things had turned out for the better since Hydra, Cal considered. New relationships. New friendships. The people of the Sultanate of Maritime Kindah had their first-ever representative government under the presidency of Bassam El-Amin, the man who had given Brendan the chance to rescue Cal from Abbas Barundi. U.N. Special Forces had intercepted King Abdullah's flight. He was in prison in The Hague awaiting trial for crimes against his people.

Cal had even received good news from Faraj, when a "Beach Bum" postcard, emblazoned with a rear view of two guys in thongs, arrived in his mailbox. The young navy ensign had somehow tracked down Cal's address. Free from naval service, he'd taken up residence in Cape Town, South Africa and gotten a job at a gay bed-and-breakfast. He was a liberated gay man now, making his own way in the world without the crutch, and the restraints, of his family's wealth. Cal tended to skim through Faraj's correspondence, however, since he still had a tendency to overshare about his sexual habits.

He spotted the cater waiter bringing the brunch meal to the table. Cal took a seat at the head beside Brendan who kissed him on the cheek while the guests went on about the gorgeous table setting. Cal had decorated it with pink tulips and white lilies and put dyed eggs in holders in front of every seat in lieu of name cards. Brendan led a champagne toast to family and friends.

Looking around the table, a big grin spread across Cal's face. There was Brendan's family and his family, and good friends like Louis, and Betsy Schoonover, and Derek who was doing his best, and little kids, and children on the way. For a moment, Cal felt like his heart would burst from the great bounty of happiness the universe had given him. Most of all, there was Brendan, who interlaced their hands and placed them on his sturdy thigh. This would be their life together. It was more than he'd ever dreamed of, and it was only beginning.

Glossary

DE RIGUEUR—proper; prescribed by fashion, etiquette, or custom

DOLMADAKIA—a Greek dish; grape leaves stuffed with rice and vegetables and meat

KATAPELTIS (καταπέλτης)—catapult

KATAPLIKTIKOS (καταπληκτικός)—amazing

KEFFIYEH—traditional Middle Eastern headdress from Kufa

KIBBEH—considered to be the national dish of many Middle Eastern countries; made of bulgur, minced onions, and finely ground beef, lamb, goat, or camel meat with Middle Eastern spices

KOUKLOS (κούκλος)—handsome

MEZZE—a Greek or Middle Eastern appetizer often served with an aperitif

OUD—wood of a tropical tree used in making incense and scents

SOTTO VOCE—under the breath, whispered

SPITI (σπίτι)—home

TAVERNA (ταβέρνα)—tavern

TOURISTAS (τουρίστας)—tourists

TRAVMATIES (τραυματίες)—injured

Author's Note

Irresistible is my first foray into romantic comedy, though readers may be surprised to know it is inspired by a story from the ancient world, as much of my work tends to be. Some years back, while drafting *The City of Seven Gods*, I was researching translated source material from the classical era, mainly for style and a better understanding of how people of the age talked about their lives. That's when I was introduced to the strange novel *Callirhoe* by Chariton of Aphrodisias, a first-century Greek writer.

One of its many curiosities is the fact that Chariton's short novel, which was only translated for wide distribution in the twentieth century, represents the first-ever extant romance novel in the world. I had read epic poems, mythological stories, and histories and philosophies of the time, but the prospect of reading an ancient Greek, full-fledged novel— well, I poured over the book like a coin collector examining a rare penny.

For me, the most shocking discovery was *Callirhoe's* structural and thematic similarity to modern-day romance. It's positively Harlequin-esque in its convictions that love can happen in an instant, love conquers all, and love will always save the day. In his introduction to the translated text, G.G. Goold notes the novel was received by critics of the time remarkably similarly to current attitudes toward romance. It was maligned as "mawkish," "pedestrian," and hardly *serious literature*. Both the literary sophistication and the foreshadowing prejudices of the classical age never fail to impress me.

Modern scholars treated Chariton's novel poorly as well, though there has certainly been a resurgent consideration of the merits of the text of late. On plotting and characterization, however, *Callirhoe* is fairly universally noted as high melodrama, unrealistic, even ludicrous, and according to the classical review site, *The Consolation of Reading*, "the ancient equivalent of a soap opera."

Those observations are, in fact, precisely the reasons I became enamored with the story. One-upping the Harlequin formula, the young heroine Callirhoe is so very, very irresistible that no man can help but fall in love with her—a circumstance made all the more absurd by her frequent asides bemoaning the gods who cursed her with fatal beauty like Helen of Troy. Her betrothed Chaereas, a handsome catch in his own right, literally fords oceans and gives up his own freedom to find her when she is robbed from the grave by pirates following a comedy of errors that leaves her presumed dead. The pirates are so frightened by her beauty, thinking her to be some favorite of the gods and therefore bad luck, they dump her at the nearest harbor to sell her as a slave. Her master, of course, falls in love with her, and eschewing convention, insists on marrying her. When Chaereas catches up, a trial is called to determine which man can claim Callirhoe as his wife. Yet the magistrate is immediately smitten by Callirhoe as well and schemes to take her for himself. It's all very campy and somehow reminded me of a Monty Python skit. Consider the novel's last line, when Chaereas and Callirhoe are finally reunited:

"As they rushed into each other's arms, they fainted and fell to the floor."

Now that's deep love.

We'll never know if Chariton intended his story as a parody or believed it to be a masterpiece. To me, it screamed out for a modern-day retelling, which turned into a gay mash-up of *There's Something About Mary* and *My Big Fat Greek Wedding*. Naturally, I had to take some liberties bringing the story into the twenty-first century. Of note, in the original, a flight of jealousy leads Chaereas to kick Callirhoe in the stomach. He strikes her in the precise place that induces coma and leads to her untimely burial. I just could not see that type of violence playing well to a contemporary audience, nor could I do that to my beloved 'Callirhoe'—Callisthenes.

I did, however, want to recreate the original story's wildly absurd tone and, in doing so, none are spared from parody: men and women, gay and straight, young and old, rich and poor, and a parade of nationalities. I apologize especially to the Greeks. My hope is readers will quickly pick up this is a story not meant to be taken entirely seriously.

About the Author

Andrew J. Peters has been writing fiction since his elementary school principal let him read excerpts from his mystery novel over the PA system during lunch period, an early brush with notoriety, which quite possibly may have been the height of his literary celebrity. Since then, he has studied to be a veterinarian, worked as a social worker for LGBTQ youth, and settled into university administration, while keeping late hours at his home computer writing stories.

Andrew is the author of eight books, including the award-winning *The City of Seven Gods* (2017 Best Horror/Fantasy Novel at the Silver Falchion awards) and the popular *Werecat* series (2016 Romance Reviews Readers' Choice awards finalist). Andrew lives in New York City with his husband Genaro and their cat Chloë. When he's not writing, he enjoys traveling, Broadway shows, movies, and thinking up ways to subvert heteronormative narratives.

Email: ajpeters@andrewjpeterswrites.com

Facebook: www.facebook.com/andrewjpeterswrites

Twitter: @ayjayp

Website: www.andrewjpeterswrites.com

Also Available from NineStar Press

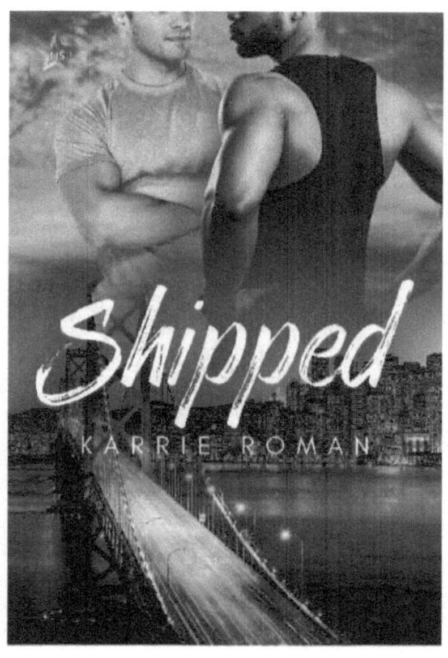

Connect with NineStar Press

Website: NineStarPress.com

Facebook: NineStarPress

Facebook Reader Group: NineStarNiche

Twitter: @ninestarpress

Tumblr: NineStarPress

9 781949 340488